PRAISE FOR

# SHORE LOSER

"High seas high jinks that will keep you turning pages to see how Danielson's going to get this wild bunch of true-to-life sailors out their next close call. Great fun!!"

— Pat Henry,
author of *BY THE GRACE OF THE SEA:
A WOMAN'S SOLO ODYSSEY AROUND THE WORLD*

"Fast moving. Pure entertainment. Forget looking for a white hat. In this shoot em' up, the good guys wear authentic deck shoes.

— Kitty James,
boating journalist,
editor of *SANTANA MAGAZINE.*

"Most fun you can have without getting your feet wet."

— R.D. Lyons,
author of *MEXICO'S HIDDEN GOLD*
and *RIDING GUTS 'N' GLORY.*

"Capt. Doug Danielson's sea-going adventures mirror the real world cruising lifestyle, not the Hollow-wood version. His characters have stepped right out of all the salty waterfront bars and sun-bleached marinas you've ever dreamed of. Best of all, Danielson uses correct nautical lingo with the everyday grace of a veteran sailor because he is one."

— Capt. John E. Rains and Capt. Pat Miller Rains,
authors of *CRUISING PORTS, MEX WX,*
and *BOATING GUIDE TO MEXICO.*

# SHORE LOSER

*To Brenda Watts UHHS Reunion 2008*

### Douglas Danielson

**TSUNAMI PRESS**
Puerto Vallarta, Mexico

Douglas Danielson can be reached at his website
www.Doug-Danielson.com
or by email at: capt.doug@prodigy.net.mx

Cover design and layout by Paul McBroome
Final editing by Dan Grippo and Joy Eckel
Portrait Photo by Lew Jennings
Picture of Russian IACC boat by Hugo Carver
Printed in the United States of America by BookSurge Publishing
Visit www.booksurge.com to order additional copies.

ISBN: 1-4196-7263-0
ISBN-13: 978-1419672637

This novel is a work of fiction. Any references to real events, businesses, organizations and locales are intended only to give the fiction a sense of reality and authenticity. Any resemblance to actual persons, living or dead, is entirely coincidental.

For **Karen**: Thanks for being there
through all the rough seas and calm anchorages.
Hasn't it been one hell of a voyage?

"Someone's rocking my dream-boat, someone's invading my dream.
We were sailing along, so peaceful and calm;
suddenly something went wrong.
**--Recorded by the Ink Spots in 1941**
**Words & music by Leon René & Emerson Scott**

# SHORE LOSER

Douglas Danielson

PROLOGUE

# SUMMER 1994

AeroMexico Flight 158 touched down in Tijuana more than twenty minutes behind schedule. A pneumatic screech announced their arrival as multiple sets of tires tore into the hot asphalt, gray smoke signaling their protest. The air travel up from La Paz had been bumpy and uncomfortable—the landing was just as bad.

Two of the passengers scrambling down the boarding ladder were Americans. Unshaven, wearing winkled shorts and dirty t-shirts, they seemed no different from many other U.S. expatriates living in exile in Baja California—running from debts, the law, the IRS, or an ex-wife. With no luggage, they passed quickly through the concrete terminal that was perpetually under construction.

Once outside, neither man spoke; both were searching for the familiar black limousine that would take them to their destination in this border city of over two million inhabitants.

ೋ ೕ

An hour earlier, Leonard Sleak, an impeccably groomed businessman with a pencil-thin moustache, left his plush office overlooking the Pacific in La Jolla, California. Two armed bodyguards picked him up in a rented Lincoln and drove the forty-five miles down Interstate 5 and through the US/Mexico border crossing.

On the seat beside Leonard was a fine leather briefcase. It was locked and he did not have the key. He had been told it was filled with marked and banded bundles of U.S. currency amounting to over $1,000,000. The money had been "laundered" through his development company and was from an investment scam that, if discovered, would shock the San Diego yachting community. He suspected the money would ultimately be used to pay off Mexican officials and move narcotics to the United States. This was a dirty business and he hated it.

Even though they passed through the border safely, a familiar acid taste invaded his mouth as he kept turning his head, looking through the rear window to see if they were being followed. Tugging at his moustache, he could not seem to get comfortable in the luxury of the Lincoln's leather interior. His left hand, resting on the briefcase, twitched spasmodically. On previous deliveries, Leonard had been calm and self-assured. This time things were different—his financial survival was at stake. If this transaction and the ones to follow didn't go smoothly, the new "investment partner" in his land development company would make his life even more miserable than it already was.

CHAPTER ONE

# RESCUE

Sometimes I feel like I've spent my whole life taking exams for one idiotic thing after another: grammar school, high school, Department of Motor Vehicles, the Navy, and now the Coast Guard. Here I am, Jake Mortensen, twenty-five years old, and just mustered out of the United States Navy. Once again the establishment, this time the Coast Guard, wanted to judge my abilities solely by the way I filled in boxes on an 8½ x 11 sheet of paper. What a man does with what he knows should be the real indication of how smart he is.

It took me two weeks to complete the requirements for the U.S.C.G. captain's exam, a test given in several parts. The Rules-of-the-Road portion was closed-book and required a score of 90 percent to pass. My hours of study paid off; it was a piece of cake. Book-learning tests have always been easy for me, and my roommate Ted Blythe's coaching helped, too. It surprised me there was no on-the-water practical examination. With my Navy sea time and the years spent on my father's sailboat, I qualified for a license for 100-ton Master. Pleased with my Navy paramedic training and Ted's reference, YachtTow hired me part time on a trial basis. By the second week in November 1994, I was riding along, learning the ropes.

"Mayday! Mayday! Mayday!" the distress call blared over the VHF marine radio late Friday morning.

"Vessel calling mayday, this is the United States Coast Guard San Diego Activities Group, Channel one-six. What is the name of your vessel, location, and nature of your distress?"

"Coast Guard, Coast Guard, this is the power vessel *Elaine II*. I am in front of the lighthouse off Point Loma, and my wife is in the water. We ran into something and we're drifting toward shore. The engines won't go into forward or reverse. Please, send help!" the male voice cried out in panic.

Ted and I were cruising by the submarine base on our way out of the main channel. We notified the Coast Guard and the Harbor Police of our position, and since we were the closest rescue vessel, they asked us to respond. Ted throttled forward and wound our engines to maximum RPM. I tugged on my wetsuit and strapped a sheathed rigging knife to my right leg.

I knew the ocean temperature was unusually cold this time of year, a bone-chilling fifty-four degrees. My Navy training had drilled into me the dangers of hypothermia. Getting the guy's wife out of the water quickly was imperative.

"*Elaine II, Elaine II, Elaine II*, this is *YachtTow I* underway to your position. We think we have a visual on you. Please, state hull color and type of vessel."

"*YachtTow I*, this is *Elaine II*. We are a thirty-five-foot Bayliner, white hull, blue boot stripe and canvas. Please, hurry! My wife's in the water and the boat's drifting toward the rocks."

"We've got you in sight. Does your wife have a lifejacket on? Have you tried to anchor the boat?"

"She's not wearing a lifejacket. I threw her a horseshoe buoy. I've tried to anchor, but the water is too deep and it won't hold. Please, please, hurry!"

Ted and I rounded Point Loma. We could see the vessel in a field of kelp about 200 yards west of the treacherous rocks on the face of the peninsula. The Bayliner was almost directly in front of the very lighthouse put there to alert boaters of the danger, an area legendary for shipwrecks.

Ted throttled down and eased into the choking, foul vegetation. Our propellers chewed up the pulpy marine plants and threw them out in our diminished wake. We could hear the waves crashing nearby on the jagged granite outcroppings.

Textbooks define immersion hypothermia as a loss of heat when a body is covered in water. Survival time depends on water temperature, body size, amount of body fat, and activity. An average person wearing light clothing in approximately 50°F water can survive only two to three hours, becoming exhausted or unconscious in thirty to sixty minutes. Physical activity such as swimming and treading water will accelerate cooling by about 35 percent. With few exceptions, humans die when their normal rectal temperature of 99.7°F drops below 78.6°F. There wasn't much time, and Ted and I knew it.

I kept my eyes on the woman struggling in the water. She had drifted about 100 feet from the vessel. Head bobbing up and down, she looked like a paper sack floating between *Elaine II* and the rocky shore. She was clinging to a yellow horseshoe buoy and appeared to be entangled in slimy branches of kelp. When Ted got me to within fifteen feet of her, I grabbed a life preserver and jumped into the frigid water. As I swam toward the thrashing woman, Ted fed out more line attached to the float. When I reached her, she was shivering convulsively. Fortunately, she was still conscious.

"Here, stop trying to swim." I yelled to be heard above the surf. "I'm gonna put this thing around your waist. Hang on to your horseshoe buoy and try not to move. This life preserver has a line attached to it, and my partner has the other end."

Using my knife, I cut away most of the kelp that encircled her and cinched the flotation device in place. Thick vegetation made swimming a challenge. Somebody once told me women's cosmetics were made from this stuff. They must have been kidding.

"You're gonna be OK!" I yelled, as I signaled Ted to pull in the rescue line.

Swimming alongside her, I cleared our path. As we approached *YachtTow I*, Ted was prepared for us. He had hung a ladder off the stern and was standing on the swim platform ready to help.

"Quickly—she's shaking," I looked up and hollered, as I started to boost her out of the water. Ted used the line attached to the life preserver to lift her. The swim step kept jerking up and down with the swell, making the climb from the water difficult. Red-white-and-blue cotton clothes clung to her body, her long brown hair tangled with leathery leaves.

"Get her into the forward cabin. She needs to get out of those wet clothes and wrap herself in a thermal blanket," I shouted above the ocean noise. "There's a towel in my backpack. Use the sleeping bag if necessary. And if she can't do it herself, you help her. Forget modesty, Ted. She needs to get her body temperature back."

Ted assisted the woman forward, while I pulled our gear and myself out of the water. After she was warmly bundled, Ted went back to the helm. Both engines had been shut down for safety while we climbed out of the water, now he lit them up again. Hearing the rumble of twin 320-horsepower machines coming to life below the cockpit floor made me feel warmer. With my wetsuit dripping all over, I unsnapped a thermos and poured a cup of coffee. It was still hot, and I handed it to the shivering woman. She could barely hold on to it, her hands were trembling so much. Then I poured a cup for myself. The hot liquid tasted good.

"*Elaine II, Elaine II, Elaine II, YachtTow I* on Channel two-two-alpha." Ted had the mike in his hand.

"*YachtTow I, Elaine II*. Is my wife OK?"

"Yes, sir. She's safely on board, getting warm. I'm going to come along your port side so my partner can get on your vessel. Put some fenders out. He will board at your swim step. Be ready to give him a hand."

"Geeze, Ted! We've got to make the transfer quickly." I pointed at the Bayliner, now less than 150 feet from the boiling, jagged shore.

A few minutes more, and *Elaine II* would enter the surf. Rescuing the woman had cost valuable time. If the saltwater intakes to our Caterpillar engines sucked up any of the leafy debris surrounding us, *YachtTow I* would also be in danger. We came alongside *Elaine II*. I grabbed the owner's hand and jumped aboard. Short and fat, he was a Pillsbury Dough Boy in a captain's cap.

"How much anchor line you got out?" I asked, as I released his puffy grip and, holding onto a horizontal rail, moved along the cabin toward the bow.

"Forty feet of quarter-inch galvanized chain and 200 feet of half-inch nylon rode. It's all out!" he yelled as he precariously followed me forward.

Thunderous surf crashed against the shore as I pulled in on the anchor line. It felt like nothing was attached. I decided not to use the windlass, but instead hauled in the three-strand nylon line hand over hand. It looked new. When I got to the thimble attached to the chain, I continued to take it up. Nothing was connected to the end; the anchor was gone. The owner stared in astonishment. I used the fid in my rigging knife to disconnect the shackle that held the chain and line together. The shackle pin had not been secured with any seizing wire.

Waves breaking behind us and against the shore were deafening. Green water bubbling with white foam surrounded us. While I struggled, Ted maneuvered his vessel in front of *Elaine II*. He backed the stern toward me as I released the chain from the line.

"Go to the wheel and straighten the rudders!" I shouted at the owner.

"Throw me the end with the thimble," Ted yelled, as he stopped *YachtTow I* and ran to the stern. "Come on! Damn it! We're out of time!"

Huge swells heaved both boats up and down. With all my strength, I threw the line toward *YachtTow I*. Ted caught it and made it fast to the towing post, as I wrapped my end several times around the anchor windlass and cleated it off. I gave him a thumbs-up when both ends of the line were secure. Then I held on to the towline to prevent it from fouling his props as he eased *YachtTow I* away, taking up the slack. Both propellers churned up big chunks of marine vegetation as we pulled away from the menacing shore—not a moment too soon, as a huge wave broke underneath us, tossing *Elaine II* around like a kid's toy. Hanging on to the bow pulpit and checking my balance, I picked up the loose anchor chain and carried it back to the stern cockpit, then joined the owner on the flybridge. A Harbor Police vessel arrived just as Ted pulled us out of danger.

"You OK? I'm Jake Mortensen," I said, patting the chubby man on the shoulder as I climbed from the ladder to a seat behind him on the bridge.

"Name's Monty Banks. I don't know how to thank you guys."

"Everything all right back there?" It was Ted on the VHF. Monty picked up the microphone.

"We're just fine here. How's Elaine?"

"She's going to be all right." We could see her in the passenger seat, bundled up in the sleeping bag. "She needs medical attention. Where do you want us to take you?" Ted was all business.

"Slip C-15 at San Diego Yacht club. I'll call ahead on my cell phone to get a doctor to meet us." I took the helm, while Monty went below. With his large girth, I was amazed he could manage the narrow ladder from the flybridge down to the aft cockpit.

Ted went on the VHF again, with the Coast Guard and Harbor Police. Both agencies wanted to know if they could cancel the mayday; Ted confirmed the emergency was over and filled them in on what had happened. He thanked the Harbor Police who were still standing by and informed them he was towing *Elaine II* to San Diego Yacht Club (SDYC), where a report would be filed. The Coast Guard thanked Ted and signed off. After he directed me to change radio frequency to VHF 18-alpha, Ted called his operations center.

"Ops Center, This is *YachtTow I*."

"Ops Center, here. Roger, *YachtTow I*. Sounds like you guys have been busy. Go ahead," came back the cheery voice of Ted's dispatch gal.

"Good afternoon, Betty. Yes, we have the vessel *Elaine II*, a thirty-five-foot Bayliner, in tow. Final destination: SDYC."

"Roger dodger, Ted. The vessel is registered with us. Monty and Elaine Banks. Nice couple. Just bought a membership. New boat."

"Thanks, Betty. Jake, you listening?"

"Roger. Jake, here."

"Jake, when we get near Ballast Point, I want to tighten up the tow."

"Roger, Ted. I'll stand by on 18-alpha. You tell me when."

Ted towed us through the kelp and into the main channel to San Diego Bay. He put out a call on VHF Channel 16, alerting all vessels of our in-tow status. As we approached the lee of Point Loma, the water flattened out. Ted throttled back in front of Ballast Point so I could shorten the towline. We continued up the main channel, turning to port at the end of Shelter Island, and reduced our speed even more as we passed the Harbor Police docks. The officers who had responded to the distress call waved as they tied up their vessel.

"*Elaine II*, *YachtTow I*." Ted was back on the air.

"*YachtTow I*, *Elaine II*. Go ahead, Ted."

As we passed Southwestern Yacht Club and approached the SDYC docks, both boats slowed, almost stopping mid-channel.

"Jake, I'm going to release the towline and come along your port side. Put fenders over the rail and get ready to tie up."

"Roger."

With Monty at the helm, I went down the ladder and toward the bow, kicking fenders over the side. Ted untied the line from his towing post; I hauled it in and coiled it on the foredeck. Monty found the dock lines and handed them forward. Within minutes the two vessels were tied together.

Ted maneuvered us down one of the many rows of boats fronting the Yacht Club. Several curious observers lined the dock, waiting to help. Both boats stopped in front of an empty slip, and I cast the bitter end of our towline to someone on the finger dock. Untied, we let the people on the dock pull *Elaine II* in, while Ted backed his vessel into a nearby vacant slip before coming over to assist.

Once *Elaine II* was secured, Monty went to check on his wife, with Ted and me following. A tall, white-haired man had boarded *YachtTow I* to attend to her. Elaine was still in the sleeping bag.

"John . . . how is she?" Monty asked.

"Little bit of hypothermia, but she's going to be just fine," John responded. A gentle, distinguished-looking man, John was SDYC's fleet surgeon. He'd been eating lunch at the marina when Monty called. "We need to keep elevating her body temperature with lots of hot liquids and a warm bath. Let's use the Jacuzzi at the pool."

Ted and I helped Monty take Elaine off the boat by locking our hands in a fireman's carry and toting her up the gangway. Monty returned to his boat and grabbed the seabag with her clothing. At the pool enclosure, her female friends took over; Ted, Monty, and I were no longer needed.

"Jake, why don't you two join me on the club patio for something to eat? I could use a drink."

"Sounds good, Mr. Banks. Give us about a half-hour. We need to secure our vessel," I replied, shaking his hand. "And I've got to get out of this wetsuit."

"Also, sir, you'll need to fill out some paperwork. Would it be better to do that at the club?" Ted remained businesslike.

"Please, call me Monty. I've got to clean up a bit, too. Let's make it an hour. If I'm not there when you arrive, just use my name and order whatever you want."

Monty shook Ted's hand and we started back to C-dock. People were still standing in front of the disabled boat, piecing together versions of what had happened. Ted abhorred Monday morning quarterbacks and, without a word, climbed on *YachtTow I* and fired up both engines. People nearby tried to ask questions as I used a dock hose to flush saltwater off my dive gear and myself before boarding. I suggested they talk to Monty.

As we motored past *Elaine II*, the crowd on the docks waved to us. I felt good inside; today my knowledge and skills had actually helped someone. Most of my SAR training in the Navy had been used to pick up missile casings and spent torpedoes, instead of saving people. Maybe going to work for Ted's company was a good idea after all.

"*YachtTow I* to Ops," Ted called Betty on the VHF radio.

"Ops to *YachtTow I*. How ya doin', guys?"

"Fine. We've delivered *Elaine II* to SDYC. If there's nothing else for us, we're coming in."

"Nothing else, Ted. Come on home."

We idled up the main channel and turned into the gap between Shelter and Harbor Islands. Taking the shoal buoy to port, we headed toward Commercial Basin, where flame-haired Betty greeted us at the dock.

"You got my paperwork?"

"Nope. We have to go back to the Yacht Club for it." Ted started hosing down the boat.

"Oh, poor babies!"

Ted said he'd finish putting the boat away. I draped my wetsuit over the transom to dry, grabbed my bag, and headed for the ramp-top restrooms and a hot shower.

Forty minutes later, we piled into Van Gogh, my VW Baja Bug, and set out for the Yacht Club at the base of Point Loma. Poor old Van Gogh—I had bought the car two years ago from a boat maintenance friend who had built the custom fiberglass body on a 1965 Volkswagen Beetle chassis. It had a souped-up engine with dual carbs, a hot cam, special heads, and a stinger exhaust. The wheel wells were modified to accommodate wide beach tires, and there were no doors, just rounded fenders that you had to step over. During construction, my friend claimed he found a cat's ear stuck to the generator pulley, hence the name. He liked the moniker and had pinstriped it on the rear fenders to show off his artistic bent.

When we arrived at the San Diego Yacht Club gate, the guard handed us guest passes. Despite everything else on his mind, Monty had alerted staff we were coming. I was impressed.

Since 1924, SDYC has been one of the driving forces in West Coast yachting. Architecturally, the main building reminded me of Coronado Peninsula's famous, old Hotel Del Coronado, with a pitched shingled roof, small dormer windows, and a widow's walk. In a way, the whole thing was like a country club, the difference being that boat slips replace fairways and putting greens—to be exact, 650 slips, plus land-based dry storage for 160 others. Internationally renowned, the club's year-round racing calendar and Junior Sailing Program have brought competitors from as far away as New Zealand and Europe.

Most yacht clubs are snobby, but the few times I have visited this club, I've always felt warmly welcomed and completely comfortable. Ted had been here many times before. I had only visited for awards ceremonies, after crewing in sailboat races from Marina del Rey or Long Beach.

The entry corridor with its polished wood deck was lined floor to ceiling with half-models of members' racing yachts. Ted pointed out the trophy alcove where the America's Cup was displayed in an alarmed glass case. The surrounding area was roped off. I just had to stop.

In awe, and remembering the story, I knew I was looking at a very special piece of history. Originally "The Royal Yacht Squadron Hundred Guinea Cup," it became known as the "America's Cup" when the ninety-five-foot schooner *America* won it in 1851—incredible when you think about it. This was not just any old, silver sporting cup. Seventy-five years after the United States fought Britain for independence, we sent a vessel to race around the Isle of Wight and proved, once and for all, we were masters of the sea. In a sense, the America's Cup became a symbol of New World sailing prowess over the Old World. The majestic silver trophy was truly beautiful.

Mr. Banks was not in the cocktail lounge or on the patio.

"The Russians are going to compete, whether we like it or not," I overheard from a stocky, casually attired man sitting beneath an umbrella in a corner of the patio deck. Waving his hand to emphasize his argument, he revealed a diamond-studded Rolex and gold wristband in an obvious display of wealth. It seemed to punctuate the rather lively conversation he was having with two other men. I could only catch bits and pieces, but they were talking about the Russian America's Cup entry and its financial problems. I wanted to hear more, so Ted and I sat down at an empty table several umbrellas away. When a steward came to take our order, we showed him our guest cards.

"You're here with Mr. Banks? Welcome! Yes, he called. He said to tell you he'd be about fifteen minutes late. Can I get you something from the bar?"

The waiter placed white cocktail napkins, embossed in red and blue with the club's pennant and latitude and longitude. Ted ordered a Corona, while I stuck to my usual, a Meyers and Coke.

I had followed the America's Cup event in the sailing magazines for years. SDYC gained prominence in world yachting circles when it recaptured the Cup in 1987—this after the Australians ended the 132-year reign of the New York Yacht Club by taking the trophy Down Under in 1983. San Diego then successfully pitted Dennis Connors and a catamaran against a mega-yacht challenge from New Zealand's Michael Fay in 1988. When SDYC hosted the event again in 1992—and Bill Koch won with *America3*—it became obvious to the yachting world that San Diego Yacht Club was a power to be reckoned with.

"If we don't help the Russians financially, we lose a tremendous political opportunity," the man said, still trying to make his point. "Even if you don't think they'll race well in the Louis Vuitton competition, we ought to ensure they at least get the chance to compete!"

"Why? Just tell me why! You're talking big bucks, Peter, and I want *our* team to win. I'll put my money on Dennis, or even the girls if I have to." The second man was older and wearing a blue blazer, white pants, and tie.

"Listen, I've seen the Russians' hull. They've installed a fore-and-aft rudder system similar to the one Tom Blackaller was working on before he died. And the wing keel is articulated with fully adjustable trim tabs."

"You've got to be kidding, Peter. Where would Russki builders get that kind of engineering? They don't know anything about this type of racing sailboat. Us . . . Australia, New Zealand, Italy, and maybe the Japanese . . . but not the Russians. Give me a break."

"I'm telling you! Elvström has built four sets of racing sails in Saint Petersburg. Borrowed some shaping technology from North that'll put other sail makers to shame. All we've got to do is come up with the money to get the sails here in time and help with the other expenses."

"You must be smoking something, Peter. It's crazy. The Russians can't possibly be a threat," the younger man at the table finally got a word in.

"In the name of Corinthian Yachting, you guys, let's help them financially and find out!" On a roll, the man called Peter Hammer continued to pitch his two listeners. "You know I'm right! Because of Yeltsin's politics, rubles earmarked for the *Age of Russia* sailing program got diverted to deal with domestic problems."

"How much?" It was the older, yachty guy again.

"Six million to do it right."

"Whew! I don't know. You're talking a lot of money, and I can't see any benefit to the donor. Maybe a tax write-off and some publicity. If it's set up right."

"Trust me, it's been set up right. I had the best tax lawyer in San Diego do it. I've already put in $500,000. Here are the papers. See for yourself."

"Who is this trustee, Leonard Sleak?"

"A businessman in La Jolla, land developer. I've known him for years—he bought my old sailboat, *Shore Loser*, when I decided to switch to power and purchase *Broad Jumper*. Honorable guy, his family's been in the area for three generations. Old wealth."

The debate rambled on, as our drinks arrived almost simultaneously with our host and his wife. She looked considerably better than two hours ago, when Ted and I had carried her up the ramp. Her hair was salon fresh, her outfit—ivory slacks and soft blue, cable-knit sweater emblazoned with gold anchors—elegant. Mr. Banks had cleaned up his act, too, but the effect wasn't quite the same. In white trousers and an unbuttoned blue blazer exposing his belly, he still had that Dough Boy look. But the crest and nametag on his jacket told us he was a V.I.P. in the club. Ted and I stood in greeting.

"Here is the lady you saved—the love of my life, Elaine. Please, sit down, boys. Meet your rescuers, dear: Jake and Ted." Monty slid a chair out for his wife and ordered cocktails.

"I can't thank you both enough. I thought I was a goner!" she said, with a tentative laugh.

"How you feeling now?" I asked.

"A little weak, but I'm OK. Looks like Monty and I were not supposed to go to Catalina this weekend."

Monty Banks explained that he and his wife had been on their way to Avalon. Some friends had lent them a mooring for three days, and this was to have been their first long trip on *Elaine II*. It was also to have been a getaway before the holidays and the America's Cup madness. Monty had misjudged the kelp beds off Point Loma and hit dense growth just as the throttles had been accelerated to twenty-five knots; the kelp became entangled in the props, and the shaft coupling bolts sheared off at the V-drives. Elaine was climbing the bridge ladder when the boat stopped abruptly, loosening her grip. Tossed overboard, she landed about fifteen feet starboard of the vessel. Knowing she wasn't a strong swimmer, Monty threw her a buoy. While he struggled to set anchor, Elaine tried to paddle back to the boat. When she got entangled in kelp, she panicked. She had been in the water almost an hour before she was rescued.

Ted jotted notes as Monty related the story. "I think I've got it all. Would you, please, check this report? Could you add your vessel information and complete the blanks I've marked?" Ted handed his pen and report across the table. Sometimes he was so businesslike he was no fun to be around.

"If you need a diver to check the shafts and propellers, I'm available tomorrow," I volunteered, hoping to lighten things up.

"Didn't know YachtTow did that kind of stuff," Monty said, as he ordered another round of drinks and requested menus. "Anybody hungry?"

I explained that I had just mustered out of the Navy and was working on a trial basis, part time, for YachtTow, and I tried to supplement my income by diving. Monty seemed interested. In addition to being a yacht club officer, we learned he was also a manager in the vessel mortgage division at First Interstate Bank.

"I'm impressed with the way you handle yourself, Jake. Are you a Coast Guard licensed captain?" He handed the paperwork back to Ted.

"Yes, sir, Master 100-gross ton," I replied, not revealing that I had just obtained the license.

"Well, this is interesting. Yes, I want you to dive and check out my boat tomorrow. But I may have another proposition for you, one I am sure you may find a bit unusual. Do you speak any Spanish?"

"A little. Mostly cusswords I learned from a Chicano friend in the Navy," I laughed.

We set a time to meet. Elaine recognized someone and excused herself, while we continued our discussion. In the background, the voices at the negotiation table droned on, as Peter Hammer tried to convince his friends to support the Russians. But what Monty had to say next got my complete attention.

"Several years ago, First Interstate made a bad loan on a big sailing yacht. We filed all the necessary documents and threatened repossession. The owner, a corporation, is still ignoring us. Since the boat is in La Paz, Mexico, I think they feel we won't spend the money to go get it. I've called everyone on my list of repo captains—nobody wants to do it, because the boat is in foreign waters. And besides, they are all busy." He was looking at me, trying to gauge my reaction. "You interested?"

"Of course, I'm interested," I responded without hesitation. "I'm pretty familiar with the Baja. My father and I used to spend a lot of time down there on his sailboat before I went into the Navy. But I wouldn't know what to charge for the job."

"I can help you with that. We'll agree on a daily rate for you and your crew, and you do it on a time-and-expense basis. Think about it." Monty was smiling. Like a fisherman, he'd set the hook. "I'll pull some information together and we'll discuss it further tomorrow."

"When do you want me at your boat?"

"How about 10 o'clock?"

"I'll be there."

Elaine's timing was uncanny, returning just as the waiter brought our food. With Monty's business chat over, she became more animated and conversational. Although they both seemed young, she had mastered the role of an executive's wife. The topics she introduced were intelligent, her opinions thoughtful, and she was very careful not to upstage her husband. On the contrary, she promoted him by conveying the feeling that he was powerful and in charge. Her obvious adoration struck me as bizarre. After all, this pudgy little guy had not only damaged their brand-new boat, he had also almost killed her. I was beginning to understand Ted's feelings when he made jokes about recreational boaters.

When I got home, the first thing I did was phone my father. His opinions were always right on the mark, and I wanted to hear how he felt about his son becoming a repo captain.

"You got to do it, Jake. It vill be good for da soul, clear da head, give you a new perspective on tings. I vish I vere able to go vit you."

"Dad, why don't you? I'd love it!"

"Vell ... dere is dis lady I haff been seeing ... Hilga. Kinda reminds me of your Ma. Met her at a Sons of Norway dinner. Pretty. You vould like her. Ve are vorking togeter on da Yuledag Committee."

"Seriously?"

"Nah, ve're yust on da committee. And ve are yust friends."

"Well, OK, if you say so." I decided not to press the issue.

Saturday morning I carted all my dive equipment over to the Yacht Club. When I got there, Monty was at his boat talking to his mechanic, Greg, who had reconnected the propeller shafts and cleaned chunks of waste out of the raw-water strainers. He didn't want to run the engines until I checked out everything below the waterline. The prop shafts were difficult to rotate by hand, and he was certain they were fouled.

It was a good thing Greg waited, because the propellers were totally ensnared. I had to exert a lot of energy to cut away the rubbery branches wound around the shafts and jammed up against the struts and cutlass bearings. I wondered if Revlon really paid good money for this stuff. It completely filled two dock carts. When everything was cleared and I could inspect them, the bronze propellers and stainless steel shafts appeared undamaged. I gave the word and Greg fired the engines. They sounded healthy.

"Let's take her for a test run," Greg said to Monty. "If anything is damaged, we'll notice a vibration."

"You got the time, Jake?" Monty asked.

"Sure, if it's not too long. I've got a very important appointment I can't miss later this afternoon," I replied. "Just give me a minute to rinse off my stuff."

Finished with squaring away my dive gear, I released the dock lines and jumped on board *Elaine II,* still in my wetsuit. Monty was at the helm, and it surprised me to see him maneuver his vessel reasonably well in close quarters. I began to modify my opinion about his boat handling.

Once we were in the main channel and past Ballast Point, he pushed the throttles forward. Not wanting to go near the kelp again, he steered for the outer entrance buoy and pushed the vessel up to twenty-five knots. Greg remained aft in the cockpit, listening to the engines. There was no detectable vibration and everything sounded normal. After a wide turn around the buoy, we came back in.

Greg and I held our breath and tended the fenders when Monty failed to reduce speed as he turned into his slip. Neither of us said anything when a portion of the bow scraped the dock. I reverted to my initial impression of Monty Banks' seamanship—his skippering skills definitely needed work. He apologized for the sloppy docking maneuver and said he'd meet me at the bar after I cleaned up. I left him to finish with Greg, while I hauled my gear up to the parking lot, showered, and changed.

When I got to the club lounge, it was brimming with sailors who'd just finished a day racing Etchels, Solings, and Stars. They were awaiting the outcome of protest hearings and posting of race results. Some of Southern California's most competitive racers were in the crowd—Dennis Conner, J.J. Isler, Dave Ullman, Bruce Nelson, and others I had seen only in sailing magazines. The remarkable mix of sail makers, semi-professional sailors, and boat designers were enthusiastically reliving the tactics, wind-shifts and mark roundings of the afternoon. It was intimidating and invigorating at the same time—something I missed while in the Navy. Nostalgia set in as I recalled the good times I had growing up racing Sabots and Lasers in the junior program at Long Beach Yacht Club. Reluctantly, I left the group in the lounge and found Monty out on the patio, where it was quieter.

"The bar's full of rock stars!" I said as I sat down.

"Oh, that's just the usual bunch, including Dennis. We have some older Cruising Club members who barely tolerate this group. They only give in because racing is so tied to the history of this club." He was frowning. "Wait until the rest of the America's Cup crowd gets here. I understand some of them are real prima donnas."

Monty paid me for inspecting his boat and shifted the conversation to the job in Mexico. He suggested I charge a daily rate of $300. First Interstate would pay all expenses, plus a bonus of $1,000 if the boat arrived in San Diego undamaged.

" I'm gonna need airfare and $5,000 up front, and how dangerous is this?"

"Should be just a normal sail back up the Baja. We've been in contact with the marina where it's berthed, and they are expecting us to send a captain down. The advance money is no problem. Of course, I'll need you to turn in receipts for everything."

"OK, I'm your guy."

"When do you think you can you leave?"

"I've got to get a crew together. Easiest would be to fly to La Paz and do it over Christmas vacation."

Monty said he would have his secretary draw up the agreement, and it would be ready for a meeting the first week in December. We shook hands, and I headed for the late-afternoon appointment I'd been dreading, the one I'd been putting off for so long.

CHAPTER TWO

# THE NAVY

"Anna, I'm really sorry . . ." I said, uttering empty words, words that couldn't change anything.

The memorial service had been a month ago, and I'd procrastinated since, hoping to muster up enough emotional fortitude for this moment. Anna was holding me tightly, her body trembling. She was whimpering, sucking in air and letting it out in broken moaning sounds. Her husband, Wally Oleson, Petty Officer First Class, was dead. Nothing I could do or say would bring him back. A big Scandinavian from Minnesota—the father of her unborn child, my best friend—dead. I still couldn't believe it.

He was one of those individuals everyone liked. That was obvious when his funeral was held in the Navy's military cemetery on the upper south side of Point Loma. All personnel from Anti-Submarine Warfare Group 35 and Helicopter Squadron 451 were there to bury him with military honors. Anna had asked me to be a pallbearer, tough duty for me because he and I had been such good friends. As I held Anna, the ceremony came flooding back. I felt detached, like I was watching a wide-screen movie rerun through my mind.

⌘ ⌘

From high atop Point Loma, the midday view of San Diego bay was vibrant and crisp, as were the smell of ocean air and the call of sea birds in the distance. A casket draped with a large American flag waited before the open grave, where over eighty Navy personnel in Dress Whites stood at parade rest while a lone bugler played *Taps*. Rifle fire reverberated in the distance as the coffin was lowered into the earth. Then the color guard, in traditional Crackerjack Dress Blues, folded the ensign and transferred it to the honor guard, the casings from the salute tucked into the folds. I will never forget the stoic look in Anna's steel-blue eyes as she accepted the small triangular package.

The accident had been senseless. Four good men lost their lives at San Clemente Island, sixty nautical miles northwest of San Diego. Navy brass labeled it "pilot error" in the press releases, but the rank and file knew differently. There hadn't been enough preparation time before the fleet was ordered to converge on the island for maneuvers.

Two aircraft carriers, *Kitty Hawk* and *Constellation,* had steamed out of San Diego harbor that foggy October morning, accompanied by three surface combat vessels, *Lake Champlain, Princeton,* and *Shiloh.* Why put so many lives in danger? This was 1994—the Cold War was over; Russia was falling apart. Why were Navy aircraft dispatched to fly low over the surrounding waters? We'd heard the rumors before, Navy pilots functioning as Coast Guard drug spotters while engaged in "war games."

Why deploy so much naval hardware? To show the Secretary of Defense that the Pacific Fleet was prepared? No, it was all a bunch of crap—bureaucratic stupidity. The real reason was this was a different kind of war maneuver, a different kind of game—this was part of the government's "war on drugs."

Drug interdiction killed Wally.

ඏ ඔ

Stroking her long blond hair, I felt Anna's tears soaking through my shirt. At barely five feet tall, she looked defeated and vulnerable in her loose-fitting maternity dress.

We embraced awkwardly in the doorway of her small apartment, a converted garage behind one of the old, two-story Carpenter Gothic houses on the Coronado Peninsula. Wally rented it when they married because it was close to North Island Naval Air Station. It was an incredible find, since almost everything on Coronado is way too expensive for an enlisted man's budget. Along with some of the other guys from HS-451, I had helped them move in just after their wedding less than a year ago. Wally was proud of the way Anna had fixed it up with "a touch of Norway," as he put it. Flower boxes adorned the windows and front porch. She had even reupholstered their secondhand furniture in tasteful blends of texture and color. They were very much in love and so happy together.

Their landlords, a retired naval officer and his wife, lived in the larger house in front. They seemed to enjoy having young people around and always showed up at Wally's monthly barbecue and beer-drinking session. It had become an after-payday ritual we all looked forward to, held on the lawn between Wally's place and the big house.

Why did he have to die? Damn it! It just wasn't fair.

As Anna wept, more disturbing images crept into my mind. I had been in the Operations building when HS-451 got the call.

ඏ ඔ

Flying over the site, it was terrible. His aircraft had been an S-3B Viking with a crew of four. The pilot lost orientation in fog, had engine trouble, and decided to ditch into the briny deep. For the longest time, the plane flew low, almost upside down. When the crew ejected, they exploded directly into the water, the impact killing everyone. Our assignment was to fly out and retrieve the bodies.

Wearing full search-and-rescue gear, two of us jumped from the chopper into the middle of the debris site. There was an oily, foul-smelling, jet-fuel slick, and junk floating everywhere. Prop wash from the helicopter hovering overhead was kicking up the sea. Saltwater foam and trash flew all around us, mixed in with aircraft rubble were chunks of flight suits containing mangled pieces of flesh. Something I thought was an airplane part caught my eye. It turned out to be a leg so broken it didn't look human. It had a tattoo—crossed anchors and wings.

Suddenly, I vomited all over my face gear. I knew that tattoo. I had helped Wally get it. The turbulent seas and churning carnage around me, whipped to a frenzy by the chopper blades, didn't help. I swallowed back the bile. By the time they pulled me out of the water, I'd decided this was *not* something I wanted to do. My days with the Navy were numbered.

෴ ෨෨

Now, he was gone and Anna's future shattered. Twenty-five years of life had not prepared me to comfort a woman under this kind of circumstance. Embraces were always a preamble to satisfying primal urges. I couldn't even remember what being held by my mother felt like, she died when I was so young.

I'm not especially religious, but any belief I might have had in a "Greater Power" was being seriously tested. Why would God, or our government for that matter, let something like this happen? What should I do or say? Here was a woman whose world had just been blown apart. She and I both knew he was dead and gone—that fact was not going to change.

"Anna, you need anything, any kind of help, please, call me," I said, searching for the right words. "You've got lots of friends. Don't feel you're alone." Attempting to divert her thoughts from Wally, if just for a moment, I asked, "When's the baby due?"

"In two months," she whispered, her reddened eyes searching mine. "Jake . . . sweet Jake, you're such a dear. I'm really glad you came by." Regaining her composure, she took two shuddering gasps for air and stepped away. Feeling like a klutz, I kissed her cheek.

"I've kept everything bottled up since the funeral. I needed to let it out," she said, sensing my awkwardness. "Just having you here has been a real help."

"That's not all you've got bottled up," I joked.

"Hope it's a boy," she said. "I just might name him Jacob. Wally would like that."

"Promise you'll call me if you need something?"

"Yes . . . I will, Jake. I promise."

With a start, I realized we hadn't moved from the open doorway for more than an hour. Pausing on the step outside, and watching as she closed the door, I caught myself holding my breath. Consoling her was one of the hardest things I've ever had to do.

As I passed the ornate verandah of the main house, a deep voice called out. It was the landlord, a big man with dignified bearing whom I knew and liked from Wally's barbecues.

"Petty Officer Mortensen, how is Anna holding up?" he asked. His matronly wife, her eyes filled with concern, was standing beside him, holding his arm. I was surprised he remembered my name. He obviously didn't know I'd quit the Navy.

"She's going to be OK, sir," I responded, almost saluting. "She had a good cry and let it all out. Even though she's a strong woman, she's gonna need help. Her parents live near Wally's, in Saint Claire, Minnesota, so I think she plans to go back there to have the baby."

"Henry, I should have a visit with her tomorrow." This woman was not like any of the self-important officer's wives I had encountered. "I think I'll bake some cookies and take them with me, as an excuse."

"Please, don't think you need an excuse, ma'am. But the cookies would be a nice gesture. I'm sure she'll appreciate it." I turned to her husband. "Sir, let me give you my phone number, in case you need to contact me. I care about her very much. Got to know Wally pretty well when we went through Anti-Submarine Warfare School together in Pensacola. Even got tattooed at the same time."

"I'm sorry you lost your friend, Mortensen. But we all know the risks when we sign up."

"Yes, sir," I replied, not wanting to get into a discussion about the difference between peacetime accidents and wartime casualties. We shook hands. "Please, keep an eye on Anna and call me if you think she needs anything. She's got a lot of difficult decisions to make."

As I drove away in my Baja Bug, twilight was descending on the peninsula, and the autumn air was heavy with cool ocean fog. Ornate street lamps blazed on one after the other, like small aerial explosions. Stopping before the one-way onto Coronado Bridge, I pulled into a gas station to use the payphone.

My stomach told me it was past feeding time, and I had promised to meet Ted Blithe for dinner at the Red Sails Inn on Shelter Island. His girlfriend, Jill, was going to introduce me to a friend from work.

Someone had ripped off the phone book from the booth, forcing me to pay for a call to Information—what an annoyance! The meeting with Anna had left me edgy. I deposited more coins and dialed the restaurant.

"Good evening, Red Sails Inn." I recognized the voice of the chubby Hawaiian waitress.

"Hello, Shina. Is Captain Blithe, the YachtTow guy, there? He may have two women with him."

"Two *pretty* women? Better get here soon, fella. You're missing out. He's sitting at the bar with a big grin on his face. Want to talk to him?"

"Don't need to. Tell him Jake Mortensen called and I'll be there in twenty minutes. Thanks, Shina."

The party had started without me—again.

I returned to Van Gogh. After I took possession, I installed a killer stereo system, halogen spots, and two chrome roll bars padded to carry surfboards. Behind the molded plastic bucket seats, I added brackets to tie down an ice chest or scuba gear. It was perfect for the beach. Wet bathing suits, dive tanks, and sand couldn't hurt it. All I had to do was hose it out. Except for the removable yellow canvas top, Van Gogh was navy blue, with a variety of surfing and sailing decals all over its oxidized body.

The vehicle did have one irritating disadvantage: when the damp coastal marine layer rolled in, the plastic seats got very wet. The gas station had no paper towels at the pump islands, and the toilets were locked. Brushing away as much moisture as I could with my hands, I sat down and turned the key in the ignition. I couldn't believe it. Ted was going to introduce me to two pretty ladies, and I had a wet posterior.

Out of time and patience, I navigated as fast as conditions would allow, over the Coronado Bridge and onto I-5 North, looking for the "Cruise Ships Use Next Exit" sign. Already late, I didn't have an extra thirty minutes to go home and change. Ted and the girls were going to be several drinks ahead of me, as it was.

Twenty minutes later, I parked, locked the stereo faceplate in the glove box, and climbed over the fender. The seat of my pants was soaked.

"This is *not* going to be good," I mumbled out loud, as I walked through the mist toward the restaurant. I opened the heavy wooden door and made my way through the bar, toward the two dining rooms filled with an intriguing mix of Point Loma old wealth, yacht club new wealth, shipyard workers, and boat technicians. Waitresses, clad in white shorts and red shirts with "Get Your Ship Together" on the back, ran to and from the kitchen or chatted with diners. Most of the customers were regulars.

"They're outside on the patio," Shina announced, as I squeezed past her into the second dining room. "How'd you get your buns wet, kiddo?" she asked, slapping the seat of my shorts with her stack of menus.

"Is it that noticeable?" I knew her comment was made in fun, but it made me even more irritable.

It was a busy Saturday night and all the tables were occupied. I spotted Ted and the two women seated on the far side of the deck, their table in front of the wall with a sea-life mural.

"Glad you made it," Ted said, standing. "How's Anna?"

"Much better. I think she'll be all right. The people she rents from are keeping an eye on her. Sorry I didn't have time to change."

"Hey, squid! You sit in something or you take a dump in your shorts?" a booming voice, like a drill sergeant, came from an adjacent table filled with marines on leave from Camp Pendleton.

"Ignore him. He and his buddies are drunk. Hello, my name is Toey—Toey Wong." Still sitting, she held out her slender hand. "Ted told us what you had to do this afternoon. I am so sorry. I bet it was really difficult."

"Hello, Toey. Hi, Jill, Ted." Shaking Toey's hand, I pulled out a canvas deck chair and sat down. "I think I need a drink."

"Meyers and Coke?" Ted asked, motioning to the waitress.

I didn't know whether to be mad at the obnoxious dumbo at the next table or happy at being introduced to Toey. Shina was right: Both women were beautiful. I had met Jill Dilly, Ted's main squeeze, several times before. She was visiting at the Pacific Beach house when I moved in, and I'd also seen her at surf parties a couple of times during the summer. In Ted's words, she was a "Three-B": blond, beautiful, and bad. She filled out a bathing suit in all the right places and was an accomplished surfer. Conversation with her was a little distracting—she talked like a "valley girl"—but, otherwise, I liked her.

Now, Toey—what a knockout! Olive complexion and freckles, she looked Eurasian. Her hair was black, straight, and pixie short. She had beautiful mahogany-brown eyes, an impish smile, and all five feet two inches of her was gorgeous. She was wearing a light-green golf shirt with a small Alameda Yacht Club burgee where you might expect an alligator. Her shorts were loose-fitting and white, her body an athletic build amply endowed above the waist. She sat with her back straight, which emphasized her chest even more—she was at least a 34-C on the mammary scale. I definitely wanted to get to know her better.

"Here, this'll get you started." Ted motioned to the waitress, who was behind me with my rum and Coke. "We better order some dinner before the rest of us get plastered."

I was almost beyond eating. We selected from the menu, and I ordered another drink. Maybe getting smashed would distract me from unhappy thoughts for a while.

Ted directed the dinner conversation toward small talk about sailing and surfing. Making fun of himself and calling on his YachtTow experiences for laughs, he even got into some of the stupid things recreational boaters do. When he wasn't trying to be businesslike, he was actually fun to be around. It surprised me he didn't mention the rescue we'd just participated in. I would have told the story just to impress the women.

When he didn't say anything about it, I decided to keep quiet about my deal with Monty and my upcoming boat repo job in Mexico. The conversation I'd overheard about the plight of the Russian boat was also bugging me. The whole afternoon was bugging me, so I clammed up, concentrated on Toey's good looks, and just listened.

I learned Jill and Toey were both teachers at a private school in University Park. Jill's subjects were social studies and phys-ed. Toey taught Spanish and marine biology. They were almost halfway through the fall semester and talked about how to keep their students challenged. The light conversation and laughter made me begin to feel there was hope for the evening.

We had almost finished eating when the Marine acted up again. I've always had a dislike for the Marines. It started when I was a teenager, growing up in Southern California, long before I joined the Navy. It goes back to the stories my father told me of how the Camp Pendleton brass tried to keep surfers from using San Onofre and Trestles, located between Nixon's "Western White House" and the Marine base, arguably the best surfing spots in South Orange County. Of course, the government claimed the surfers were a security risk. Dad and his friends suspected the officers wanted to preserve the beaches for their own use.

"Hey, china doll! Why don'ja come over here and spend time with some real men?" Now he was *really* smashed, and his buddies were trying to quiet him down. "Got some USDA grade sausage I'd like to show ya."

More drinks came: fruit juice for the ladies, Mexican beer for Ted, and another rum and Coke for me. I was beginning to get a buzz on, and the Marine's behavior was becoming increasingly irritating.

"Shit! Bet I can show ya a better time than that squid," he bellowed, staggering to his feet. I couldn't believe it! He was coming over to our table. "Did'ja see the tattoo on his leg? Crossed flippers with an anchor—gimme a break! How about it, china doll? Wanna see a real man's tattoo?"

"This is *not* going to be good!" I said to myself.

He put his big hands on the back of Toey's chair to steady himself. When I saw how terrified she looked, I lost it.

"Get your mitts off her, you stupid jarhead!" I shouted, my chair falling over as I stood up. My damp shorts had stuck to the canvas seat.

The Marine straightened to his full six feet, his muscular chest covered in a gray t-shirt bearing the gold USMC emblem and the words "Pain Is Weakness Leaving The Body." His pants were green and khaki camouflage, like GI Joe's, with lots of pockets.

All around me, there was yelling and screaming and the scraping of tables being moved. From the corner of my eye, I saw women trying to pull their male companions out of harm's way. Some of the men held their ground, anticipating a show, hoping for the blood and gore that might follow. Waitresses and bus boys scurried to remove anything breakable.

This was exactly what the leatherneck was angling for, a fight to show off what he'd learned in boot camp. Wanting in the worst way to wipe the smirk off his face, I planted a right hook alongside his jaw, followed by my left fist to his belly. He grinned and looked surprised, rather than hurt. Whereas my Navy SAR training had put me in good condition to save lives, his Marine combat training kept him in shape to end them.

We did an awkward little dance, shuffling around, punching and jabbing, trying to discover where the other was most vulnerable. Finally, impatient with the sparring, he lunged. I reacted with a lightning-bolt knee lift to the groin, just before his fist sledgehammered into the side of my face.

The momentum of his punch thrusting all 230 pounds at me, gravity took over, my back slamming against the deck. I rolled out of his path and stood up just as his knees crashed into the planking. Doubled over, head down, he clutched his privates.

It took all my strength to swing my hands, clenched together, from between my legs, upward against the underside of his jaw. The crunch of bone against bone told me I'd hurt him big time. In obvious agony, he rose, his eyes squeezed nearly shut in concentration. I thought I heard Toey screaming as his blood-splattered fists pummeled my ribcage in a blind rage.

Somehow, I landed several more jabs to his face. It may have been my imagination, but his chin felt squishy, and I know I saw red pumping out of his nose as Ted and the Marines pulled us apart. Then, I lost consciousness.

CHAPTER THREE

# TATTOO

"Do you feel like some breakfast?" Toey asked softly. "It is Sunday morning. Come on, Jake, do you feel like getting up?"

Bright sunlight filtered through the gray and peach, floral living room drapes, hurting my eyes when I tried to open them. My head was throbbing, I think more from a hangover than from the fight. My chest and ribs were sore.

There was a sheet under me and a cuddly blanket on top. All I had on was my underwear. As I tried to sit up, I noticed the knuckles of each hand were wrapped with gauze. A large cloth bandage was taped above my left eye.

"How'd I end up on your couch?" I asked. "This isn't at all what I had in mind when we met last night."

"You were in no condition to do anything else," she giggled. "Here, let me put something on that bruise."

Her hair was neatly wrapped in a white towel. Sitting beside me, she held an ice pack against my left cheekbone. The cold felt good and seemed to reduce the pulsating in my head.

A red robe with black symbols and gold embroidery only somewhat concealed her contours. She smelled wonderful, as if she had just taken a bubble bath. As she leaned toward me, two erect nipples exposed themselves for a second, before retreating behind the silken material. I wanted to reach out and touch her as she tended to my wounds, but my hands were all wrapped up. What if I just lowered my head and nestled it in her bosom?

"That obnoxious Marine was trying to kill you!" Realizing I might have observed too much, she pulled her robe tight and stood. "You messed his jaw up pretty good."

"How'd I get here?" I repeated. Positioning the ice on top of my head with one hand, I pulled the blanket onto my lap with the other to cover the effect she was having on me.

"Ted and Jill helped me put you into your car," she replied, delighted by my predicament. "I live just up the street from the Red Sails. We had to get you out before the police and MPs got there. Thank goodness, the manager and waitresses know us and helped."

I fidgeted and listened in silence.

"Ted felt it best to bring you right to my place. Jill and I drove you here, while he stayed behind to pay the bill and leave his name and phone number with the manager, in case there was any damage. Not long after we left, the MPs arrived and hauled off Mister Ugly."

She took a deep breath and continued. "Ted got here as quickly as he could and carried you up the stairs to my couch. We did not know whether you were really hurt, or drunk, or both. He checked you out to make sure you had no broken bones. After he and Jill left, I cleaned you up and bandaged your wounds. You were a mess."

"Thank you, Florence Nightingale," I said. Her stilted speech made me wonder if English was her first language. "Not your usual kind of first date, huh? I'm sorry. I sure ruined the evening."

"You did not do anything wrong. That stupid Marine was the one acting inappropriately. He was the jerk." Clutching her robe, she bent down and kissed my cheek. "And, besides, Jake Mortensen, you were defending my honor. Not many men would do that!"

"Oh, I bet they would. Did you undress me or did Ted?"

"Now, how about some breakfast?" she laughed, ignoring the question.

"Sure but I think I better clean up first. I'm not exactly dressed for formal dining."

"OK, the bathroom is down the hall on the right. I washed the blood out of your pants and sweatshirt. They are drying in the shower. There is soap and a clean towel in there, too."

Toey's décor impressed the heck out of me. Her small living room was furnished with a rattan couch, matching rattan chairs, a teak and brass coffee table, and two teak lamp tables. A black-lacquered hutch in the corner opposite the couch held a television and stereo. The artwork on the walls was modern Oriental.

Wrapped in the blanket, I headed to the bathroom, past her bedroom with its neatly made bed. I imagined how different things might have been if I hadn't gotten into that fight last night. And, remembering the tempting sights and smells of Toey from a few minutes ago, I began getting aroused, again. It was time for a cold shower.

Of course, her bathroom was as neat as the rest of the place. Inside the glass shower enclosure, my clothes hung over the tub. Now dry, the bloodstains were almost invisible. She'd done a great job.

Undoing my bandages, I examined the damage. Man, I hadn't been this banged up since falling out of old Mrs. Sappington's apple tree. I had minor bruises on my chest, ribs, and left cheek, but my knuckles got the worst of it, like I'd been pounding against concrete. I had to assume my opponent's face was worse.

"You've really done it this time, Mortensen!" I exclaimed, removing the bandage above my left eye to reveal a blackish-blue goose egg. Using my right hand, I pushed my chin from side to side. It was OK. The damage wasn't half as bad as I felt.

I stepped into the shower and adjusted the controls to splash cool water over all five feet ten inches of my bruised body. I must have let the tap run fifteen minutes. Lathering up, I noticed the soap was the same fragrance I'd smelled on Toey. It triggered an image of us bathing together, spreading the slippery stuff all over one another. Just as I was becoming excited again, the soap started stinging. So much for fantasy. I rinsed, toweled off, and got dressed.

Leaving the blanket neatly folded on the couch, I found Toey in the kitchen, chopping onions. I sat at the small glass table she'd arranged with placemats, silverware, apple juice, and a bowl of fruit. The *San Diego Tribune* lay folded on a chair. Noticing the headline, I picked it up.

"This morning's breakfast is bacon and scrambled eggs, sir. I usually have just a fruit plate. But you look like you need more than that," she said.

While I was showering, she had changed into light-emerald-green shorts and a mustard-yellow pullover, both baggy. Her hair was bouncy and curled in toward her chin. She had an apron around her waist, with a big red dragon and some Chinese letters on it.

"Please, don't go to any trouble," I said, embarrassed at all the attention. "After all you've done, I should be taking *you* out to breakfast. Did you read this article?"

"The one about Bill Koch putting together an all-women's America's Cup team to challenge Dennis Connors?"

"No, the one about the drug bust in Ocean Beach. That's near where Ted and I go surfing a lot. Police are linking this to a new crime organization moving into town. The head shop they're referring to is right up the street from the municipal pier."

Putting the paper down, I returned my attention to Toey. "What do the characters on your apron stand for?"

"They say: Do Not Bother Cook!" Waving the spatula at me, her face lit up again. I couldn't get over how pretty she was. Even her loose-fitting clothes couldn't camouflage her figure. I watched as she scrambled the eggs, adding onion, tomatoes, and cheddar cheese. The bacon was being kept warm in the oven. When the eggs were done, she took her apron off, and brought everything to the table.

Until that moment, I hadn't realized how hungry I was. "You're a pretty good cook!" I mumbled, my mouth already full.

"And you are a pretty good eater, sir." Then she added, "When we are finished with breakfast, I should put new bandages on your hands."

"No, they're OK. Honest. Flesh abrasions seem to heal faster when they're exposed to the air. You're making too big of a fuss."

"Jake, you never answered my comment about *America3*, the all-girl boat. Do you think they have a chance to win the Challenger's Series?"

"Come on, Toey—against Team Dennis Connors with all their experience—you've got to be kidding."

"No, I am not kidding. They have Leslie Egnot as skipper, and she is an Olympic medalist. Dawn Riley is a Whitbread Around the World yachtswoman, and J.J. Isler is a match-racing champion. The crew is pretty impressive. You have to admit that."

"Let's change the subject, OK? This is kind of like discussing politics and religion," I said.

"Oh? What do you want to talk about, then?"

"Anything but a competition of women against men. That's not what sailing is all about. It's a team sport. The best men and women sailors should be working together to keep the Cup in San Diego. That's what I think. And besides, men and women should make love, not war."

"OK, you win. Ted says you just quit the Navy. Is that true?" she asked. "How is that for changing the subject?"

"Trying to trade one nautical topic for another?" I laughed. "Yes, it's true. A whole bunch of things happened lately that bothered me. It was time for a change." I was sorry she'd brought up the Navy. I wanted to learn more about her.

"Well, I know about Wally and the crash. What else is there?" she continued.

"If you really want to know, I'd already put in for early retirement before the accident. With accumulated leave and vacation time, I was able to opt out before my tour of duty was up.

Wally's death and the way the Navy handled things just confirmed my decision. They called it "pilot error." That's just a chicken excuse. Nobody talks about the brass that sent all those men out on maneuvers in pea-soup conditions. It's peacetime, for heaven's sake! And, on top of it all, they were really out there searching for druggies. That's the Coast Guard's job. Nothing in the Navy makes sense anymore."

"It cannot be that bad, Jake."

"Want to hear another one? They made me Petty Officer Second Class when I re-enlisted three years ago. My pay rate stayed at E-5 for the entire time, yet my scores were the highest in the Wing on all my Sea-Air Search-and-Rescue stuff. I was prepared to save lives. I've got commendations up the wazoo and still got passed over for advancement.

"I took the E-6 exams three times, but promotions always went to the guys who were brownnosing and had decided to re-up. Unfortunately, they're the same clowns who end up running the Navy, at least from the enlisted man's point of view."

"Wow. I'm sorry I brought it up."

Afraid my griping might mess up any chance of Toey ever wanting to see me again, I felt I needed to leave before I said something really asinine. Fortunately, the phone rang just as I was dreaming up a graceful exit.

"It is Ted Blithe." Her eyes full of curiosity, Toey handed me the receiver.

"How ya doin', pal?" Ted's familiar voice snapped me out of my anger. "You able to drive? Or you want me to come get you?" he asked. "I'm off work at four."

"Thanks anyway, Toey's taking good care of me. She's a great nurse— and pretty, too!" I saw her smile and decided to press my luck. "I'm gonna try to talk her into going to the beach with me. I'd like to soak up some rays before the fog rolls in this afternoon. Thanks for the thought, Ted. I'll see you at the house tonight."

"Do you really want to go to the beach all banged up like you are?" Toey asked, hanging up the receiver.

"The sun and saltwater will do me good. If you don't have anything else planned, how about it?" Helping her clear the dishes, I said, "Let's go to Pacific Beach. I need to stop by my pad on the way to pick up some things."

"OK, I could use a break. If you load the dishwasher, I will change into a bathing suit. Give me a few minutes."

"Hurry," I said, anxious to see her in a swimsuit. I finished racking the dishes and waited in the living room.

Moments later she appeared in her frumpy breakfast outfit, carrying a canvas bag and small cooler. Purple sunglasses were perched on her head.

"Where's your swimsuit?" I asked, barely concealing my disappointment.

"I am wearing it underneath, silly. Shall we go?" she suggested, lowering her glasses.

My Baja Bug was parked in front of Toey's garage, next to Shelter Island drive. I recognized where we were immediately, just a few blocks from the restaurant. Carrying her bag and cooler while Toey locked up, my muscles felt sore and my head and ribs still hurt. Just the thought of taking this beautiful feminine creature to the beach, though, was plenty of incentive to forget any aches and pains.

Twisting the ignition key and stomping on the gas pedal brought Van Gogh to life. Reattaching the faceplate on the stereo, I inserted a Bob Marley tape and adjusted the volume. The sun was out, I had my Ray-Bans on, and the world was looking a whole lot better.

"I have to make sure everything is locked securely when I leave," Toey said, climbing over the fender and into the bucket seat next to mine. "A couple of bikers moved in next door, and I do not know much about them yet. They are kind of rough-looking—big, hairy guys with lots of tattoos."

We drove, listening to Marley and the Whalers sing about world peace and love. Eventually I turned onto Mission Boulevard near the roller coaster and followed it out to Crystal Pier and the funky seaside community of Pacific Beach.

"Now that I'm not living on the Navy base at North Island, this is my home. I love this place," I said, as we rumbled down the crowded street, the sidewalk filled with scantily clad roller skaters, blond surfers, and sunburned tourists.

"When I was very young, my father and mother used to take me to the ocean all the time. Mom emigrated from Denmark when she was a teenager, and Dad said the only thing about her home country she ever talked about was how cold and rainy it was. She couldn't get enough of California sunshine and beaches—winter or summer, it didn't matter." I said, breaking for a stop light.

"After she died, my father made sure we continued to go to the beach every chance we got. It helped him keep his memory of her alive. But I'm talking too much."

"No, go on, please."

"My father taught me to swim and surf. He was pretty good on a longboard. Three places that really stick out in my mind are Santa Monica, Venice, and Huntington. They always had a carnival atmosphere, I guess because of the piers and all the people, and Pacific Beach is a lot the same. You can still find surfboard shops, juice stands, saloons, kite vendors, tattoo parlors, palm readers, and even a roller coaster."

"And narcotics dealers? I have heard there are also a lot of drugs and crime," she said. "Are you not afraid to live in this neighborhood?"

"Come on, every place has its good and bad points. Pacific Beach's reputation isn't as bad as Ocean Beach. Remember the newspaper article? And, besides, I live a couple of blocks inland, outside of the commercial area."

I turned down an alley and parked in the carport space with Ted's name on it. "Here we are: Jake and Ted's bachelor digs. We have two other roommates. I'll introduce you to them if they're around."

Our beach pad is typical of townhouses in many Southern California coastal communities—only as wide as the double carport, extending from the alley to the busy street in front. Architecturally as unimaginative as a chicken coop, it's a tan, two-story, stucco box with four bedrooms, a couple of balconies, and a rear walled-in patio.

As we entered the concrete backyard, I prayed the house was clean. Clay pots filled with barren ficus stalks and withered wandering Jew stood in silent memorial to Ted's beautification attempts. An overstuffed couch, redwood picnic table, cast-iron barbecue, and numerous surfboards cluttered the small area.

Jan and Dean surfing music blared from a portable tape player. One of my roommates, Buddy Wright, was using a vibrating sander on a longboard supported between two sawhorses. He switched off the noisy machine as we approached. I introduced Toey to him.

"Pleased to meet you, pretty lady," he smiled, setting the tool on the board and wiping his hands on his baggies. A confirmed bachelor, Buddy kept in great condition by running on the beach every morning. He was a health-food nut, abstained from drinking, was passionate about surfing and sailing, and certainly didn't look his forty-five-plus years.

"Buddy's a sailing instructor, gives lessons under contract at some of the hotels on Mission Bay. He gets paid to play," I said. "He's also an experienced ocean racer and crews on some of the maxi-sleds. He's sailed in the Trans-Pacific Yacht Race to Hawaii three times."

"What position do you work when you crew?" Toey asked, pushing up her sunglasses. I could see she was impressed. Maybe I had over billed him.

"Sheet trimmer and, sometimes, foredeck," he replied, pausing to see if she understood.

"Wow! That is a lot of work." Her expression showed respect. "I crew on a Schock 35 called *Tsunami*. It is mostly PHRF stuff. I do foredeck or handle the running backs because I am so light. We are pretty competitive."

"I'm thinkin' I know the boat. Tall rig. Maxi-roach on the main. Goes to weather and reaches like a champ. Owner's name is Mike," Buddy replied, as he picked polyester resin from his hands. "You guys usually win your class. Yeah, I know the boat well."

While they continued talking sailboat racing, I went into the house and changed into swim shorts. I put a couple of beach towels, a sweatshirt, and suntan lotion into my knapsack. Thankfully, Toey had stayed outside. Compared to her apartment, mine was a cluttered pigpen, like a frat-house after a party.

On Sundays and Mondays, it was Miles' responsibility to clean up the place, since he usually didn't work those nights. Also in his forties, Miles Tripp was not my favorite roommate. A heavy drinker and smoker, he played jazz piano for a living but, most of the time, he was out of work and out of money. These days, he entertained at one of the saloons in Pacific Beach.

I found him stretched out on the couch, newspapers scattered on the coffee table and the dusty floor. He was watching television.

"Hey, man, heard you got roughed up last night," he said, a glass of my Meyers in one hand, a thin, brown cigarette in the other.

"You heard right. But I'm OK." I was trying not to let him get to me, yet I had to confront him with how annoyed I was. "Damn it, Miles, I almost brought a female guest in here. You're smoking inside the house. You know that's a no-no. And the place is trashed. How come?"

"Sorry, man. Chill out!" His eyes were bloodshot, and his voice sounded strange. "I played a multi-set gig last night, man." He took a long drag on his cigarette before dousing it in his drink.

"Louie and John showed with their horns. It was heavy, man. We jammed till the bar closed . . . lotsa tourists, lotsa tips. Didn't slip into the sheets till four A.M. Just got up." His hand was shaking so badly, he could barely hold his glass.

"Well, get off your duff and get this place cleaned up before Ted gets here!" I admonished. "You know how he likes things neat and tidy."

"Sure, kid, I'll have the place spiffed up before he's home," Miles answered, not moving.

Disgusted, I went into the kitchen to pack Toey's cooler with drinks and ice. Then I went back outside, still bothered by Miles. She and Buddy were still talking sailing when I re-joined them on the patio. I decided to interrupt.

"Buddy, you're his friend. Is Miles feeling all right? He looks like he's on something."

"Whoa, dude, he's just tired. He didn't get into a fight like I heard you did, but he did play a long show last night. I'll keep an eye on him. You kids go to the beach and let me handle it." Buddy sounded defensive. He always did when it came to Miles.

"It was nice meeting you, Buddy. I will be sure to look for you on the water at the next regatta."

Every square foot of sand below Crystal Pier was covered with bodies. Locals and tourists combined in an exuberant tapestry of bold colors, shapes, and odors. Pacific Beach is populated by two kinds of natives: passive and active. For the most part, the passive locals are good-looking, golden-brown individuals, who smell of coconut oil and have elevated sunbathing to an art form. Typically, they are scantily attired in colorful fabric, accentuating gym-prepped physiques. Most wear Oakley or Porsche wrap-around sunglasses. Active locals are the ones doing stuff: surfing, roller-skating, or playing volleyball.

During the summer months, there are also pinkos, easily identified by the large hats they wear to shield their fragile skin. Pinkos speak with urban accents and are obviously from the northern latitudes. Their children dig, construct sandcastles, and run back and forth to their parents, kicking sand on sunbathing passives. Usually unfamiliar with the ocean, some pinkos—both parents and kids—are afraid to enter the surf. Instead, they repeatedly run to the edge of it, scream, and speed back to the safety of their multi-colored umbrellas.

Toey and I picked out a clear spot near the volleyball nets and spread our towels. Active locals, engaged in noisy cheering, occupied most of the area.

In California, beach volleyball is played with teams of two and is extremely competitive, strenuous, and demanding. As practiced by athletic blond surfer types, it's a game of killer instincts. We watched as one competitor set the ball high in the air, allowing his teammate to slam a powerful spike at the opposition. A defender dove for it, his hands plowing into the sand inches away from where the ball firmly touched down. Unsuccessful in saving the play, the player extracted himself from the trench he had dug with his body, as an admiring crowd cheered his effort.

About this time, Toey took off her baggy outfit. Oh, my gosh! Although her Day-Glo lavender bikini was modest enough, the bottom in the popular French cut, and the bra sufficiently large to contain, but not restrain, her bosom, I was certainly not disappointed. Neither were the guys around us.

"Close your mouth and stop staring, silly. What did they do to you in the Navy? Surely, you have seen a girl in a bathing suit before."

"Girl? That's an understatement! I'm looking at a beautiful almost-naked mature woman," I said. "You want some Ban de Soleil on your back?"

This day at the beach was off to a perfect start. Just lying alongside Toey and looking at her set my imagination in motion. And spreading the lotion over her brown-freckled skin definitely strained my self-control. I hoped to have a similar effect on her when she returned the favor.

"Tell me about this tattoo," she asked, smearing lotion along my legs. Crossed flippers and an anchor were prominently displayed on my left calf.

"Got it when I finished Navy SAR School in Florida and Wally came out for my graduation. He'd received his orders and was being assigned to an S-3 Viking Squadron on North Island. We blew the doors off Seville Quarters in Pensacola. You know, the classic Navy walk: a bar for every taste. We partied and sampled them all that night to get up enough courage to have our "tats" done. He got his for ASW. I got mine for SAR."

"I am sorry. I didn't mean to bring up those memories again." Her kneading hands felt soothing on my tight muscles.

"Hey, don't be sorry. I'm glad I have those memories. He and I had some great times together and helped each other through some tough stuff. I'm gonna miss him."

We finished basting each other and tried to get serious about improving our tans. While she lay on her back soaking up rays, my thoughts became erotic again—nonsense stuff, like how a swimsuit top is such an incredible piece of engineering, if you think about it. At one point, I contemplated putting her quick-release clasp to the test.

Instead, I pulled on my short-sleeved O'Neil wetsuit, and ran into the surf. Although the Pacific Ocean off the coast of San Diego stays a cool 68°F most of the year, and the air temperature was in the 80s, the water couldn't have been more than a chilling 60 degrees today. The breaking waves invigorated my recovering body, while sedating my over-stimulated nerves. There was very little undertow, yet a good southerly swell had developed. I guessed it was caused by a late-season tropical depression down off the Mexican Baja coast, but I hadn't seen a weather forecast for days. I body surfed until my muscles couldn't handle anymore, and I started to get the shakes.

Toey was content just to work on her tan and read. Dense land-radiated fog started to filter out the sun around 4:30. It became cool and damp, ending an otherwise flawless Southern California Sunday. People began packing up, abandoning their beach encampments. The volleyball games were over, and the contestants had gathered to drink beer, congratulate the winners, and poke fun at the losers.

Toey pulled a jacket out of her canvas bag, while I shed my wetsuit and put on a sweatshirt. My body was so numb, I was feeling fewer of the effects from the previous night's encounter with the Marine. In fact, after spending the day with Toey, I was feeling pretty damn good and hopeful things might continue into the evening.

"Jake, it looks like everyone is vacating the beach. Shall we go, too?" she asked, obviously getting cold. "I had a great time."

"Damn, I was wishing this day wouldn't end." I stood up and started shaking sand out of our towels.

"I know, I was feeling the same way. But you need to work tomorrow, and I have parent/teacher conferences I should prepare for."

We climbed up the bluff to the promenade and walked past the many beach-oriented businesses. The sidewalk was crowded—everyone had migrated from the sand. Enticing smells from the food establishments beckoned, and I couldn't resist. I was hungry and hoped Toey was, too.

"Why don't we stop and get something before I take you home?" I asked, also wanting to prolong our time together. "We haven't had anything to eat since breakfast."

Placing my hands on her shoulders, I turned her into the doorway of the Busted Surfboard Saloon. We went upstairs to the outside deck overlooking the action.

Our waitress wore an abbreviated navy dress over a skin-tight spandex bodysuit. As she took our order, it was hard to ignore her reasonably decent figure. I guessed her to be in her late forties or early fifties. Her facial features were hard, her skin leathery. With her sun-bleached gray hair pulled into a youthful ponytail, she chewed a wad of gum so large it affected the way she talked.

I'd been in here several times, drunk and foolish with Ted, and hoped she wouldn't recognize me. I didn't want anything to mess up what was left of my day with Toey. My worries proved pointless, however; she was so busy trying to keep all the orders straight she had no time to think about anything else.

We ate uninterrupted. "Buddy says the Russians are going to compete for the America's Cup. Is that true or is it just a rumor?" Toey asked after a long silence.

"Buddy should know. He keeps up on that kind of stuff a lot more than I do." I pushed my plate away and took a sip of my drink. "I can't imagine them getting through the first round of the Louis Vuitton Challenger Series."

"The world is changing, Jake. Who can tell what has been going on over there; everything has always been kept so secret. The paper reported there is a group here in San Diego trying to raise money for them."

"Yeah, I know. Ted and I overheard some men talking about it when we were at San Diego Yacht Club last week. A guy named Peter Hammer was making a hard sell."

"Oh?" Then she looked devilish. "Buddy also thinks the all-women crew has a chance."

"There you go again. You're not gonna leave it alone, are you?" I said.

"Buddy should know, right?"

"Right."

Afterward, I drove Toey through the busy Sunday traffic back to her apartment. Parking in the front driveway, I saw her neighbors' garage door was open. Two big men were inside, working on motorcycles.

"Jake, I had a wonderful day. Thank you."

I helped her climb over the fender and started to pick up her bag and cooler from behind the seat. Kissing me on the cheek, she took her things. "I can handle this stuff," she said, starting up the stairs. At the top, she turned and said, "Call me, please. I think I like you, Jake Mortensen."

"But I didn't even get your phone number." I must be losing my charm. If it were any other eligible chick, we would be in the sack by now. I didn't even get a chance to ask her if she would go to Mexico with me to get the boat for Monty. The men next door polishing their Harleys must have thought I was a wimp.

"Ted and Jill have it. I bet they will give it to you . . . if you ask nicely," she said. Then she turned and entered the apartment I had slept in less than ten hours ago. I hoped I would get another chance soon. Next time, I vowed, circumstances would be more favorable.

It was now past 7 P.M. Ted was waiting for me when I returned to the house. The living room and kitchen were picked up and even looked clean—he'd obviously jumped on Miles' case.

"Well, tell me about Toey. You score?" He was standing in front of the refrigerator, devouring a chicken leg, a lascivious grin on his face.

"Not even close. But she sure got my attention!"

"Jill and I thought you'd like her. How about going out for a drink? You can tell me about it."

We walked the two blocks from the house back to the Busted Surfboard, where there was still a lot of activity. Even though it was Sunday night, most of the small shops along the promenade were open. For most businesses, the summer months and fall weekends are the busiest times of the year.

"Weren't you in here earlier, hon'?" the middle-aged waitress greeted me as we sat down by the bar. "That was one exotic lady you had with you!"

"Yeah, that was me . . . and her." I was surprised the gray ponytail remembered us. Dinner traffic had slowed and the bar business had picked up.

"What'll you have, guys?" she asked, the wad of gum still wobbling around in her mouth.

Ted kept the booze coming, as I described my day with Toey in great detail. Then he filled me in on the night before and the outcome of the fight. Apparently I broke the other guy's jaw. Glancing at my knuckles, I saw they were scabbing over—exposure to saltwater had helped. Then I expressed concern that Miles might be back on drugs. We both knew he'd used pot and harder stuff in the past.

"You may be right. I thought he was a little spaced out when I came in this afternoon. I'll say something to Buddy about it." Ted squeezed another lime into the neck of his beer bottle. "I've always let Miles be Buddy's problem. If it weren't for their friendship, I'd just as soon tell Miles to take a hike. Seems like they knew each other in Vietnam. They were both in the same platoon."

As soon as my glass was empty, another Meyers and Coke appeared. With Toey no longer a distraction, I couldn't help admiring the tightly clad figure serving us. For a mature woman, her body was firm and trim. I guessed she worked as an aerobics instructor or something similar during the day.

"Now that I'm out of the Navy, I need to change my way of living, Ted." The rum was loosening my tongue. "Right now, I'm too unsettled to have a relationship, particularly with someone like Toey."

"Wow! She must've got to you bad. Sounds like you're getting serious. You in love, dude?" Ted laughed. "Or in lust? Maybe it's just overactive hormones. If I weren't happy with Jill, I'd be interested. Toey's definitely a looker!"

We continued talking and drinking. Ted was the older brother I never had. He could find humor in any situation, and when I was down he would laughingly remind me, "If the world didn't suck, we would all fall off!"

At least ten years my senior, he kept himself in good shape and still held his liquor pretty well. He owned the house we lived in—Miles, Buddy, and I rented from him at a very reasonable rate. It helped him cover the mortgage. I looked up to Ted. He seemed to be totally in control of his life.

We were both getting pretty plastered when he came up with a crazy idea. "You're a sailor, right? You want to change your life, right? Well, friend, it's time to get a new "tat"! I know just the place. The guy's a real artist."

Ted paid the bill and we staggered out, the fog in our brains about equal to the moisture in the atmosphere. As we navigated erratically, Ted sang the chorus from the Pirates of the Caribbean ride at Disneyland. People stepped to the opposite side of the promenade to let the two drunks pass, arm in arm.

Around a corner in the next block, we found a blinking neon sign announcing, "Tattoo Parlor." Sam, the proprietor, had that Hell's Angels look: he wore two large brass earrings, a full beard covered his pockmarked face, and the top of his head was cue-ball smooth. If the images covering his huge body were evidence of his tattooing skills, he had real talent. The studio walls were papered with scraps of flash showing additional designs.

In my drunken stupor, and with Ted's prodding, I selected a picture of a square-rigged schooner under full sail. Underneath it was an empty banner that would contain words of my choice. I wanted something that didn't sound like motherhood or apple pie. The only meaningful phrase I could think of was "Always Leave A Clean Wake."

CHAPTER FOUR

# RACING MACHINE

Joining the U.S. Navy, and then mustering out, have to be two of the most significant days of my life. I signed up when I graduated from high school in 1988, slightly over six years ago. The economy in Southern California was entering a recession—jobs were scarce—and, at the time, I thought I had no other option.

What I really wanted to do was follow in my father's footsteps and become a carpenter. I yearned to build things, see the fruits of my labor. When I applied to several of my father's contractor friends, I discovered most were struggling to keep their businesses afloat.

Framing jobs were hard to find or nonexistent. New home construction in Orange County had fallen off by 75 percent—in Los Angeles and San Diego counties, it had stopped completely. The only continuing activity seemed to be in desert communities like Riverside and San Bernardino, where the land was less expensive.

Thoroughly discouraged, I couldn't picture myself living inland, hours from the ocean I loved. The Navy seemed to be the right solution—the only solution. I liked to surf, scuba dive, and swim, so the course of duty I selected was Sea-Air Search-and-Rescue. This seemed to fit with my pacifist philosophy.

The first of many disappointments with the military way of doing things came when my Navy recruiter told me I had to be attached to an Anti-Submarine Warfare unit if I wanted to be guaranteed entrance into SAR school.

Now, at last, I was a civilian again. The Navy had dangled all sorts of carrots to try to get me to re-enlist—things like new responsibilities and an increase in pay. I wasn't remotely interested. I'd already become disenchanted with military life—Wally's death had clinched it.

More attractive options presented themselves. During the last few years, the California economy had started to rebound. Jobs were becoming more plentiful, and the America's Cup was about to be held just outside San Diego Bay. International publicity, enthusiasm within the yachting community, and expectations of tourist dollars were driving a resurgence of business activity along the waterfront.

Even so, without the security of the Navy and a full-time job, times were scary for me. I wanted to live and work near the ocean, but didn't have a clue about how to find a paying position in the boating industry.

There seemed to be an abundance of part-time and semi-volunteer stuff, but nothing that would generate steady income. Days spent walking Shelter Island and Commercial Basin looking up friends of friends, hoping to connect with a genuine job lead or an introduction to a potential employer, had dead-ended for me.

After weeks of coming up empty, I resorted to using my scuba-diving skills and began doing underwater yacht maintenance. The underside of a poorly cared for vessel sitting in saltwater can get pretty ugly. In spite of the use of anti-fouling paint, slimy marine growth, barnacles, and other sea life tenaciously attach themselves to a hull if it's left untended for more than a month. Because of ever-tightening EPA restrictions, coatings legal for use in California appeared to be less and less effective.

Barnacles and other crustaceans can swiftly damage a diver's equipment. In just one week, my tanks were scratched, a quarter-inch wetsuit was torn and abraded, and my protective gloves were shredded. I needed to reassess the profitability of scraping the crud off the bottom of someone else's toy.

The women in my life weren't lighting my fire, either. I phoned Toey several times, but when I tried to ask her out, she was always friendly but too busy working to go on a date during the week. And on weekends, she was tied up grading papers or crewing in a sailboat regatta. I felt a polite brush-off in the works. Maybe she had the hots for the skipper of *Tsunami*. Anyway, our future didn't look promising.

I yearned for female companionship. When Anna called one morning, I jumped at the opportunity to visit her. She wanted me to help her pack; she would be leaving for Minnesota at the end of November, the baby due around Christmas. I spent several evenings helping her organize her belongings for shipment east. I would miss her as much as I already missed Wally—the way things were going, maybe more. I was beginning to feel very alone and depressed.

"I've got to find some steady employment," I moaned, hoping Ted was listening. It was the third Friday in November and we'd met for a drink at the Busted Surfboard. "What I make diving doesn't begin to cover the cost of wear and tear to my equipment. The part-time stuff I do with you helps, but it's not enough."

"Ever think of going on full time with YachtTow? I know you like the work." Ted signaled the waitress for his second beer. "I can give you the stuff you need to study for the towing exam. Only hitch is, you have to drive back up to the Coast Guard service center in Long Beach to be tested again."

"I can handle that." Ted's comments were intriguing—after a strenuous day scraping slime from yacht underbellies, I was definitely interested.

"Hornblower Dinner Cruises is always looking for qualified captains. You've already got the 100-ton Master's ticket," Ted continued. "And YachtTow, Vessel Assist, and SeaTow are looking to double personnel before the Challenger and Defender series start. They're anticipating increased boating activity because of the America's Cup. You need a towing endorsement to work for any of them . . . so why not spend part of tomorrow with me again and see if you really like it? I promise we won't have to rescue anybody this time."

At dawn, Saturday, raw sunlight burst through my bedroom window, ending any hope of sleep. After showering and shaving, I quickly dressed and went downstairs, looking forward to a day on the water with Ted. The brass Seth Thomas ship's clock on the wall chimed six times; otherwise, the house was unusually quiet.

I found Ted at the breakfast table, talking on the phone to his dispatch center, getting instructions. As I was about to learn, YachtTow handles a busy schedule of towing activities, in addition to responding to emergencies. While requests for assistance, like the rescue off Point Loma, always take priority, it's the ongoing maintenance and commercial contracts that are the bread and butter of the towing business.

"Got to make a stop at Knight and Carver shipyard on the way in," Ted said, getting up to check on the coffeepot. "Need to pick up a tow order and look at their haul-out schedule and docking situation. Can you drive?"

"Sure. Aren't some of the America's Cup foreign teams setting up over there?" With all the design controversy in the press, I was interested in seeing at least one of the sleek racing machines up close.

"Yeah. I think the Australians, the Japanese, and the Russians," he replied, filling a thermos. "The rest of the entrants have compounds scattered around San Diego Bay. Get a cup for coffee and grab your backpack. Let's go."

I drove out Mission Boulevard onto Sea World Drive. We crossed over the channel that permits access to the Pacific for deep-draft yachts leaving Quivira Basin and Mariner's Cove. The Islandia Hotel and its marina occupy the entire north shore of the small yacht harbor. We turned in at the frontage road circling around to the shipyard on the opposite side.

San Diego County is home to several full-service yards catering to the pleasure boat and yachting community. The Knight and Carver facility in Quivira Basin is one of the largest and oldest construction-and-maintenance yards in the area. It has the capability of building and repairing custom vessels up to 200-feet long; more importantly, it's located away from the hustle and bustle of Shelter Island, with easy access to the open sea and the America's Cup racecourse. That's why the Australian, Japanese, and Russian syndicates selected it.

When we arrived, the police had barricaded the street, and the shipyard was alive with activity. Quite a few cars were parked along the road, and people were milling around on the parkway grass, drinking coffee and talking.

"What's going on?" Ted asked the officer controlling traffic.

"Russian race boat just arrived," he answered. "You got business here?"

"Yes, I'm Captain Ted Blithe," Ted replied, handing over his YachtTow credentials. "I have an appointment with the yard manager, Bill Sweetwater. My crewmember, here, is Jake Mortensen." I pulled out my driver's license.

The policeman took our documents and made a call on his car radio. After a few minutes, he came back and told us we were cleared, but only as far as the shipyard office. He let us drive beyond the barricade, and we parked about fifty yards from the entrance.

As we climbed out of my car, a huge tractor-trailer rig was backing precious cargo toward an even larger crane. People in hardhats were standing around talking and pointing at the bright-red racing hull. Yellow webbing slings were being positioned on either side for lifting.

As with other America's Cup vessels, the underside was covered with heavy, white plastic to keep the keel and rudder configuration secret. A gold hammer and sickle emblem and Russian lettering were displayed in the center of the plastic camouflage. The mast was not yet rigged, but padded and secured along the length of the deck. It looked as if a lot of the deck hardware—winches and fittings—weren't installed yet.

In spite of its unfinished state, this boat was special, designed to meet new International America's Cup Class Rules initiated in 1992. To delight the media, TV spectators, and ESPN, IACC boats are formulated for performance and speed, a big jump from twelve-meter yachts that raced in previous America's Cup events. These new seventy-five-foot-long machines are the most technologically advanced racing yachts ever.

And here I was, standing in front of one being entered by a country I had been trained to defend against. I was dumbstruck with awe.

Ted waved at Bill Sweetwater standing next to a wildly gesturing, stocky, balding man in a suit. Bill, a slim, weathered guy in his fifties, was trying to calm the agitated businessman. I recognized the guy as the promoter I'd seen at San Diego Yacht Club. We headed toward them.

"Morning, Ted," Bill greeted us as we approached. "Lots of excitement around here. The Russians have arrived. Meet Mr. Peter Hammer. He's partly responsible for this circus."

"Now, wait a minute. I just want to see they get a fair shake. *Perestroika*, you know," the chunky man said, veins sticking out on his neck as he acknowledged us. His tieless shirt was unbuttoned, exposing gold chains and a hairy chest. "You people from the organizing committee or the port authority?"

We introduced ourselves all around, and Bill explained we were here on another matter. Then he excused himself to talk to us.

"Don't you walk away from me, Sweetwater. Gawd damn it! My investors and I have collected a lot of money so the Russian team can use your yard. Their vessel should be your number one priority—your only priority."

"Damn, if he don't act like he owns the friggin' place," Bill mumbled, leading us around the truck and crane and away from the bystanders. "I'm beginning to dislike that pompous asshole!"

Ted's lanky friend showed us where we should put the sixty-foot motor yacht we planned to bring over from the Islandia Marina later that day and promised to have some people on hand to take our lines when we arrived.

He also hoped to have the Russian boat situation under better control. It was to occupy a secured part of the yard, now being set up for that purpose. The Japanese and Australian boats, which had arrived a month before, were on a property west of the Knight and Carver yard, with their own docks and a ten-foot-high fence with a large gate to give access to the crane.

In stark contrast, the Russian syndicate had made no advance arrangements, yet the shipyard was jumping through impossible hoops to accommodate them at the request of Mr. Hammer and the America's Cup organizing committee.

"These teams are fanatical about security and keeping their hull designs a secret," Bill said as we walked back. "The Japanese and Australians are very well-organized. I don't know what to make of the Russians yet. Part of the crew is from St. Petersburg Yacht Club, but they seem to be low on funding. With all the political upheaval in their country, who knows?"

"What's Mr. Hammer's part in all this?" Ted wondered out loud.

"I'm not sure. Fundraiser, I guess," Bill shrugged. "So far, he's paying for everything with cash. Peeled off a stack of hundreds this morning to make an initial payment. Mostly did it for show in front of the press, I think. Belongs to several yacht clubs. Kind of a high-flyer, big-spender, promoter type."

"Yeah, we've seen him around," I said.

"His grandparents were Russian immigrants, and he speaks the language. I'm told he has raised quite a bit of money to help cover the Russian team's expenses. I don't think they're going to be able to compete, though; they're too far behind schedule."

"I think I agree," said Ted.

"All I really know about Peter is that he owns an eighty-two-foot Hatteras Convertible named *Broad Jumper*," Bill continued. "We did some fiberglass modifications to it several years back when it was brand new—added some extra fuel tanks so he could go down and fish Cabo. Also used to own a fifty-foot sailing yacht before he switched to power. He's pretty active politically within the San Diego boating community. Other than that, I'm not sure what he's all about."

"OK, Bill, you've got your hands full. We'll see you early this afternoon," Ted said. "What channel should we use on the VHF to talk to you?"

"Hail us on Channel 9 and we'll switch to 72," Bill responded, patting the portable radio attached to his belt.

As we were leaving, Peter Hammer yelled at Bill. The intense little man had several Russian crew surrounding him—they appeared upset over where the lifting slings were being positioned on the vessel's hull. Like an orchestra leader conducting a rock concert, Hammer was waving his arms and jumping up and down. At that moment, I wouldn't have taken Bill's job for any amount of money.

We climbed into Van Gogh and drove over the hill to the YachtTow docks in Commercial Basin. Ted stopped at the dispatch office at the head of the gangway to pick up more papers, introducing me again to Betty, the freckled redhead operating the phones and radios.

Two thirty-one-foot twin-engine Ray Hunt-designed Bertrams were moored at the docks. Each had been retrofitted for YachtTow's purposes by adding a towing post in the center of the aft cockpit. A hard, fiberglass dodger covered the helm and passenger seat. Both hulls were yellow, with the black YachtTow emblem on the sides. A heavy, corrugated band of rubber fendering was attached to the gunwales.

On the cowling in front of the passenger seat was an assortment of electronic equipment—radios, direction finder, and navigation gear. In the cuddy cabin down forward were a first-aid kit, oxygen bottle, life vests, and other safety and life-saving apparatus. Lines of various sizes were stowed in large deck lockers behind the helm and passenger seats.

"Get ready to cast off," Ted said, warming up the twin 320-horsepower Caterpillar marine engines. "Let's go do it!"

I released the dock lines and climbed on board. Ted eased the gears into forward, and we motored out past the shoal markers and green buoy identifying the entrance to the mooring basin. Once clear of shallow hazards, we turned to starboard and headed for the main channel.

It was midmorning and sailboat activity was increasing. A gentle November breeze was blowing, permitting easy tacking back and forth within the protected waters of North San Diego Bay. Fishing-charter boats had preceded us by several hours; they were probably already at the fishing grounds. Some would work the edge of the kelp beds north of Point Loma, while others would venture into Mexican waters and fish the area around the Coronado Islands.

Ted pushed the throttles forward as we passed Ballast Point and skirted the restricted area at the sub-base in the lee of Point Loma. Several fishermen in small, outboard-powered runabouts and inflatables had ignored the government's prohibition and were anchored in this area, the hope of a good catch taking precedence over harbor rules.

We saw a father and small child in a fourteen-foot aluminum rowboat, anchored in the middle of the busy commercial channel. Intent on tending their lines, they seemed oblivious to the boat traffic.

"That kind of stuff drives me crazy," Ted said, pointing at the small aluminum skiff. "Bet there isn't a lifejacket on board and the kid doesn't know how to swim."

Shaking his head, he advanced the throttles enough to kick in the turbos. A powerful whine came from below the fiberglass floorboards as the big marine engines increased RPM. The Bertram was capable of thirty knots on her deep-V hull and cruised around twenty-five to twenty-six knots.

"Aside from stupid boaters, the biggest problem around here is kelp." Ted eased our boat a bit to starboard, out of the main channel. "At this speed, you have to be careful and stay seaward of the kelp beds," he said as we were passing Point Loma. "I can usually see where they are by the glossy flatness of the water. Even then, there's lots of loose crap floating around. As our friend, Mr. Banks, discovered, it's best to give the whole area a wide berth."

"Yeah, I see what you mean." Doing twenty-four knots, we flew by a large, mahogany-brown branch and churned it up in our wake. "How they planning to conduct the America's Cup competition out here with all this junk?"

"Guess they'll have to set up in deep water, away from the kelp. That should make it interesting. The marks of the course will have to be anchored by some very long ground tackle." Ted pointed to one of the vessel's depth sounders. We were abeam dangerous, submerged New Hope Rock and heading up the coast toward Mission Bay. "I'm registering forty fathoms—that's 240 feet!"

"What about spectators?" The organization of the event was starting to intrigue me.

"Race committee boats will probably be the only ones anchored. They'll have to use long steel cables. My understanding is that spectator boats will be assigned to specific areas a predetermined distance outside of the racecourse."

Looking at his watch, Ted pushed our speed up to thirty knots. We made the seven-nautical-mile run from Point Loma to the Mission Bay entrance channel in about fifteen minutes.

"Here's a piece of trivia. We're now passing two of the most notorious drug-dealing areas in San Diego County," Ted announced, slowing the boat to five knots as we went down the waterway that parallels the flood-control bulkhead into Mission Beach. "Over there on the right is Ocean Beach and Dog Beach. On the left is Mariner's Cove."

"I know," I said, nodding. "Those places are off-limits to Navy personnel. We got warnings posted all the time."

Ted called the Islandia Hotel Marina on the VHF radio as we entered Quivira Basin, telling them we were here to pick up the sixty-foot Ocean Alexander, *Papa's Toy*, with orders to tow it across to the shipyard. The dock master agreed to meet us at the slip and help us with the lines. He said the captain, Larry Kleinschmidt, was on board and ready for us.

Apparently, on an outing the previous weekend, *Papa's Toy* had overheated and sucked a valve in one of her two 8V92 Detroit engines. Unable to maneuver in tight places with just one engine, the captain had called YachtTow to help get her into her slip.

Later, the owner, Police Commissioner Virgil Lee Klean, decided to have the shipyard perform other routine maintenance while the machinery was down. A member of Southwestern Yacht Club, he wanted his vessel in top shape so he could use it as a spectator boat during the Louis Vuitton Challenger Cup events. Otherwise, it would have been a simple matter to repair the engine with the vessel in her slip.

As we approached, the boat's burly, blond captain was standing on the bow with a towing bridle already rigged. Ted shouted some recommendations, cautioning Larry to do everything slowly, and established which VHF channel to use for inter-ship communication. I made the bridle fast to our hawser and stood clear of the towing post.

Using the Bertram's powerful engines, Ted exerted just enough tension on the bridle to start the Ocean Alexander moving out of the slip. When he was underway and completely in the fairway, Larry used his bow thruster to turn the large vessel. We repositioned our boat, took up the slack on the lines, and began the tow.

Both Ted and Larry were confident boat handlers, and the entire transit to the shipyard's docks was uneventful. I marveled at how little radio conversation was needed between the two of them to get the job done. They did most of it with hand signals.

With *Papa's Toy* safely tied up, the three of us went up the gangway to the office to finish the paperwork. Bill Sweetwater was waiting for us, much more at ease than earlier.

"Finally got the Russians settled in," he said, shaking our hands. "Boy, are they a confused lot. No money, no organization, and Hammer's meddling sure doesn't help. I hope we see results from his fundraising campaign soon. Otherwise, I'm afraid Knight and Carver's gonna take a bath on this one."

"Well, don't try to make it up on *Papa's Toy*," Larry joked. "You know how my boss is pretty tight with his money."

As we left, I noticed it was quiet around the Russian boat, except for two reporters who were taking pictures and jotting notes.

"You guys made moving *Papa's Toy* look so easy," I said to Ted and Larry in admiration.

"All in a day's work, Jake," Ted replied, smiling. "How about it, Larry? Can we drop you off somewhere?"

"Thanks, anywhere at the Islandia Marina. OK? It don't really matter."

The three of us climbed into the YachtTow boat. Then, leaving Larry at the end of his dock, Ted and I headed back out to sea. "Let's go get something to eat," he said, pushing the throttles forward as soon as we'd cleared the end of the jetty.

Later that evening, Ted and I dropped into the Busted Surfboard to have a cool one and recap the day. We got into a heated debate over the fate of the Russian boat and why someone like Hammer would be raising money for it. How come he wasn't supporting one of the American teams?

In the middle of our conversation, Buddy Wright joined us at the bar. He didn't usually drink, but he liked the ambiance of the Busted Surfboard and knew he could find us hanging out there most evenings when we weren't at home. I thought he also had the hots for the ponytailed gum-chewer.

Tonight she wore 1960s-style, hip-hugger bellbottoms that were snug and shimmering gold. A loose, white tank top just covered her breasts and exposed her flat, well-tanned midriff. Enormous red and gold enamel fish hung from her earlobes, and half a dozen charm bracelets jingled on her wrists. Smiling at Buddy, she took our drinks and led us to a quieter spot across the room, her tight little rump undulating as she preceded us. While placing the drinks on our table, it looked as if she bent over on purpose, just so Buddy could peak at the contents of her blouse. I heard him call her Wanda when he ordered a glass of iced tea.

"Damn! She likes you, Buddy!" I couldn't help myself. "Be careful. When they get over forty, they get a little desperate."

"Oh, really? Don't worry about me, man. She's just fun to be with." He laughed and blushed. "I can look out for myself, kid."

"How's our roommate Miles doing?" Ted asked, redirecting the conversation. "Some days, I think he's back on pot, or worse. Other days, I think I'm wrong, but it's bugging me." He was addressing Buddy. "You've known him longer and better than I have. What do you think?"

"I'm not sure, Ted. I was gonna say—the last time he was messin' with drugs, he was working long hours at a club downtown in the Gas Lamp District. I was thinkin' the same guys playing horn with him now were working with him then—Louie and John." Buddy held up his glass and motioned to Wanda for a refill. "Your guess is as good as mine."

"He's playing at a place a couple of blocks from here. We ought to go check out his act," I interjected.

"Good idea. Let's eat first." Ted also tried to get Wanda's attention. "I don't think the entertainment starts until nine." From the saloon's high-cholesterol menu, Ted and I each ordered a steak and mashed potatoes, which came smothered in thick, brown, onion and mushroom gravy. Buddy chose a Caesar salad. Unusually quiet during dinner, he kept glancing in Wanda's direction, watching her scamper between bar, kitchen, and patrons. Finally, he blurted out what was on his mind.

"I was gonna say—is there a problem if I ask Wanda to go with us? She gets off at nine." His expression dared us to say no.

"Only if you make sure she behaves herself." Ted couldn't resist the jab. "You, too. I don't want you both embarrassing us on the dance floor with obscene, geriatric gyrations."

Frowning at Ted, Buddy got up and went over to where Wanda stood at the barmaid's station. I could see her smile, nod her ponytail, and giggle. She seemed excited, as if no one had asked her out before.

Despite his age, Buddy was good-looking, had wavy blond hair, stood six feet tall, and kept remarkably fit. Until now, I'd thought he was a confirmed bachelor. Imagining the two of them having sex, I smiled and almost chuckled out loud. I wondered if she kissed with the wad of gum in her mouth.

"Ain't lust grand?" Ted laughed. "They're made for each other. He's got all kinds of attractive young babes drooling over him when he teaches sailing, and then he falls for a Jane Fonda wannabe. Go figure!"

We put on serious faces when Buddy returned. Without a word, he sat down and attacked his salad. In silence, Ted and I finished our overcooked meat. Periodically, I let out a snicker and Ted chuckled. Buddy continued ignoring us. When dinner was over, he ordered a glass of wine.

At 9:10, Wanda announced she was off-duty. Since the bill was paid, we all stood up to go. "I'm Jake Mortensen and this is Ted Blithe," I volunteered. "We've been in here so often, I feel like I know you, but we don't know your name." Buddy was speechless.

"Gertrude Wanda Duet. Pleased ta meetcha guys. My friends call me Wanda or Trudy. I prefer Wanda." She smiled, locked her hands behind her back, and rotated her upper torso from side to side, sending her blouse swinging. "I teach aerobics at The Spa when I'm not working here." So, I'd been right. I was looking forward to seeing her in action on the dance floor.

The four of us wandered over to Dizzy's Office, an intimate jazz club on a narrow side street. It had a postage-stamp dance floor, ringed by tiny cocktail tables with black-and-white checkered tablecloths. The place was empty, except for a sprinkling of couples sitting down front and a few suit-and-tie types leaning against an upholstered bar.

Miles was playing something smooth and easy on the piano, while the two horns seemed to be warming up—they sounded good. Two cocktail waitresses in sexy, French chambermaid outfits were working the tables. One met us at the door and ushered us to a good spot near the trio.

I think Miles saw us as we sat down, but he made no acknowledgment. His head and upper body rocked back and forth, elbows stiff as he played, a brown cigarette clenched in his teeth. Smoke drifted from his nostrils as he stared somewhere beyond the dance floor, squinting occasionally. The man was into his music.

When John on the sax, and Louie on the clarinet, loosened up, the sounds kept getting better and better. They really had talent. The first set lasted an hour and a half. Buddy and Miss Duet got up several times to shuffle around to mellow music from the thirties and forties. Ted and I were content to drink and watch.

Buddy surprised me. My middle-aged roommate had all the right moves. Wanda was the clinging type. With her arms around his neck, she plastered her lithe frame against his. Their bodies moved in unison, as if stuck together.

The ridiculous smile on Buddy's face told me he was totally enjoying the moment. The two got so slithery and sultry, it looked like they were going to do something indecent right on the dance floor.

Miles also took notice, smiling and nodding to the horn players, who suddenly switched to a 1920s jitterbug. The tempo change caught the couple off guard, and it was apparent they were having some difficulty adjusting to the new rhythm.

When the selection was finished, Miles announced a thirty-minute intermission, and the musicians disappeared from the stage. During the set, Dizzy's Office had filled up with a mixed bag of tourists and locals, some there to listen and dance, others just to drink. The sweet aroma of marijuana filled the room.

It took Buddy and Miss Duet a while to make it through the crowd to our table; his face was contorted into a witless expression that made him look like he was in pain.

"You having back problems, old man?" Ted started in, ribbing his friend without mercy. "Wanda may be too much woman for you! Looked like you were hobbling around out there."

"You guys mind your own business," Buddy snapped, his pained grimace changing to a frown. "I'm all right."

As if taking Ted's remark as a signal, Wanda scooted her chair next to Buddy, leaned her body against his, stuck her hand up under his Hawaiian shirt, and started rubbing his back. Her eyes projected devilish thoughts as she whispered in his ear. Buddy looked startled and embarrassed, clearly not knowing how to deal with the attention he was getting.

Almost on cue, Miles arrived at our table. Ted and I weren't quite sure how to react to our roommate's seduction at such close proximity, so the piano player's appearance was welcomed. Looking dapper in a striped shirt with a white, button-down collar, a wide paisley tie, cords, and wingtip shoes, Miles ran his hand through his wavy brown hair, pulled over an empty chair, and sat down. The brown, wrinkled cigarette he was smoking *was* marijuana—the smell was unmistakable.

"Gee whiz, mister, you sure play good dance music," Wanda quipped, breaking the silence. "Buddy and I could have kept right on going if it wasn't intermission."

"Maybe *you* could have, dear, but my old friend, here, was having trouble keeping up. Name's Miles. What's yours?"

"Wanda. Gertrude Wanda Duet is my full name." She held out her hand; Miles ignored it.

The look on Ted's face told me he was uncomfortable with Miles smoking grass in front of us. I felt the same way and sensed Miles was probably on more than that. Still engrossed in Wanda, Buddy showed no reaction.

"Sorry, friends. Got to start the next set," Miles announced, getting up. "Thanks for catching my act tonight. Buddy, you take care, man." Then he added, "Looks like you're in capable hands." Laughing, he walked back to the stage.

"You two lovebirds keep right on dancing, or whatever. I'm going to call it a night." I put money on the table to cover the tab and stood up.

"Me, too," Ted said. "Don't bother to get up, Buddy," he chuckled. "Wanda, now he's your responsibility. Make sure the old man gets home safely."

"Safely, sure. But I won't guarantee his condition," she smiled. "I don't know how much stamina he's got."

Miles' second set was beginning as we elbowed our way toward the door. Looking back, I could see Buddy smiling and shaking his head at Wanda. The musicians launched into a George Shearing number and the audience cheered—to hear good jazz and smoke pot were the reasons most people were here. If Miles had anything to do with it, they weren't going to be disappointed tonight.

CHAPTER FIVE

# SURFERS AND BIKERS

Working with Ted all day Saturday had been just the kick in the butt I needed to head off in a new direction. Not only was I impressed with his professionalism, but also his work seemed varied and challenging. Best of all, I saw a way of being out on the ocean and getting paid for it. I resolved to get my towing endorsement the first of the year, after I got back from La Paz.

Dying to tell someone about my new goals and the Mexico trip, I decided to call Toey. It seemed like a long time since I'd last talked to her.

"Hello, Jake. How are you doing?" she responded, her voice soft. I imagined her wearing just her silk kimono.

"I'm doing great. How about you?"

"School and students have been really demanding." She sounded down. "I am sitting here grading papers and trying to adjust my lesson plan to be at a logical stopping point before Thanksgiving."

"Speaking of the holiday, a bunch of us plan to spend this Friday at the beach. Would you like to come with me?" I held my breath and waited.

"Yes, I would like that. I need to get out of this dismal apartment, and I would like very much to see you again." She perked up a bit. "Are Ted and Jill going to be there? I have been so busy with my students, I have only talked to Jill a few times since the first week of school. I feel terrible. The campus is not that large."

"Ted's working Thanksgiving Day so he can be off on Friday. Jill's coming. Buddy's got a girlfriend, name's Wanda. They'll both be there, too. Buddy doesn't eat meat, but he's determined to be in charge of the barbecue, don't ask me why.

"Jill's making potato salad, and Ted and I are bringing refreshments and munchies. Miles might even show up, and others will be dropping by." I stumbled on, "Can I pick you up early? Like eight o'clock in the morning?"

"Sure. In fact, I will have breakfast ready." Now she sounded excited, too. "What can I bring?"

"Nothing, just you and your swimsuit. I'll pick you up bright and early Friday. Breakfast would be great but, please, don't go to any trouble."

We said our goodbyes and hung up. I promised myself things would end up differently with Toey this time. Last time, with the fight, everything was pretty much a disaster.

Hoping to make the next three days go by as quickly as possible, I contracted to clean six boat bottoms before Thursday. People wanted their vessels ready for the holiday, so finding the work was easy. Over the last few weeks, I'd left business cards at several yacht brokerage firms on Shelter Island and had been turning jobs away.

At night I studied for the towing exam, and sometimes Ted quizzed me. I was having a little trouble remembering the subtle differences between the international and inland lights and shapes for towing vessels and barges.

By Thursday afternoon, I was ready for a break. At Wanda's suggestion, Buddy had made Thanksgiving reservations for 6:30 at the Busted Surfboard. She was working the evening shift, so she'd be able to serve us.

Ted was going to get off around 4 P.M., unless there was an emergency. The plan was for Ted, Buddy, and me to meet at the saloon around 6. Miles had to entertain at Dizzy's Office later that evening, but he said he'd try to join us for a while if he could wake up in time.

Wanting to get out of the house, I decided to leave for the restaurant a half-hour early. The promenade was crowded with surfers heading home, skateboarders, and a few tourists peering into the windows of closed shops. All that remained of the Thanksgiving Day sun was an amber glow out toward San Clemente Island.

"Hi, Jake! Happy Thanksgiving!" Spearmint-chewing Wanda greeted me at the door. "You'll have to wait at the bar. I'm sorry, I can't seat you upstairs until your reservation time. Meyers and Coke?"

"You got it." I couldn't believe the costume she was wearing—kind of a modified Pilgrim's getup with an extremely short black skirt. She wore white seamed stockings and a white ruffled low-cut bodice, generously displaying her cleavage. A black, Amish-type scarf covered her head, the gray ponytail poking out from underneath. Her big-buckled black pumps had three-inch heels.

Paper cutouts of turkeys, pumpkins, and cornstalks hung from orange and black crepe paper attached to the ceiling. Though festive, the saloon felt more like Halloween than Thanksgiving. When Wanda placed my drink on the table, she leaned over enough to expose the contents of her frilly top.

She was totally uninhibited. Men liked that she flirted with them, and I'm sure she did it to increase her tips. For an uneasy moment, I tried to imagine how Toey and Jill might react to her at the beach party.

It was past dark, and the saloon was filling with holiday patrons, most of them from the neighborhood. When Buddy and Ted arrived, I was on my second drink. Trying not to look overtly interested, I was enjoying Wanda's playful antics with the customers. She was, unquestionably, the best-looking of the three waitresses on duty. I delighted in watching her provocative, athletic figure flit from patron to patron like a busy bee.

She bent over several times while serving customers, I think for our benefit, exposing black ruffled panties. I didn't detect any jealousy in Buddy. He seemed to be enjoying the show as much as everyone else.

Noticing my roommates had arrived, she came over and—with a squeal—deposited her perky rear on Buddy's lap. Throwing her arms around him, she kissed him passionately. He seemed embarrassed, but not surprised.

"Happy Thanksgiving, hon'. You too, Ted." She winked at both Ted and me. "Have a table for you guys in a few minutes. I'll bring your drinks first." Chewing rigorously on her gum, she wriggled around in Buddy's lap for a moment, smiled, got up, and headed for the bar.

"Better be careful, old man." Remembering the night at Dizzy's Office, I couldn't resist commenting. "We don't want you walking around like a cripple again."

"Shut up, Jake!" Buddy wasn't amused. "I don't want to hear any more about that."

Miles never showed up.

When it was our turn for a table, Wanda ushered us to the outside deck overlooking the beach. We all jockeyed like adolescents for a view of her stockings and underwear as she led us up the stairs.

In keeping with the Busted Surfboard's tradition, our holiday meal came smothered in heavy brown gravy. Since tonight was "all-you-can-eat night," Wanda delighted in ensuring our plates stayed loaded. I had seconds on turkey and mashed potatoes, but when the pumpkin pie with whipped cream appeared, I complained it was too much.

"Buddy needs it to keep his stamina . . . and other things . . . up," Wanda quipped. "You guys want anything else to drink?"

"No!" we all said, almost in unison. Buddy asked for the check, and each of us contributed our fair share. As he was counting the money, I thought I saw him put in more than the normal tip. When we got up to leave, Wanda whispered something in his ear, and his expression brightened.

6:30 Friday morning found me restless in bed, after tossing and turning all night. For some reason, when I eat a lot of turkey I get gas. It's happened after every Thanksgiving as far back as I can remember.

Opening the medicine cabinet, I plunked an Alka-Seltzer into a glass of water, watched it disintegrate, and guzzled it. Letting one last pungent blast from my troubled bowels, I went downstairs to greet the day. Ted was rummaging around in the kitchen cupboard under the sink.

"You're up early. Lose something?"

"Oh, Jill just called. She needs a big pot to boil potatoes in. I thought we had one under here that we used for lobster. Sometimes she really pisses me off. I can't believe she waited until this morning to make her potato salad."

We emptied the contents of two shelves onto the kitchen floor before finding the large kettle. Since Ted's day was off to a bad start, I offered to pick up the drinks and snacks for the party. I told him I was having breakfast with Toey at her place and to call me if Jill needed anything else.

I hoped they both would be in better moods by the time they got to the beach. I didn't want anything to go wrong on my first real date with Toey. En route to her place, I stopped to stock up on beer, munchies, and soft drinks. When I arrived, she had granola and fruit on the kitchen table.

"You look great," she said after we'd eaten. Reaching across the table, she took my hand and examined my knuckles. "No one would ever know you were in a fight."

"It's been over a month. Come on, now. Let's forget that." I had hoped she wouldn't bring it up. "I'd like to start over. Can we pretend it didn't happen?"

"OK. But it was scary." She stood up and kissed me on the cheek.

In tan, cotton walking shorts and a long-sleeved, purple sweatshirt with "Newport to Ensenada 1992" and "Tsunami" stitched in gold, Toey was as beautiful as I'd remembered. I couldn't take my eyes off her as she cleared the table.

"We better get going," I said. "We're in charge of saving a place on the sand."

"I will be ready in a minute—just need to get my sunglasses and a windbreaker. Oh, I almost forgot: Jill called and asked if we could pick up some paper plates and napkins." I followed her into the living room, where she motioned toward the door. "I have to lock up. Meet you down at the car?"

While we were eating, the driveway next to Toey's had become a motorcycle convention. Three big Harleys and two tricked-out Yamahas were parked in a row. Glistening chrome and candy-apple lacquer accentuated the expensive machines, their owners nowhere to be seen.

"How you getting along with the bikers?" I enquired as we drove away.

"They give me the jitters," she replied. "It seems like there are always a couple of motorcycles parked in front. They play loud music and make a lot of noise at the strangest hours. The neighbors have called the police several times. It is not a good situation. I hate the mess dogs make, but I am thinking of getting a German shepherd for protection."

We stopped at the market to pick up ice and the things Jill had asked for. Then we headed for Ocean Beach, where the best surf break is between the jetty and the pier. Parking in the metered lot, we started lugging stuff toward the shore.

"Who plays the guitar?" Toey asked when I lifted the case from behind the seat.

"I do," I said. "Got to be in the right mood for it to sound good, though. It helps if everyone's had a little too much to drink, me included."

Sandwiched between the Pacific Ocean and Point Loma, saddled with an unsavory reputation from the sixties and seventies, Ocean Beach is a community time has forgotten. Downtown and along the beachfront, an eclectic mix of mom-and-pop shops occupy converted wood-and-stucco cottages and beach bungalows. During the 1960s and 70s, it was kind of the Haight-Ashbury of Southern California.

"This is one of my favorite surfing spots," I said, as we lugged our stuff across the sand. "This place is the only old-time beach town remaining on the entire California coast. I think it should be preserved. Maybe someday an official body will declare Ocean Beach an endangered habitat, like the redwoods."

"Are you going to preserve the panhandlers, too?" Toey's brow wrinkled. "That one in the parking lot was young enough to be in grammar school."

"Come on. You've got to overlook that kind of stuff. This place is still a mecca for surfers of all ages who ride the waves just because they're there. Maybe he just needs money for bus fare back home—look on the positive side."

We found a spot with a good view of the surfing area and set up camp. Marking our territory, Toey arranged blankets, beach chairs, and towels, while I started working on the surfboards.

Ted and Jill arrived about 10:30. Jill seemed in good spirits; Ted did not. After toting all their stuff to our encampment, he went to work preparing his board.

"Like, wow! You guys sure picked a gnarly spot," Jill said, peeling off clothing. As she stood stripped to her two-piece suit, I remembered Ted's description, and she was definitely "Three-B." "Hey, all. Like, surf's up. Look at that awesome break! The waves are smokin'!"

Ted and I didn't wait for Jill. We put on our wetsuits, attached board-leash Velcro cuffs to our ankles, and headed for the water. I wanted to get in as many rides as possible before too many people got in the way. And Ted wanted to work off the morning's frustration.

I swam my board out, putting some distance between us. It pleased me that I might be in better shape than Ted. I paddled into the first wave and was going down the line, when Ted dropped in right behind me. But then the wave started rolling, and we rode it together. He was riding the crest in my wake, and I was afraid I might fall and embarrass myself. Ted finally turned out, leaving me a solo ride clear to the beach. It was the best wave I caught all morning.

Buddy and Wanda showed up with the barbecue and fixings about noon. Ted and I had just returned from surfing; Jill was still in the water. Toey was improving her winter tan and holding down the fort. She had been lying on her back and rolled over onto her stomach as the others arrived.

"Hi, everybody. Sorry we're late," Wanda said. "Buddy was having a hard time. Couldn't fit into his bathing suit, so I had to help him."

Ted laughed out loud, I snickered, Toey didn't know what to think. Buddy made himself busy setting up the barbecue and avoided eye contact with everyone. Wearing a floppy straw hat and lime-green workout clothes, Wanda went over to introduce herself to Toey. I held my breath.

"Hi! I'm Gertrude Wanda Duet. My friends call me Wanda." She extended her hand down to Toey. "You're the pretty, little Chinese lady I saw with Jake at the Busted Surfboard. I work there."

"Hello, Wanda. My name is Toey, Toey Wong," she responded, propping herself on her elbows and adjusting her sunglasses with both hands.

"Shit! You've got great boobs, honey. You an exotic dancer or a stripper or something?" Plopping herself down on the blanket next to Toey, she continued, "Damn, I wish mine were that big. I'd get better tips!" Wanda put her hands under her own breasts and pushed them up.

Ted and I decided to join Buddy at the barbecue. Out of the corner of my eye, I saw Toey sit up and pull on her purple sweatshirt, though it kept hanging up on her protruding chest.

"No. I am a teacher, Wanda. Just be happy with the way you are." Toey's tone was matter-of-fact. "These things are really a nuisance. I can never get anything to fit right. And men are always making passes at me. Jake knows, because he had to defend me one night."

"Wow. I never think about things like that." Wanda said, pushing her breasts together. "Maybe if mine were just a little bigger . . ."

Feeling I should rescue Toey, I walked over to where they were sitting. She smiled gratefully as I approached. Wanda was taking off her sweats, her fluorescent-orange bikini barely covering the essentials. It was the same color as Navy life rafts and safety gear. Costume jewelry dangled from her wrists and earlobes.

"I'm gonna start the charcoal around three. How's that sound?" I said, interrupting their girl talk. "If you're going in the water, you should do it now. Jill's still out there."

"I am ready. How about you, Wanda?" Toey stood up and stepped into her purple wetsuit, after placing her sunglasses in a beach bag.

"Hell, no! I never learned to surf. Buddy wants to teach me, but I think I'm too old to learn," she replied, rubbing coconut oil on her already bronze legs. "You kids go on. I'll stay here and keep the riff-raff away from our stuff."

We all paddled out just beyond where the swell was noticeable, and there was Jill. Over the next hour, we spent most of our time sitting on our boards and waiting. Finally, Jill and I caught one last rolling breaker and rode it all the way to the beach. When we got to shore, she'd had enough, and I didn't feel like conditions were going to improve, so we unhooked our safety leashes, cleaned the boards in the ocean, and started back to camp.

"Have you met Wanda?" I asked, thinking it was now or never.

"No. But Ted's totally warned me about her. Like, I know she works at the Busted Surfboard and sees Buddy."

"She's watching our stuff. I'll introduce you."

When we arrived at camp, Miles was talking with Wanda, who was spicing their conversation with passages selected from a romance novel. Miles, clad in navy swim trunks and a light-blue Monterey Jazz Festival windbreaker adorned with piano keys, was nervously running his hand through his hair, a wrinkled cigarette hanging from his mouth. I greeted him and introduced Jill to Wanda.

"Pleased ta meet ya. Boy, you and Ted sure go together. You look like real live Ken and Barbie dolls." Wanda, being complimentary in her own special way, had her thumb stuck in her paperback to mark her place. "Wanna hear some trashy romance stuff? I think it's giving Miles a hard-on."

"No," I laughed. "I'm going to start the barbecue. Miles, would you give me a hand?" It was better to let Jill get acquainted with Wanda on her own. It had worked with Toey.

By the time Toey, Ted, and Buddy came ashore, Miles and I had the coals well stoked. The three die-hard surfers huddled around the barbecue while removing their wetsuits and toweling off. Then Buddy went to work on the food. Wanda and Jill set up the serving line.

People wandered over and introduced themselves. Most had surfed with us and were part of the regular Ocean Beach bunch. I couldn't believe the amount of food being set out. Jill's potato salad, the munchies Toey and I picked up, Buddy's shish kabobs, and leftovers Wanda had brought from the restaurant: turkey, stuffing, pumpkin pie, and yams.

When dinner was over, Ted started a campfire and intensified the flames with the barbecue coals. I pulled out my Mexican guitar and started tuning up as the sun was dropping. When the air cooled, most of the beachgoers cleared out. Only a few groups like ours remained, huddled around small fires scattered between the jetty and the pier.

Though Toey had on her sweatshirt and jacket, she draped an arm over my shoulder and leaned against me for protection against the chill. I liked having her next to me as I strummed out chords in the key of C, John Denver stuff. Jill and Ted and Buddy and Wanda huddled together in couples, making Miles the odd man out. After a while, I noticed he'd disappeared, probably to have a "cigarette."

I continued playing mediocre music on my six-string. Every now and then, someone hummed along, but most of the time we just stared out at the ocean. Even normally exuberant Wanda was quiet. Sounds of the surf and the squawking seagulls in search of thermals contributed to a feeling of reverence. Silently, we all hoped to witness the elusive green flash as the sun exhausted its last burst of energy and disappeared beyond the horizon. Then it was time to go.

"What happened to Miles?" Buddy asked as he packed. "One minute he was here, and then he's MIA."

"Bet he felt uncomfortable as the only single," Wanda said, kissing Buddy on the neck. "He's probably gone home."

We racked surfboards atop our cars and drove back through Ocean Beach. On the way out, I thought I saw Miles' beat-up Chevy in the Dog Beach parking lot. But I wasn't sure enough to circle back and check it out. Besides, I was anxious to get to Toey's apartment, hoping something might develop.

"Does Miles usually just disappear like that?" she asked. "It was strange how it happened."

"I don't know. He's kind of a creature of the night." I was trying to keep her from worrying. "He'll show up. He's probably already home. How'd you get along with Wanda?"

"I like her. She is really very smart, uneducated but intelligent. She puts a totally different perspective on things."

"That's for sure!" I agreed, laughing. "Inappropriate at times, too."

"Oh, come on! The things she says do not shock me. She has a good heart," Toey said, laughing. "At Buddy's age, he could do much worse. They enjoy each other. That is all that really matters."

"Did I tell you I'm going to Mexico to repossess a boat for First Interstate Bank?" I said, finally sharing the news.

"Jake, you must be crazy!"

"No, I'm not crazy. Monty Banks set it up. It's a job."

"You do not know what you are going to find down there." She sounded apprehensive. "People do not like to give up their possessions, and even if the bank provides you with the legal right to take the boat, someone is bound to resist. It could be a risky and dangerous undertaking."

"How's your Spanish? I was going to ask you to go with me," I pressed on.

"My Spanish is very good. I teach it, remember?"

A real goof on my part—even so, she began to waffle.

"Come with me, Toey. It's *not* gonna be dangerous. All we have to do is sail it back to San Diego. Think of it as a trip to Mexico, all expenses paid."

"I do not know . . . I can only go if it is over Christmas vacation. How long do you think it will take? Where is the boat? Who else is going along as crew?"

"Thought I'd ask Buddy or one of my Navy friends. Ted has to work over the holidays, or I'd ask him. The boat's in La Paz. I plan to go down a few days ahead of my crew to locate the vessel and clear the paperwork."

That Toey would even consider going was encouraging.

We pulled into her driveway and saw three Harleys parked next door. Heavy-metal music blasted from her neighbor's stereo. Once inside her apartment, the noise was still oppressive. It was the base rhythm that was the most annoying, vibrating the heck out of everything.

"Idiots! You want me to go over and say something to them?"

"And get beat up again? I do not think so, Jake." On her tiptoes, she pulled me to her and kissed me. "I do not want things to end up like last time."

"Neither do I," I said, stroking her silky hair. I could feel her breasts against my stomach as she hugged me. I tipped her chin upward to kiss her again.

We moved to the couch, our hands exploring beneath bathing suits as we continued to kiss. I was beginning to fondle her breasts, and she had just placed her hand on the bulge in my lap, when the phone rang.

"I am so sorry, Jake, but I have to get the phone," she whispered.

"Please. Let it ring."

"It could be about Miles," she said and gently pushed me away. In total frustration, I released her.

Of course, it *was* about Miles. Buddy had stopped by the house with Wanda and heard a message on the answering machine. Miles was being held at the downtown San Diego jail on narcotics possession charges.

Buddy had tried to reach Ted at Jill's apartment and, when there was no answer, he decided to call Toey's. Buddy pleaded with me to go help him get Miles out of the slammer. Bailing out a pot-smoking roommate was not what I had in mind for the evening.

"You have to do it, Jake." Tears welled up in Toey's eyes. "No matter what he has done, you cannot leave him in jail. It is a terrible place. Awful things happen."

She was right, though I didn't want to admit it. I gave her a lingering kiss and headed out the door into the moonless night.

By the time I got home, Buddy had returned from dropping off Wanda. It took us two hours to find a bail bondsman because of the holiday weekend. It was 3 A.M. Saturday before all the paperwork was completed.

When finally released, Miles looked terrible, his hair messed up and his face bruised. For the first time, I noticed his skinny arms riddled with scars, the telltale needle tracks revealing a lifetime of heroin use. He was doubled over and could barely walk.

"Thanks for bailing me out, man," he moaned. "Never go to jail wearing just a swim suit. Had to fight off every faggot in the joint!" He held his stomach and forehead, as if he was going to barf.

Buddy and I got him home and into bed. Thanking us again and again, he said he'd tell us the whole story later, but now he just wanted to get some rest. We left him in his misery, both hoping to get a few hours' shut-eye before the night became day.

At 10 A.M. my snooze was interrupted by the phone downstairs.

"Good morning, Jake. You sound like you just woke up." It was Toey.

"I did," I said, trying to yawn silently.

"Were you able to get Miles out of jail? I have been so worried. I could not sleep. Is he all right?"

"Yes, but it took us until after three this morning, and he was in bad shape. Looked like he was coming off something." I held the receiver against my shoulder with my chin, struggling to fix coffee. "Don't know the whole story yet."

"You must have had a rough night. I am really sorry." Her voice was so soothing. "I called to see if you wanted to come over later. I feel like cooking a real Chinese dinner."

"Only if you teach me how to use chopsticks," I teased. "What time?"

"About 5:30?"

"I'll be there."

"Oh, and Jake, I've decided to go to Mexico with you . . . if you still need crew."

"Boy, do I need crew!" Funny, I'd assumed she was already going. Anyway, Toey's call put me in a wonderful mood. Tonight we were going to finish what we had started, I just knew it.

Miles emerged from his room around one P.M. I was sitting in the living room, studying for the Coast Guard towing exam, when he stumbled downstairs. He could hardly walk and was still wearing the swim trunks he'd worn in jail. Bruises were evident on his back and shoulders. Someone had really thrashed him.

"You gonna be all right?" I helped him navigate. With one hand on his stomach, he groped for the arm of a chair. Beads of perspiration rolled from his forehead, his face contorted in pain.

"Don't know, man. Never had cramps this bad, and I never get this way from happy sticks. Must've bought into some bad stuff. I really fucked up this time."

Usually, when I'm around someone sick, I have a lot of compassion. Not this time. In disgust, I listened to him relate what happened after he left the beach party. I was right. It *was* his car I'd seen in the parking lot at Dog Beach, where he'd gone to score some heroin. Apparently, the police had staked out the area and busted him during the buy. Miles said he'd learned his lesson this time. Yeah, right, and I'm Santa Claus on a surfboard.

On the way over to Toey's, I stopped for some flowers, a last-minute impulse. I felt very strange after I'd bought them. I don't usually give women flowers.

I parked Van Gogh and saw the neighbor's driveway was empty, the garage door closed, and the apartment quiet. I hoped they were gone for the weekend.

When I presented Toey with the bouquet, she acted surprised. She reminded me of a Chinese princess—silver necklaces with large jade stones complemented her heavily embroidered, red sheath. Following her into the kitchen, I held the flowers while she looked for a vase.

"Your motorcycle neighbors gone?"

"They left last night shortly after you. Someone called the police again, and they all disappeared. It has been quiet all day, thank heaven." She arranged the flowers and set the vase on the counter. "Please, sit down and let me serve you, sir."

She'd obviously gone to a lot of trouble. The table was set with woven-reed placemats, china plates, wooden chopsticks, and small brass-wire baskets with long, twisted handles. A highly polished, bronze Mongolian hot pot sat on a ceramic trivet in the corner.

Lamb sliced paper-thin was arranged on a platter. Various sauces, cabbage, spinach, cellophane noodles, bean curd, and cooked noodles were in individual bowls. The moat of the hot pot was filled with a clear broth. Toey lit the Sterno under the shiny metal chimney and then filled my teacup from an ornate china kettle.

"We will have tea first. If we drink it during dinner, the oil and the food will destroy the taste. This is jasmine. Do you like it?"

"Yes. Why don't the tea cups have handles?" I asked, taking a sip.

"Because, Jake, if the cup is too hot to pick up, the tea is too hot to drink."

"OK, Toey. I'm in your hands. This all looks wonderful. Please, tell me what to do."

"Eat, silly. Pick up a piece of lamb with your chopsticks and cook it in the broth. When it is just tender, dip it in the sauce and eat it."

When we'd finished the meat, she added the vegetables to simmer in the broth. When they were cooked, we scooped them out with the wire baskets.

She served a golden rice wine that tasted very much like sherry. After we'd finished the vegetables, cooked noodles were added, becoming noodle soup served to conclude the meal. For dessert, she'd made Walnut Sweet, a hot pudding mixture of ground walnuts, dates, granulated sugar, and cornstarch. Everything was delicious.

"Do you like the wine?" she asked, refilling my glass from a ceramic urn.

"Yes. I think I'm getting drunk. What is it?" I took another sip of the amber elixir.

"It is very special. It comes from Shaoshing in the Chekiang province of China. This urn has been aged over ten years in underground cellars. It is called *Hua Tiao*, which means 'Carved Flower.'"

"Is it expensive?"

"I do not know." She stood and kissed my cheek. "My father gave it to me to save for someone very special." Unclasping the jewelry from her slender neck, she reached for my hand and led me out of the kitchen. "I think the dishes can wait."

I agreed, and took her in my arms. I was lost in her kiss, overcome by the exotic fragrance of her skin, anxious to resume where we'd left off the previous night. She led me past the couch, down the hall to her room. Beside the bed, I kissed her again. With her breasts pressing against me, I unzipped the back of her dress. She was wearing nothing underneath.

CHAPTER SIX

# MEXICO

When morning came, I was half awake, trying to persuade myself I was still asleep. Warm rays of winter sunlight percolated through Toey's bedroom curtains. She was curled with her back to me, her small rump tucked against my side. I heard her breathing the slow inhale and gurgling exhale of a deep, contented sleep.

I slipped out from under the comforter. As I swung my feet to the cold hardwood floor, my elbow almost toppled the nightstand lamp. I grasped its china base and froze, listening for any change in the gentle rhythm of Toey's breathing. Like a cat burglar, I gathered my clothes from the floor and tiptoed to the bathroom.

While I was showering, Toey got up and began rummaging around in the kitchen. She was in a terrycloth robe and cutting cantaloupe when I entered the room. She spun around and kissed me. I hugged her and kissed back—I wanted the pressure of her against my chest.

"You hungry?" she asked, pulling away.

"What do you have in mind?" I said.

"Not that, silly. Food! Fruit and cereal?" She pulled her hair out of her face, her eyes sparkling.

For a moment, I considered luring her back to bed. But things were moving too fast. Getting prepared for my Monday meeting with Monty and the Mexico trip was my priority. Breakfast was the sensible alternative.

While I was eating, Toey showered. When she returned in slacks and a sweatshirt, I'd already tidied up the kitchen.

"Why, thank you, Jake. You did not have to do the dishes." She smelled freshly desirable.

"Hey, I wanted to. What do you have on your agenda for today?"

"I need to work on my lesson outline. There is only one week of school left before Christmas vacation. What do you want to do?"

"Why don't we go over to my place and do some planning? All the Mexico charts and books are there. I can bring you home right after lunch."

"OK. But let me follow you in my car. That way you will not have to run me back." I sensed she was making sure she could escape if I had an ulterior motive.

Toey's Toyota was in pretty good shape, compared to Van Gogh. Bright yellow, it was easy to keep in my rearview mirror as we drove toward Pacific Beach. When we arrived, we parked both cars on the busy boulevard in front, next to Miles' Chevy and Jill's red Pontiac Fiero. I guessed Buddy and Ted's wheels were parked in the alley carport.

"Looks like the whole gang's here. Who's in charge of the party?" I asked as we entered.

My exuberance contrasted with the tranquility of Ted and Jill sitting quietly at the dining room table, Jill grading papers and Ted adding up marks and entering them in a spiral-bound ledger. Toey and I walked through the living room, where Miles held down the couch, snoring to a football pre-game program.

"Like, happy Sunday," Jill said, speaking first. "No party here, just Miss Dilly's study hall."

"Buddy and Wanda are out in back, working on a surfboard. Buddy's convinced her she has to learn how to ride." Ted was grinning. "A surfboard, I mean."

Jill poked him in the ribs with her elbow, then turned toward us. "Like, what's happening with you guys?"

"I've agreed to go to La Paz and pick up a yacht for Monty Banks," I said. "Gonna do it over Christmas vacation. Toey's agreed to help. Anyone else want to go?"

"Why don't you ask Buddy? As far as I know, he hasn't committed for any sailing school stuff, and he was going to take some time off, anyway."

Ted would've been my first choice, even if Jill had to tag along, but I knew he had to work over the holidays. Toey sat down at the table, conversing with Jill, while I went out back to talk to Buddy.

Wanda's bubbly chatter greeted me as I opened the screen door. "Hey, Jake, how ya doin'? How's your pretty little Toey?" She was wearing her lime-green sweats and chewing away.

"We're both great. How about you guys?"

"Buddy's convinced me to try surfing. This is going to be my very own board." She bumped him in the thigh with her rump. "Right, honey?"

A 1960s vintage Stewart longboard was supported between sawhorses—they were sanding out fiberglass repairs Buddy had made to the bottom. Wanda's hands were powdery, and her sun-worn face smudged with white. The messy work didn't seem to faze her.

"You're going to have to wait for the water to warm up," I suggested. "The ocean's wintry cold right now."

"Yeah? I don't want Buddy freezing his equipment off, you know. It's working pretty good right now." She smiled, chewing lustily and butting him with her backside again. Buddy rolled his eyes in feigned embarrassment.

"I've got an idea! Why don't you two come to Mexico over Christmas vacation with Toey and me? All we got to do is pick up a sailboat and sail it back. The water's warmer, and all expenses paid. Bring your boards. It could be quite a party." As soon as the words came out, I couldn't believe I'd included Wanda in the invitation.

"You really mean it?" she asked. "I can get the time off. I know I can. Shit, the restaurant owes me. Buddy, you planned to be off anyway. Remember? You said no classes until January. How about it, honey? Let's go!" She hugged Buddy's neck, a cloud of fiberglass dust rising above them.

"Yes, I mean it. I'd like both of you to go with me." I laughed, wondering what Toey would think. "We're going to pick up a Gulfstar 50 ketch. Should be a piece of cake to sail it back. Right, Buddy?"

"I'm game," he said. "What's the deal?"

I explained briefly and suggested they clean up and come inside. I felt it was important for the four of us to sit down and plan with the charts.

"We're going to party in Mexico!" Wanda blurted as we entered the dining room. "Toey, you and me and the boys. Ain't that great?" Her exuberance woke Miles. He moaned a grudging acknowledgement and retreated upstairs. I assumed he had to play later that night.

Toey looked at me with surprise. She knew I was going to ask Buddy, but Wanda she wasn't prepared for. Thankfully, she took it in stride. Interested in what we were up to, Ted and Jill set aside their papers to pore over charts with us. Looking at the coastal maps with this group, especially Wanda, was a big mistake.

"Well, I'll be damned. I never noticed *that*!" Wanda said, staring at the San Diego to Cabo Colonett chart. "Look here, Toey. What's *that* make you think of?"

Toey, and all of us, saw where Wanda was using her finger to trace the outline of Point Loma as it curved southward from the Cabrillo Monument and the entrance to San Diego Bay. The similarity to a flaccid penis was hard to ignore. Toey and Jill blushed, Ted and I laughed nervously, Buddy looked at the ceiling, and Wanda chomped on a fresh wad of gum and just smiled.

I moved the subject away from San Diego and its distinctive geography; the giggling and snickering continued as I tried to get us back on track. It was beginning to sink in: Captaining this irreverent group was going to be tough.

As we settled back down to business, I learned that, except for Transpac, most of Buddy's ocean sailing experience had been confined to coastal waters off California. Ted and I were the lone sailors with first-hand knowledge of the Baja. Ted had been to Cabo San Lucas numerous times on powerboats. However, I didn't realize he had also captained a fifty-eight-foot Bertram Convertible Sportfisher before joining YachtTow. The owner liked to do big-money Mexican billfish tournaments, especially the Bisby in Cabo. We identified all the anchorages and places to hide if the weather turned bad. Whenever we came to a chart with Point Loma, Wanda laughed.

As lunchtime approached, we all walked over to the Busted Surfboard. Business was slow on this off-season Sunday. Wanda used the opportunity to ask her boss for the time off. Other waitresses agreed to cover for her, so he said it was no problem. I was stuck with her.

I knew that Buddy and Toey's sailing abilities bordered on professional, but Wanda's experience was unknown, so I asked the question. "Wanda, you ever been on a sailboat?"

"Yup. Hell, yes! Used to sail Skimmers on Mission Bay. Was vice president of the association for a while." She looked at me like I should have known. "Also worked a day-fishing boat out of Commercial Basin for a couple of years. Shit, I was the galley slave. Name of the boat was *Happy Hooker*. I developed a cast-iron stomach from cooking underway."

I couldn't tell if she was putting me on or not. I caught a surprised look on Toey's face, but the tip-off was when Buddy grinned. He knew where I was going with the questions; he also knew how Wanda would handle them.

Throughout lunch, we talked about travel arrangements. I planned to call everyone after I met with the bank, signed the contract, and got money. The airline tickets could be purchased on Tuesday, so I suggested we get together for a dinner then, to discuss any last-minute stuff.

My meeting with Monty Banks was scheduled for 11:30 Monday morning. His upper-floor office in an ostentatious shiny-green tower in Mission Valley was easy to locate off Interstate 8.

I turned into the palm-lined driveway and found a parking space between a vintage white Mercedes and a silver BMW 320i. Intent on making a good impression, I wore crisp white slacks and a navy polo shirt, and arrived fifteen minutes early.

When I presented myself to the pretty receptionist, she pushed a button that summoned Monty's secretary from behind walnut-paneled walls. Grace, a pleasant matronly woman, escorted me to a small, ornate conference room. When I sat down at the oval glass and rosewood table, she handed me a manila folder and offered me a soft drink.

All the papers were ready for review, yellow Post-its attached to identify each document: delivery contract, copy of ship's papers showing First Interstate Mortgage as the lien holder, court order for repossession, and a letter from the bank authorizing me to be in possession of the vessel for the purpose of returning it to California.

"Hello, Jake. I see Grace has you all fixed up." Monty entered the room in a rumpled white shirt, skinny tie, and gray slacks. He extended his plump hand in greeting. "Any questions?"

"Yeah, a few."

"OK, but first let's wrap up the signing of the agreement so you can get your money. How much do you need for travel?" He was tucking the portion of his shirt dislodged by his belly back into his pants. "We'll go to lunch, while Grace completes the paperwork."

"I'm not sure. A hundred and fifty dollars times four people?" I felt stupid for not having checked the cost in advance.

"Grace, please, call a travel agent and verify the airfare from San Diego to La Paz. We need a check for that amount, plus marina charges, and the $5,000." He looked at me. "Be sure to keep all the receipts, Jake."

"Yes, sir."

Everything looked straightforward. In legalese, the document pretty much described what Monty and I had discussed at the Yacht Club. Grace was a notary, so I showed her my California driver's license for identification. After I signed the contract, she had me sign her book. Monty endorsed the agreement on behalf of the bank and gave the contract back to Grace as we left. I kept the folder with the other documents.

"We'll be back in an hour, Grace. Please, have everything ready when we return." I was surprised he would make her work through lunch. I had all afternoon, and this didn't seem like it was that important a deal.

In his silver BMW, Monty drove us to a restaurant on the opposite side of I-8. A huge glass greenhouse, the inside of the eatery was filled with ferns and other hanging plants. When the manager greeted Monty like a long-lost friend, I suspected the bank might hold a mortgage on the place.

We were led to a private booth at the far end of a large, curved glass enclosure. I felt like I was in an expensive nursery; all the plants, including orchids and cymbidiums, looked exotic and lush. In rebellion against the overwhelming vegetation, I ordered a well-done steak.

"Fire away. Let's see if I can answer what questions you have." Monty didn't waste any time getting down to business as he attacked a huge slab of medium rare roast beef.

He informed me that until one week ago the vessel had been berthed at Marina de La Paz. He had talked to Mary, the marina manager, in the morning, and she told him the vessel was gone, but had been seen anchored at various places around La Paz.

Since the boat owed six months' slip rent, she had filed a notice with the Mexican port captain's office. The vessel would not be allowed to check out of his jurisdiction—or the country, for that matter—until the fees were paid. Monty was sending money with me to secure a release from the marina. He emphasized I should check in with Mary immediately upon arrival, since she would be a good source of local information and could help me with the authorities.

The vessel was a Gulfstar 50 ketch, recently observed in fair condition. Of course, there were no guarantees of what we might find. Its name, *Shore Loser*, struck me as odd for a corporately owned boat. It was the kind of name a cruiser would choose. It might also predict the reaction of its caretakers when we repossessed it. I couldn't decide if I liked the sound of the name or not. I was sure I had heard it before.

When we returned to Monty's office, Grace had everything ready. "Here are the signed contracts and checks, Mr. Mortensen. I need your signature on the receipts for the money. I am also going to need the names of your crew and their résumés." I looked at Monty.

"It's just a formality. The insurance company needs it in order to bind coverage," he said.

"What do you mean?"

"In case you guys get hurt, or killed, or disappear, or something. We want to be sure the value of the boat is covered if you don't make it back. Actually, we would probably be better off financially if you didn't. Just kidding!"

I had an uneasy feeling as I gave Grace the information about my three friends. When she read their names and experience back to me, it reminded me of newspaper obituaries. I recalled Toey's warning, when we first discussed going to Mexico. The potential danger associated with our mission was beginning to sink in: We were going to a foreign country to steal a boat, and then we were going to make a run for the border, about 950 miles away.

Grace tucked my checks and documents in a large manila envelope and sealed it. I shook hands, thanked them, and made a hasty exit before I could change my mind.

Most of Tuesday was spent running around, making last-minute arrangements and getting stuff for the trip. Spread out among several marine hardware stores and the travel agency, I dropped over a thousand dollars.

By evening, I was ready for a break. Buddy and Toey had agreed to meet me at The Red Sails Inn around 7. Wanda had to work. At 6:30 I stopped to pick up Toey, just as she pulled into her driveway.

"Hello, Jake. Are you early or am I late?" Her arms were full of books and papers. She looked exhausted.

"A little of both. Here, let me help you." I took what she would give me and followed her upstairs.

The adjacent driveway was still empty. I asked how things were going. "They are gone," she said. "I will tell you the whole story at dinner. Can we go? I am ready to let my hair down." We walked the few blocks to the waterfront restaurant.

"No fights tonight, Jake, promise?" Shina, the happy Hawaiian, teased as we entered.

"OK, but you make sure there are no Marines in here on leave," I laughed.

She led us to a table near the fireplace. I told her we were expecting one more, gave her our drink order, and Toey began her story.

Sunday night, the police had raided the biker's apartment, found drugs, and identified three stolen motorcycles. Several of the bikers resisted arrest, and a fight ensued. Apparently, the officers had to call for backup, and the apartment sustained a lot of damage. On Monday morning, Toey had to miss school to accompany her landlord to the courthouse, where he filed an eviction notice, and they both signed complaints.

"I am scared, Jake."

"Don't be. They're locked up, so they can't do anything." I reached across the table and held her trembling hand.

"What if someone posts bail, and they all get out? Like you did with Miles? They may think I had them arrested."

"That won't happen. If they got into a fight with the cops, they're in big trouble because of their own actions, not yours." Since I didn't really know what would happen, I added, "Think positively. You'll be with me in Mexico, partying for two weeks and stealing a boat."

"Yes? Like this is going to be a vacation?" Her eyes were locked on mine, deadly serious.

"Monty assured me, everything is going to go smoothly. All we have to do is sail the boat back to San Diego. Like my father said, it'll be good for the soul."

"Maybe you are right, Jake. I really do need to get away from this place. Thinking on the positive side, this will give me a chance to practice my navigation skills, something I do not get to do when I am racing. And I get to spend some time with you. I am really looking forward to that."

"There you go." I squeezed her hand.

Buddy joined us, and I distributed the airline tickets and confirmations for the rooms booked at the Los Arcos Hotel. Since I was flying down early, I'd pick each of them up at the airport when they arrived.

"On the off-chance we miss each other, the Los Arcos Hotel is a landmark on the waterfront, three or four blocks from Marina de La Paz. Any taxi driver knows it," I said, trying to make the whole thing seem a breeze.

By the time we finished eating, Toey's mood was much lighter. Both she and Buddy seemed charged up about the upcoming adventure. On the way home, Buddy was going to stop by the Busted Surfboard and fill Wanda in. We knew she was anxious to go and, party animal that she was, probably was already packed. I walked Toey back to her place after dinner and shared a lingering kiss at the bottom of her stairs.

"Call me if your rowdy neighbors come back. Van Gogh and I will come right over."

"This is not funny, Jake Mortensen. You are not going to be in town."

"I'll be here through tomorrow night. After that, call Ted. I'll explain what's happened." I really didn't think there would be a problem. "Don't worry. I'll have him check up on you."

"I am sorry, Jake. Please, take care of yourself. I will be all right."

When I got home, nobody was there. Figuring Ted had joined Buddy at the Busted Surfboard, I decided to hook up with them. Sure enough, they were downstairs, Ted drinking beer and Buddy iced tea.

"Hi, Jake! The usual?" Wanda came flouncing over from the bar.

"Yes, please. You ready to go to Mexico?"

"You bet your bippy, honey. Got my bags packed already . . . don't I, Buddy?" She gave Buddy a familiar nudge. In contrast to Toey, Wanda always seemed to be in a good mood, never upset with Buddy—never upset, period.

Wednesday was spent packing. I decided to take all of my scuba stuff, removing the pressure valve from my aluminum 90 so I could take it on the plane. The tank, BC, regulators, eighth-inch wetsuit, weight belt, knives, and other gear filled one multi-compartment dive bag. My clothes, personal kit, navigation gear, charts, foul-weather jacket, and inflatable safety harness fit snugly in my Navy seabag.

Wednesday evening I called Toey to check up on her. As far as she knew, her former neighbors were still in jail. Because of the damage they had caused to the apartment, her landlord's attorney was doing his best to keep them behind bars. He'd filed all kinds of charges and was taking them to court.

She sounded more confident and seemed to be looking forward to the trip. I was relieved. I was going to have other things on my mind— like finding a boat in a foreign country and taking it away from whoever was on board. From prior experiences in Baja, I knew the Mexican police would be no help.

I flew to La Paz Thursday afternoon on Mexicana Flight 241. The Spanish-speaking crew was courteous and attentive and, best of all, the booze was free. I was reintroduced to Bacardi *Añejo*, a tasty, dark Mexican rum.

Our descent over the mountains into the barren valley north of the city was bumpy, and at one point I thought we had hit an air pocket, because we dropped toward the runway. At the last moment, we zoomed in full throttle, the passengers cheering when we touched down.

On the ground, it took half an hour to clear immigration and collect gear. At customs I was told to press the button on an apparatus similar to a traffic signal, and a red light flashed "Alto." Impatient tourists backed up in a line behind me as the agent went through my luggage, questioning everything.

In my broken Spanish, I tried to explain I was here to do some scuba diving and was staying at the Los Arcos Hotel. I told him I didn't like to rent gear maintained by someone else, so I had brought my own.

He left, I assumed, to get a supervisor. I turned to the angry crowd behind me, held up my hands, and shrugged my shoulders.

Fifteen or twenty minutes later, the customs agent returned with another officer, who spoke some English. I wished Toey were here, her knowledge of Spanish would have been helpful. The new official had me move my luggage to another table, while his partner started processing the irritated people behind me.

"*Señor*, you got a problem! Why so much stuff? It looks new. You are trying to smuggle things into Mexico to sell, yes?" His English was actually very good. He was wearing a holstered pistol, which he adjusted periodically.

"No, absolutely not!" I decided to selectively tell him the truth. "I am here to pick up a sailboat and deliver it back to the United States. I need all this equipment, in case I have to do maintenance underway. Some of it is for safety."

I pulled out a copy of my U.S. Coast Guard license for effect, and he examined it.

"OK. You look like an honest *gringo*. I will get some papers for you to fill out. You will have to pay a fee for the trouble. Your passport, *por favor*." He held his hand out. I thought I saw him wink at his partner as he turned back to his office.

Another half-hour passed before the second agent returned. The papers he carried described my luggage and equipment in Spanish—the document had been signed and stamped "Importación Temporal" in blue ink over the typing. I added my signature to five copies, one copy was returned with my passport.

"Now you have to pay, *señor*." He extended his hand.

"*Cuantos*?"

"Fifty dollars U.S., *señor*."

"Do I get a receipt?" I asked, pulling a bill out of my wallet and handing it over.

"*Gracias, Señor* Mortensen. That paper is your receipt." He smiled as he took the $50. "*Bienvenidos a México.*"

"*De nada,*" I mumbled, as I gathered up my things.

Throwing my seabag over my shoulder, I picked up the heavy dive bag and headed across the tiled lobby. A thin child ran up to me. Barefoot and dressed in a torn flannel shirt and dusty blue jeans, he reminded me of the "Save the Children" ads on television. His hair was jet black, and he looked part Indian. I wondered if his skin was really very dark or just dirty. I guessed he was about ten or twelve years old.

"Carry your bags, *señor*? Need a taxi?" He took my dive bag and could barely handle the weight. I liked him immediately.

"*¿Cómo te llamas?*" I asked.

"Francisco," he answered, struggling with the heavy luggage, as he dragged it backward across the floor using both hands. "Call me Pancho."

"My name is Jake. You know the city pretty good, Pancho?"

"*Sí,* you want me to find you a pretty *señorita*?"

"No!" I laughed. "But I do need a guide. How much for the afternoon, say four hours and dinner?"

"How about one dollar an hour? I am a good guide, *Señor* Jake. You will see. It is a good price, no?" He was out of breath and grinning from ear to ear.

"OK, you got a deal. Time starts when we leave the Los Arcos Hotel. Let's get a cab." The dive bag was so much bigger than he was, I felt guilty letting him handle it alone.

Pancho and I pushed through the dust-covered, aluminum and glass doors. An assortment of taxis were lined up, most of them older Chevrolet station wagons painted maroon and white.

Pancho yelled something in Spanish. An equally thin, older man, wearing leather sandals and an oil-spotted shirt and pants, came to take my other bag. The first car in line, one of its headlights broken and faded lettering on its side, was his.

"This is my uncle, Rodrigo. He does not speak English, but he is a good driver. You are staying at Los Arcos, yes?"

"Yes, Los Arcos—down by the waterfront."

His uncle lifted the dirt-covered tailgate, and the two of them loaded my gear into the aging wagon. Several Quaker State oil containers were nested in the empty wheel well normally reserved for the spare tire; the tailgate latch was broken. To secure the door, Rodrigo attached a piece of bailing wire to the bumper. Striped serapes upholstered the sagging front and rear seats; the headliner and door panels had gone AWOL.

Since there was no inside handle, Pancho opened the passenger door for me, then slammed it shut, and climbed in front with his uncle. As Rodrigo started the engine, a cloud of black smoke belched from the tailpipe and a loud knocking telegraphed from under the hood. The billowing exhaust engulfed the taxi behind us—an oily smokescreen grew as we pulled away from the curb.

Gray concrete transitioned to black asphalt, which became dirt washboard when we left the vicinity of the airport. Pancho's uncle expertly negotiated potholes and rocks of varying dimensions. As we neared town, the pavement returned and improved.

Arriving at the hotel, Rodrigo hopped out, opened the hood, and added oil, leaving Pancho to help me with my bags. Los Arcos was an attractive Mexican colonial hotel with balconied rooms, two interior courtyards, and a lot of history. Guidebooks described the bar as a once-favorite hangout for the likes of John Wayne and Humphrey Bogart.

A wide half-flight of steps led up from the street level to the lobby. The reception desk staff gave Pancho a peculiar look, so he decided to wait outside, leaning against the fender of his uncle's cab while I checked in. As the bellman showed me to my room, he warned me to be careful of "street children." When I laughed and told him Francisco was my guide, he rolled his eyes and repeated his admonishment.

Changing into shorts and a t-shirt seemed like a good idea. Then I checked my money and documents and separated enough to pay off the marina and still have some extra. Carrying my canvas briefcase downstairs, I locked the majority of the money in a safe deposit box and exchanged some dollars for pesos. Even if it wasn't worth much, the multi-colored Mexican money was beautiful, so different from the monotonous green U.S. currency.

Outside, Pancho and his uncle were waiting. "Where do you want to go, *Señor* Jake?"

"Marina de La Paz." I climbed into the Chevy, and we were off in a plume of smoke.

Mary, the marina manager, was expecting me. She had the slip charges itemized and a bill prepared for the bank. I paid her in U.S. traveler's checks. So far, nobody wanted pesos here—they wanted U.S. dollars. Mary told me Monty had called this morning and left a message for me to return his call.

With the bill paid, she said she'd be glad to go to the port captain, process the necessary documents, and help me obtain a clearance permitting the vessel to leave Mexico. She would need crewmember passports and visas to complete the paperwork.

Using her phone, I called collect to the States.

"Hello, Jake. How are things going?" Monty asked.

"Good and not so good. Everything is OK with the marina. However, I haven't found the boat yet. No one seems to know where it is."

"Any ideas?"

"Yeah, I'm going to pay some street kids to help me locate it." Looking out the office window, I could see Pancho talking to another youngster in the parking lot.

"That's resourceful. Good luck. Keep me posted." He seemed disinterested.

"Will if I can. I still don't know how all this is gonna play out."

I thanked Mary for her help and made an appointment to return Saturday, after my crew arrived. She suggested I ask around at The Dock restaurant next door. It was usually full of sailors and waterfront workers, and someone might have seen *Shore Loser*.

She described two men, Chuck and Bart, who had been on the boat when it was in the marina. I asked her to keep my intentions secret from the boating crowd. I didn't want them to know why I was here, and I sure didn't want word to reach Chuck and Bart through the boater grapevine. I told her my chances for surprising them seemed better if I worked through Mexican informants. She agreed.

Back in the cab, I had Pancho's uncle drive me to all the places a vessel might berth. Over the next two hours, Rodrigo added engine oil four times. We drove the entire waterfront from the Hotel Gran Baja to the Pemex dock at Punta Príeta. At Marina Palmira, I bought the three of us dinner and explained to Pancho why I was in La Paz.

"You find *Shore Loser* for me, and I'll pay you $50 U.S. You must keep this a secret, though, or no money. *Comprende?*"

"You a cop, *Señor* Jake?" he asked suspiciously.

"No. I'm a ship's captain."

"OK. One hundred dollars, and I'll find the boat. And I take you to it! Deal?" It was then that I realized I'd just teamed up with a very young hustler.

"No. Fifty dollars when you find it and take me to it. Another fifty dollars if you help me get it out of here. Take it or leave it."

"OK, *Señor* Jake. Deal?"

"Deal!" I said, and shook his small hand. I wondered just how old he really was. Rodrigo had been silently eating, I'm sure he hadn't understood a word that was said.

We returned to Los Arcos, where I made arrangements for Rodrigo to take me to the airport Friday to pick up Buddy and Wanda. Saying "*Hasta mañana*," I paid Pancho for his efforts and headed for the bar. I could hear Pancho yelling, "*Gracias, Señor* Jake," as he and his uncle departed. An *Añejo* and Coke was going to taste mighty good.

By reading guidebooks, I had a pretty good thumbnail sketch of La Paz. The capital of Baja California Sur, it is a city of almost 200,000 people. Famous for deep-sea fishing, it attracts over 100,000 visitors a year in search of marlin, sailfish, swordfish, yellowtail, mahi-mahi, and tuna.

Most of the city is on a hill overlooking a deep inlet. A long sandbar, El Mogote, shelters the bay from the Sea of Cortéz. Just fifty miles north of the Tropic of Cancer, La Paz's climate is sunny and mild most of the year. The sea can be observed from almost any point in town. Usually, the sunset is a blazing spectacle of red and yellow, making the water appear scarlet, and so the nickname Vermilion Sea.

From my barstool overlooking the beach and anchored sailboats, La Paz looked pretty and peaceful. Out there somewhere was *Shore Loser*— but where? Motioning to a lovely *señorita*, I ordered myself another rum and Coke.

CHAPTER SEVEN

# THE BOAT

"*Señor* Jake! *Señor* Jake!" Pancho was gasping for air as he ran toward me, his arms and legs flailing about like a rag doll.

I had jogged almost the length of the waterfront. Not used to the strange city noises, I'd tossed and turned all night. By sunrise, my body demanded some hard-core exercise, and a run along the beach malecón, with its rock seawall and palm trees, seemed like a good idea.

I figured I must have done about fifteen blocks before stopping to adjust my shoelaces. Poor Pancho. I wondered how long he had been trying to catch me.

"Hey, calm down, Pancho." I lifted his skinny body onto the seawall. He was wearing the same rags as yesterday, and I detected a wheeze as he labored for air.

"I saw you when you left the hotel, *Señor* Jake . . . You run too fast."

He stopped talking and tried to get his breathing under control. I waited silently as he sat with his hands on his knees, his little chest heaving in and out.

"I found the boat!" Looking up at me and sucking air through his teeth in a hissing sound, he was grinning from ear to ear.

"Sorry for the chase, Pancho. Tell me about the boat. Where is it? Can you take me to it?" How had he located it so quickly?

"My uncle Juan saw the boat in Bahía Pichilingue, out by the ferry terminal, two days ago when he was selling his fish to one of the *palapa* restaurants. You owe me fifty bucks!" he said, extending his right hand, suddenly breathing normally.

"Not until I see it! You think it's still there?"

"Yes! Yes! Juan can take us." He had climbed down from the seawall and was pulling me.

We walked back to the beach opposite my hotel, where he introduced me to a man mending a net.

"This is my *tío*, Juan. He does not speak any English." Pancho's newest uncle gave me a toothless smile and a right hand that was missing two fingers.

"How much for Juan to take us out there?" I was beginning to understand the game and wondered how many "uncles" Pancho hustled for.

"Ten bucks. Just for fuel. I pay the rest. We made a deal, yes?" Pancho looked worried. Either he didn't trust me or he didn't know how far he could push. He was scratching the back of his head, and I wondered what was in his dark hair. It looked like it hadn't been washed in a long time.

"OK, Pancho. Let's go."

Juan's boat was one of the white and blue *pangas* tethered in the water, the name, *Rosita*, painted in flowery red letters on both sides of the bow. He pulled it closer to shore, where the water was knee-deep, almost waist deep for Pancho.

I carried my little helper on my shoulders so he wouldn't have to get wet. When I smelled him, I knew I'd made a mistake. A saltwater bath would have done him good.

Juan's boat could have used a good scrubbing, too. The bilge water was full of oil, silvery scales, and fish guts. Two twenty-liter plastic containers held gasoline, in addition to the rusty five-gallon metal fuel tank in the stern. Several empty oil containers floated in the bottom of the boat. An eighty-horsepower four-stroke Yamaha hung off the transom.

We climbed aboard, and Pancho began bailing with a cut-off plastic water bottle. Juan tilted the engine enough to immerse the prop and backed us into deeper water. When we were clear of mooring lines to the other boats, he lowered the engine and twisted the throttle to full on. I thought the bow of the boat was going to rise out of the water, but the launch settled into a level plane, and we sped down the buoyed channel paralleling the malecón and the city waterfront. I guessed we were making twenty knots.

Once past the city, we turned into the channel just beyond the entrance to Marina Palmira and headed along a sandy coastline toward the Pemex tank farm at Punta Príeta. A huge oil tanker had just pulled in, her lines were being made fast to the pier and mooring buoys.

At the speed we were going, I was not sure we could avoid interfering with the tugboat working at her bow. I hung on to the gunwales on one side of me and prepared to leap overboard if necessary. At the last minute, Juan banked radically to port and kicked a six-foot wake against the mooring buoy and the tug. Pancho pointed his finger at me and laughed as if he had just played a prank on his best friend.

Passing Punta Príeta, we turned to starboard and lined up with the next landmass, Punta Colorado. Wet and salty from the sea spray, Pancho resumed bailing. As we sped along, barren coastline fell away to form what looked like a small, unprotected bay. The tank farm spread out on a desolate bluff behind us. We were now beyond the buoyed channel, which had ended at the Punta Príeta lighthouse.

After the next bluff, I could make out what looked like a large inlet, extending to the right of a low sandy point ahead. Juan corrected course to take the shoal buoy and sand spit on his port.

"There is Pichilingue. See the ferry from Mazatlán?" Pancho was standing up, holding on to the bowline and pointing. "It comes all the way from the mainland once a day."

I could barely see the big vessel in the morning haze, docked at the far end of the deep, narrow bay. Several palm-frond *palapa* restaurants dotted the long beach; half a dozen *pangas* were anchored in the water or hauled up on the sand. A speedboat was towing a parasailer high above us. But no sailboats. Disappointment covered Pancho's face.

"Maybe they moved to the other side. It is better for yachts. No big commercial boats," Pancho said, then shouted something in Spanish to his uncle.

Without reducing throttle, Juan turned *Rosita* hard to port. In one wide, banking arc, we circled back, racing along the length of Isla San Juan Nepomuceno toward the next small bay, and there it was—a lone sailboat, easily fifty feet long. It was anchored just north of some small powerboats moored along the causeway connecting island to mainland. I asked Juan to slow down. He stopped. I think he only knew two speeds: stop and fast.

"Listen, Pancho. I don't want them to know I'm here. Have Juan go quietly by the back of the boat so I can check the name. Then let's head for the beach."

Pancho told his uncle. We quickly accelerated—just the opposite of what I wanted. But it was too late. We came within ten feet of the boat, our churning wake almost swamping a rubber dinghy tied to the boarding ladder. I could clearly observe the lettering on the transom: *Shore Loser*, San Diego, CA.

Someone sat up in the cockpit as we sped by and gave us the one-finger salute. I waved back, hoping Chuck or Bart, or whoever it was, assumed I was a tourist. I wished Toey were here to make it look more convincing, like a couple joyriding, enjoying the sights.

Juan went about beaching his *panga* with the same finesse he'd used to pilot it all morning: toward the shore at full speed. Fortunately, there was little surf. He tilted the engine at the last moment, the *panga* slid ten feet up onto dry sand, and we disembarked without getting our feet wet.

Our landing placed us in front of a dilapidated hut several yards up the beach and opposite the yacht. Two small, dark-skinned children dressed similarly to Pancho ran to him and started talking. I walked to a *palapa*, ordered a *cerveza*, and sat at a rickety wood table. The beer was warm, but it didn't matter. It was wet, tasted good, and that's what I needed.

From the kids on the beach, Pancho learned *Shore Loser* had moved into the anchorage the prior morning. The two men on it had come ashore in the afternoon, drinking until very late. According to the children, the gringos were loud, vulgar, and mean to the family operating the bar. Rumor was they were on cocaine.

The information Pancho got gave me a clue about what I was up against. It didn't sound good.

I was anxious for my crew to get here; Buddy and Wanda were arriving this afternoon, and I needed to get back to the hotel. I gave Pancho his first fifty dollars and, with everyone's help, we pushed the *panga* back into the surf.

Later, when Rodrigo appeared in front of Los Arcos at the appointed time, I was disappointed Pancho wasn't with him. Maybe I shouldn't have paid him so quickly. The knocking of the taxi motor was unrelenting; we drove to the airport wondering if we'd make it. Once parked at the end of the taxi line, Rodrigo ran to a friend's car for more oil. As I walked into the terminal, I felt a tug at my pants.

"Hey! *Señor* Jake. When do we go get the boat?" It was Pancho, still in the same grubby clothes. Either he wore them for effect as he worked the crowd, or they were all he had. I really wanted to find out more about my new, young friend.

"Maybe tonight, maybe tomorrow." I still didn't have a plan.

"Jake! Jake Mortensen. We're over here!" A familiar feminine voice ricocheted across the tile and cement lobby.

I turned and couldn't believe Wanda's tourist-from-hell getup: floppy hat, cheap costume jewelry, stilettos, and tight gold lamé pants. I wasn't sure I wanted to admit knowing her, but waved back anyway. Buddy pushed the customs button and got a green light. Although they had two surfboards and big bags, officials let them pass.

"I was gonna say—that was quite a landing, man. I was thinking I was back in Nam," Buddy said, grinning and resting his luggage as we shook hands.

"Must have had the same pilot I did," I said, nodding at Pancho to help Wanda. "Yeah, it felt like landing on a carrier when I came in, too. Meet my young friend, Pancho."

We loaded their stuff and climbed into Rodrigo's taxi. He had obviously worked on the engine—oil and grease were smeared all over hands, arms, and shirt. Pancho rode in the back with the suitcases and surfboards. During the bumpy trip to town, Wanda and Buddy wanted to know everything about La Paz and if I'd seen the sailboat. I was reluctant to tell them I still didn't have a firm plan. We'd have to make it up as we went along.

While I checked them into the hotel, Pancho went off to arrange for a boat. I told him I was anxious to get back out to *Shore Loser* before dark. Before I left to go to my room and change, I encouraged Buddy and Wanda to dress for the beach and bring their surfboards. A strategy was taking shape. I packed my towel and jacket, went to meet Buddy and Wanda in the lobby, and we walked across the street to where Juan and Pancho were waiting.

The afternoon wind had built up a moderate chop in the channel. Pancho seemed as intent on getting back to *Shore Loser* as I was and urged his uncle to hurry. The weight of two extra people helped level the *panga* as we skimmed along doing a wet twenty knots.

When we rounded the low point at Isla San Juan Nepomuceno, I pointed to the anchored vessel. Buddy and Wanda nodded.

"Pancho, do you know the family at the beach restaurant in front of *Shore Loser*? Can they be trusted?"

"*Sí*. I know all these people. Sometimes I help my *tío* sell fish to them. They are good persons."

"OK. Let's go in there." I pointed to the *palapa* where the two men had been drinking the previous night. We had about an hour before sunset. I turned to Buddy and Wanda. "OK, I want you guys to act like tourists as we go by the boat."

Wanda was perfect. She took off her shorts and windbreaker. Juan and Pancho's eyes became big as saucers when they saw she was wearing a fluorescent-pink micro-bikini. Standing up, she waved her jacket overhead and started yelling.

We roared by the stern of the anchored yacht, and two heads popped up in the cockpit. Both Chuck and Bart were on the boat, with their dinghy tied to a stern cleat. Wanda sure knew how to attract attention! As we headed for the restaurant, I was positive the "caretakers" of *Shore Loser* would soon get into their inflatable and follow us in. I knew I didn't have much time.

"Listen up, you guys," I said as soon as we had ordered drinks. "Pancho, I want you to go talk to the owners and look like you work here. Wanda, when those two boat bums come in, make friends with them. Try to find out what their plans are. Tell them we're all gonna party in town tonight. I've got to figure out a way to lure them away from the boat. I'm sorry, but at the moment you are the only decoy I've got. Pancho, where is the surf good?"

"Nothing really good around here. *Yo no sé*. Maybe down by Los Muertos."

"If anybody asks, we just came from Muertos. Come on, Buddy, I've got an idea. Let's put the surfboards in the water and look like we're cleaning them. Remember, Wanda, you're the attraction. Get as much information as you can. Everyone, be careful and alert."

About fifteen minutes after Wanda got settled, the two men pulled the dinghy to the stern boarding ladder and climbed in. They had taken the bait. As they pulled their boat ashore, Buddy and I waved from the water.

One of them was grubby and in his early twenties. The college emblem on the front of his yellow tank top said UCSD. Short and stocky, he looked like a weightlifter, not a student. In contrast, the other guy was a skinny six-footer of about thirty. His prominent Adam's apple bobbed beneath a short copper beard, and he was shirtless, making it hard to miss the skull-and-dagger tattoo on his right bicep.

Ignoring us, they were more interested in finding out what Wanda was all about and hot-footed it through the scorching sand right to where she was sitting.

"If you two are game, here's my plan." Buddy and I were lying on our boards, head to head. It seemed stupid, but I was whispering. "You and Wanda talk them into going back with us in the *panga* for a night on the town. When we get to Los Arcos, I'm gonna pretend I'm ill and beg off. While you guys are partying, Pancho and I will come back out here and move the boat."

"That's what I was wonderin'. You think it'll work?"

"It will, if you get 'em both good and drunk. But be careful. Take them to a bar or disco where there are a lot of people. When they're totally smashed, pour 'em in a taxi and send them out to the ferry terminal. The road ends there. They'll have to walk to the beach and swim out to the boat. When they discover the boat's gone, nobody will be around. This way no one will get hurt." I was proud of myself. The plan actually sounded feasible.

"Where you gonna take *Shore Loser*?"

"I'll tie it up at Marina de La Paz. I don't think they'll look there— they owe too much back rent. I'll sleep on the boat and meet you for breakfast at the restaurant in the marina."

"What time?"

"Eight o'clock? You got enough money for tonight?"

"Yeah, no problem. I'm thinkin' your idea may just work."

We paddled back to shore and stowed our surfboards in the *panga*. Buddy joined Wanda and her two admirers. I went to see Pancho, who was in the back, talking with the restaurant owners. I divulged my scheme, including the part where he and I would come back to get *Shore Loser*. He grinned and nodded, explaining in Spanish to the couple.

"OK. Give me two *cervezas* so I look like I came over here for a reason."

Leaving Pancho to finish clueing-in the owners, I walked over to the party table.

"Jake, meet Chuck and Bart. They own that beautiful yacht out there." Bart was the young, husky guy, Chuck the older and taller. Wanda, playing her roll to the max, continued, "They want us to go sailing with them. Isn't that great!"

"Hey, wait a minute, doll. We invited you, not the whole damn fuckin' beach." Even though Bart said it laughing, he made it clear he was not happy Buddy and I were there.

"I was gonna say—I've got an idea," Buddy offered. "When we get done here, why don't we all ride back in the *panga* and do up the town."

"Yeah, let's party! Bet Chuck and Bart can show us the best spots. How about it, guys?" As she talked, Wanda stood up and wiggled her almost-nude torso. She winked at Buddy.

"Sounds like a great idea to me," I joined in. "Let's do it!"

We downed a couple more *cervezas* and had some *ceviche*. Buddy kept pushing the La Paz party theme. Since I was paying, Chuck and Bart drank three beers to each of ours. The sun set over the mountains west of us, turning the water blood-red, just like in the travel brochures.

Everyone had a one-more-for-the-boat *cerveza* before we helped Bart and Chuck drag their dinghy off the beach.

"We got to stop at our boat first." Bart passed his hand over his unshaven face. "Need to do something, change clothes, and lock things up."

"Better hurry, you guys!" Wanda had them mesmerized.

"We'll pick you up on our way out," I said.

Getting the *panga* launched necessitated the help of the couple who ran the restaurant. It was heavy, and the receding tide had beached it high and dry. It took the strength of six adults to haul it back into the water. When we reached the yacht, the two would-be Lotharios were ready.

"Damn Mexicans. Hold the fuckin' boat still, will ya!" Bart yelled. I thought he was going to fall into the water as he stabbed the air with his foot, trying to find the gunwale of the *panga*.

"The whole scene's movin, man." Chuck sang out, following Bart over the side of the sailboat and down into the launch. "The world's fluid, plastic, elastic . . . fantastic!"

Both were acting crazy, which suggested their reason for going to *Shore Loser* included more than changing clothes. The ride back to town seemed to take forever. Now that it was dark, everything took on a different meaning with the daytime landmarks gone. I tried to memorize the relationship of lights on shore. Punta Príeta was the only recognizable navigation light until we turned into the channel in front of the Pemex facility.

Chuck and Bart jabbered almost incoherently, using single syllables, mostly foul language. Wanda and Buddy tried their best to keep the conversation centered on their night on the town. I didn't talk much so my feigned illness would seem plausible later.

Juan and Pancho also kept quiet, until we approached the beach in front of Los Arcos. Pancho stood lookout in the bow as we threaded through moored *pangas*, shouting directions to his uncle, who had tilted the engine. The *panga* ground to a jarring stop as it hit the sand.

"I was gonna say—why don't you guys wait for us in the bar while we unload our gear and change?" Buddy was talking to the men, as he handed me one of the surfboards. "Start a tab. Wanda and I'll be there shortly. Don't know about Jake, here. He's not feeling too good."

"You need any help with your stuff?" Chuck asked, slurring.

"Nope," Buddy quickly replied, and the two men made themselves scarce.

We grabbed our gear and followed them across the street toward the lobby. Pancho was standing in knee-deep water next to the bow, while his uncle held the stern. I wanted to tell my young assistant that the wait might be as much as an hour but thought Bart or Chuck might hear me, so I didn't.

The tiled corridor outside Buddy and Wanda's room reverberated with our footsteps. We said nothing until closing the door behind us.

"You two were great!" I whispered.

"They're like some of the younger guys who come into the Busted Surfboard, shit-faced and trashed. I don't like them! You really sick, Jake?" Wanda headed for the bathroom. She didn't know the whole plan. I had only told Buddy and Pancho.

"No, I'm fine. I'll tell you when you come out."

"Hurry up in there. The evening's getting away from us," Buddy said after her. "I was thinkin' we came down here to party, remember?"

She came out about five minutes later, wearing an opalescent halter top and an incredibly tight, black leather miniskirt. I could not believe she had accomplished a shower and change so quickly. She continued working on her hair, while Buddy took his shower and I explained what they had to do next. I was counting on them to keep Chuck and Bart occupied so I could steal *Shore Loser*.

"Damn it, Jake! You know they're snortin' nose-candy, don't you?" Her mouth was packed with gum, which she nervously put through its paces.

"Just keep pouring the alcohol into them. Get them away from here as quickly as you can. As soon as I see you guys leave in a cab, I'll go back to the *panga*."

"How do we explain you're not with us?"

"I was gonna say—we tell them the kid got sick. Can't hold his liquor and begged off. We'll think of something," Buddy said, walking into the room in khaki pants and a Hawaiian shirt, his blond hair parted in the middle and slicked back. He looked like an aging surfer ready to luau.

I went to my room knowing they'd both excel at their parts, hoping they would be careful. Now to steal the boat, my role required preparation. Flashlight, dive knife, and personal kit went into my backpack, along with a towel and change of clothes.

From my balcony, I watched until the four of them got in a cab and pulled away. Wanda, laughing and talking—a real trooper. I could not imagine asking Toey to do what I was expecting of Wanda. They were two entirely different women.

Pancho met me as I crossed the street with my bag. "*Señor* Jake, I see your friends get in the car with the bad men. Are they going to be OK?"

"Hope so." I gritted my teeth, knowing I had placed them in danger. "Let's go. We've got a boat to steal," I said, forcing a laugh.

As we ran the *panga* back to the anchorage, I re-familiarized myself with the shore lights. Pancho was helpful, identifying each cluster of illumination as we sped by. When we pulled alongside *Shore Loser*, it was pitch black except for the buttery mercury vapor glow behind the spit of land between us and the ferry terminal. Chuck and Bart had not even left an anchor light on. I hoped the batteries were charged.

We tied the *panga* outside the dinghy and climbed on board. Breaking into a sailboat is easy. Everyone leaves keys in a winch handle pocket, beneath a lazarette hatch, or under a winch cover. I found them in the port winch handle pocket.

Down below, I used my flashlight to find the main battery switch and turned it to "all." When the cabin lights came on, I was in shock. The inside of this once-beautiful yacht was beyond filthy—garbage and stuff was everywhere. Pancho and I were appalled. I looked under the galley sink to see if there were any trash bags and, of course, there were none.

"Pancho, you and your uncle put as much of this stuff as you can up forward. *Por favor.*"

While Pancho and Juan worked, I stuck my head in the engine room. Things were messy there, also—oil in the bilge and unsecured tools—but not too bad. I made a mental note to have Buddy tidy up the equipment before we left for Cabo San Lucas.

After checking fluid levels in the main engine, I held my breath and pushed the ignition button. The big Perkins caught fire immediately and sounded healthy. At least the main power plant was in operating condition. I decided to examine the generator in daylight, after we docked.

Together, Juan and I lifted the 6-hp Evinrude off the dinghy transom and clamped it in place on the ship's stern rail. We used the stern davits to hoist the dinghy out of the water and secured it. With the navigation lights on, I crossed my fingers and looked to see if they all worked. They did. The radar also functioned. Pancho helped me roll up the dodger's dirty plastic windows for a clear view forward from the wheel. We were ready to haul anchor.

"You know where Marina de La Paz is?"

"*Sí*, I do."

"Have your uncle meet us at the fuel dock. If the guards give him a problem, Juan should tell them I have *Señora* Mary's permission." I turned on the circuit breaker for the anchor windlass, climbed out of the center cockpit onto the deck, and moved toward the bow. When the anchor was up, I ran back to the wheel, shifted into gear, and pushed the throttle forward.

Juan's *panga* roared away without running lights and disappeared into the darkness.

It seemed like it took us hours to navigate back to La Paz. The fact that the radar, autopilot, and depth sounder worked made the trip relatively easy. Attentive Pancho told me where the water was deep and warned me when I was approaching a shallow area. He seemed much older than he looked—he was good company, and I was developing an affection for him. I worried about how Buddy and Wanda were faring with Chuck and Bart. I hoped everything was going as planned.

"Watch out! *Señor* Jake, over there! A boat! Move right."

"Thank you. I see it."

We were passing the beach in front of the Los Arcos Hotel when several anchored vessels loomed up in front of us. I barely saw them—large, shapeless voids blotting out the lights on shore. We missed the first one by less than five feet. If Pancho hadn't warned me in time, my repo-captain days might have ended on the first night.

Unknowingly, I had steered *Shore Loser* into an anchorage area just before the marina. None of the vessels were illuminated. Guessing they were fishing boats, I slowed down until I barely retained steerage. Then, with Pancho's guidance, I worked my way through the fleet back to the main channel.

"Wow! You've got good eyes, Pancho. OK, show me where the fuel dock is." I had stopped *Shore Loser,* and we were rapidly drifting backward with the current.

"Over there. See the lights? It is the entrance to the marina. The dock is this side. *Mi tío* is standing on it. You see him?" Pancho was pointing through the anchored vessels.

"OK, grab those lines back there by the dinghy and put them on starboard—I mean, right. Right side, Pancho. When we get next to the dock, give the lines to your uncle and tell him to tie us up."

The current was ripping pretty fast—maybe as much as two knots—as I approached the wooden pier. I had to use the engine to hold us in position until Juan made the lines fast to cleats. When we were tied up, the security guard showed me where I could plug in for 110-volt power. Pancho helped me rummage through the junk in the stern lazarette until we found the cord.

It was after two in the morning when I gave Pancho his second fifty dollars and paid Juan for the use of his *panga*.

"You have any friends who work on boats?" I was thinking of the mess below.

"Me! I do!" was his quick reply.

"Should have known. OK, be back here at nine o'clock and bring a friend. You can help me get this boat cleaned up."

"How much?"

"Ten bucks for you, five for your friend."

After Pancho and Juan left, I went below to find a couple of blankets. Even though it was going to be cool sleeping in the cockpit, I preferred that to the filth and grime below. It didn't take me long to nod off.

The creaking of the wooden docks woke me later in the morning; I think it was from the motion of a passing vessel churning up a wake. My eyes blurred from straining to look at my watch—seven o'clock. I grabbed my bag, locked things up, and had just started walking past the other tied-up boats toward the buildings on land when a voice yelled at me.

"Hey, man, isn't that Chuck and Bart's *Shore Loser*?"

"Nope," I said. "Not anymore. New owner," and kept walking.

Someone came out of the shower, and I grabbed the door before it slammed shut. Slip renters are normally issued a key to access docks, toilets and showers. I'd forgotten to ask Mary for one when I talked with her on Thursday. Most of the hot water had been used up, but so what—the shower felt great.

After changing into clean clothes, I went next door to The Dock restaurant, and ordered coffee. Buddy walked in about 8:30, alone. Immediately concerned, I asked, "Where's Wanda?"

"She's beat, man. We didn't get back to the hotel until two or three this morning. What a weird night!" He ordered black java and started looking at the menu.

"Tell me about it. You guys OK?"

"Yeah, but you owe us big-time! Those two are a couple of dorks. When we finally put 'em in a cab, they were totally out of it. I'm thinkin' they've got to be feeling pretty rough along about now. Bet they slept on the beach. Where's *Shore Loser*?"

"Tied up over there. I got here about the same time you got back to the hotel," I said, pointing through the open window toward two masts on the outer side of the marina. "Let's eat, then I'll take you down. I'm afraid we've got a ton of work to do before we can leave."

After breakfast, I checked in with the marina office. Mary had just arrived. Her gray hair, pulled back into a bun with a pencil sticking through it, and the wire-rimmed glasses perched on top of her head made her look like a country school teacher.

"Good morning, Mary. *Shore Loser* is tied up to the fuel dock and needs to take on diesel."

"I see you found her. Good for you," she said, running her finger over a chart of the marina. "Here, move the boat to slip B-15, on the outer row. Please . . . as soon as you are done fueling . . . so it won't interfere with other vessels." She took my deposit and gave me two gate keys.

"I'm concerned word's gonna get out that we've brought the boat back here. Will you alert security to be on the lookout for Chuck and Bart?"

"Yes, I will, but I hope you're planning on leaving soon," she frowned. "Where's your paperwork?"

"It'll be ready after I pick up the last of my crew at the airport this afternoon."

"OK, I'll take the documents to the port captain as soon as you get them to me. If I'm lucky, I hope to have everything done by the end of the day."

Using Mary's phone again, I placed a collect call to Monty. After I finally got through, Grace pulled him out of a meeting. When I proudly announced I had the boat, he sounded strangely blasé.

"When do you expect to leave La Paz?" he asked, his mind apparently somewhere else.

"Don't know, probably tomorrow. We're waiting on paperwork."

"Good. When you arrive in San Diego, take the boat to Knight and Carver Yacht Center. I'll make arrangements and let them know you'll be there in about fifteen days."

"OK."

"Call me if you run into trouble. Good luck, Jake. And . . . be careful."

Pancho was waiting for me at the marina gate with his friend Jesus, who was a little older but just as skinny. They followed Buddy and me down to the yacht. When the fueling was complete, they helped us move to the assigned slip. I was glad the current was slack—it made maneuvering in tight quarters a lot easier.

When we were tied up, Buddy wanted to return to the hotel and check on Wanda, so I asked him to bring back trash bags and cleaning supplies. Then I organized the boys to help me bring up everything from down below, and I made arrangements through the marina office for a diver to scrape the bottom.

By the time Buddy returned with Wanda, the boys and I had pulled everything out and transferred it onto the dock. Though obviously hung over, Wanda got right to the task of cleaning out the galley and heads. I felt guilty, but didn't comment.

Buddy and I separated anything that might belong to Chuck and Bart and bagged it, while Pancho and Jesus hauled away the rest. By the time I left to meet Toey at the airport, *Shore Loser* was looking much better.

Rodrigo was waiting for me in the marina parking lot. We smoked and knocked our way to the terminal as fast as his taxi would go. We were fifteen minutes late getting there; I was hoping Toey wouldn't be angry.

Because she was so short, I had to look hard to find her in the customs line, hidden between other arriving passengers. She had only two small duffel bags and, fortunately, got a green light. When she got to me, she gave me a big hug and a kiss.

"Mmm, that was tasty. How was your flight?" I was more than glad to see her.

"It was good. How are things here? Did you find the sailboat?"

"Yes, we did. Buddy and Wanda are cleaning it." I described *Shore Loser* to her on the taxi ride back to Los Arcos.

We entered the lobby arm in arm and laughing. Hotel staff greeted us with typical Mexican flair, treating us like special guests, as mariachi music played in the background.

"What the hell have you done with my boat! Where are your two fuckin' friends?" Bart, crazed and reeking of alcohol, charged across the lobby and accosted us.

As he grabbed at my shirt, I set down Toey's bags and shoved him away. He pushed back with a ferocity that nearly knocked me over.

"Get your hands off me!" I put all my weight into blocking him. "What're you talking about?" I played dumb and Toey backed away.

"You know exactly what I'm talking about! Our boat was stolen last night while we were partying with your shit-head friends!" he shouted, his face mere inches from mine, the veins in his neck bulging and his breath a distillery. "You bastards are all in cahoots, and if I find out how, you're all fuckin' dead meat!"

"That sounds like a threat to me. You better be careful what you're saying."

"Goddamn right, it's a threat! Motherfucker!"

Hotel staff clustered around us. When the manager came running, Bart realized this was not the right venue for his accusations and backed away. Seeing the opportunity to teach him a lesson, I turned to the manager.

"*Señor*, we are guests in your hotel. This terrible street person is trying to pick a fight. We don't need this. We're on vacation. This lovely lady is frightened. If this guy shows up again, please, please, call the police immediately." With Toey's arm around my waist, we looked like innocent newlyweds.

"I will see that it is under control, *Señor* Mortensen. He will not bother you anymore. Not here!" Behind the manager, several hotel staff were ushering Bart down the steps to the sidewalk, roughing him up as they went. He yelled something obscene, but I couldn't make out what.

"Jake! What was *that* all about?"

"Consider yourself introduced to Bart," I said, letting out a sigh.

"He looked dangerous, Jake. You promised me there would not be any danger." She was seething. "You said this was going to be a safe, enjoyable sailing trip."

"Calm down, Toey. We're out of here tomorrow. Then everything will be fine—just fine!" I said angrily and picked up her bags.

After depositing Toey's luggage in our room, I grabbed my briefcase, then stopped and withdrew the money in the safe deposit box. Neither of us spoke. We took a cab to the marina, making several stops en route—I needed to be certain we were not being followed. Toey avoided looking at me and concentrated on the passing sidewalk and buildings.

At the marina office, I gave our visas and ship's documents to Mary, who said she'd do her best to complete everything by the end of the afternoon. Since it was Saturday, she mentioned she might have to pay the port captain for "overtime." I told her about Bart and asked her to do whatever was necessary so we could leave La Paz as soon as possible.

On the boat, the atmosphere was much better. Pancho and Jesus had swabbed the deck and were polishing the stainless.

"Hi, Toey. You missed all the fun! These guys were harvesting penicillin everywhere—musta been afraid of the clap," Wanda laughed, mopping perspiration from her brow.

"Hello, Wanda," Toey smiled and, then, got serious again. "I just met one of them, and I did not like it." She grabbed a stanchion and lifted herself up onto the deck, giving me a chance to watch her perky behind with mixed emotions.

"Welcome to La Paz, pretty lady!" Buddy stuck his head up through the companionway and handed out cold *cervezas*. Another positive sign, he'd mastered the refrigeration.

"We saw Bart at the hotel," I announced, following Toey into the cockpit. "He suspects we took the boat, but can't prove it. Wonder where he got *that* idea?"

"He is a foul-mouthed creep." Toey's face flushed. "Jake told me what you guys had to do last night—that must have been really scary."

"Hey, it's over. Now we just have to put some distance between us and everything will be fine," I said, attempting to put everyone at ease.

While Pancho and Jesus squared away outside, I ran a hose into the water tanks. Wanda and Toey started a provisions list, noting food, bedding, and other necessities. A functioning generator was more evidence of Buddy's efforts in the engine room. Though it was cranky on start-up, the machine put out the proper voltage.

In the midst of our preparations, I heard a knocking on the hull. It was Mary.

"Here you are, Jake: stamped crew list and exit Zarpe to San Diego. You must leave within forty-eight hours, sooner is probably better. Word around town is Bart and Chuck are out to get you. They tried to press charges with the port captain, but luckily I'd already filed against them for leaving without slip payment, so their credibility is gone.

"The port authorities are aware you are here to repossess the boat. In case you have to stop in Cabo, here's a letter saying all obligations have been paid and you're free to leave Mexico. It is in Spanish, explains the circumstances, is signed and stamped by the La Paz port captain, and is addressed to you as captain of the boat."

Mary agreed to have her staff take the trash bags filled with Chuck and Bart's personal belongings and hold them until after our departure. I told her we still had to provision and wanted to get a good night's sleep before leaving in the morning. She said she had a map of the market and hardware store locations in her office, so I gave Toey and Wanda shopping money, and they followed her back up the dock.

When Buddy and I were satisfied with things in the engine room, we hoisted the sails and checked each for damage. The main and genoa were a little old and tired, but the mizzen looked newer, and we figured all the sails would hold up for the voyage.

When the ladies returned in two hours, Buddy and I were satisfied *Shore Loser* was ready. The sun was heading for the horizon, and I wanted to head for dinner. Pancho and Jesus agreed to continue working and guard the boat in our absence. I told them to run and get security if Bart or Chuck appeared.

Even though the hotel was nearby, we were all tired and took a taxi. Because my briefcase held all our money and documents, I kept it with me. Getting out of the cab, I thought I saw Bart lurking in a shadowy corner. Had he staked out the hotel, waiting for our return? And if Chuck wasn't with him, where was he? Did they know where *Shore Loser* was? I felt uneasy and shared my concern.

"I was wonderin' the same thing. Let's eat here at the hotel," Buddy suggested. "But how are we going to get our stuff to the boat without them seeing us?"

"I'm not sure. We can talk about it at dinner. Let's meet in thirty minutes, in the bar."

Toey and I entered our room, neither of us in any hurry to turn on the lights. Toey's embrace preceded a torrid, lingering kiss.

"Oh, Jake, I have been so worried about you," she murmured, as she caressed my neck. "I am sorry I got so mad. It is just that awful person, Bart, almost ruined everything."

"You're forgiven," I said, lifting her off the floor. "I'm so glad you're here."

Her body was sweetly fragrant from working on the boat. As I pulled her to me again, her breasts grazed my chest. We explored each other, moving in slow motion to preserve the moment, as we removed one another's clothes.

CHAPTER EIGHT

# ESCAPE TO CABO

"Bet I know what you two have been doin'!" Wanda stated the obvious. "How come they take longer than us, Buddy?" she said, laughing and giving him a peck on the cheek.

Toey blushed as we sat down. I'd learned to count on Wanda to say exactly what was on her mind—the connection between her mouth and brain had no discretionary filter.

My crew had chosen a window table overlooking the street and the beach. Thankfully, the novelty of being in a foreign country seemed to have kept them preoccupied. The restaurant seemed more elegant than I remembered. Carved high-back chairs complemented chiseled wooden beams, their red velveteen cushions matching the draperies tied back at the large windows.

"What are you guys drinking?"

"Orange juice!" Buddy and Wanda answered in unison.

Our orders were taken by a waiter in a showy silver and black mariachi costume, sans the *sombrero*.

"I was gonna say—don't look now, man, but one of your favorite people is behind you." Buddy nodded toward the bar.

"Which one?"

"Chuck. His back is toward us. He was here when we came in."

"Hope this isn't going to be a repeat of the earlier Bart episode. Did you talk?"

"Nope. Didn't want to get something started."

"Strange," Toey whispered, "he does not look as frightening as Bart."

"OK, I've got an idea." The wheels of inspiration had renewed their spin. "Wanda, after we order dinner, I want you to go over to Mister Chuck. Thank him for showing you the town last night. Tell him you're sorry to hear about his boat. And tell him you and Buddy are going to Cabo tomorrow—by car."

"If I get into trouble, you guys'll come rescue me, right?" Wanda winked and wiggled, but a wrinkled brow suggested she no longer enjoyed her assigned part.

"Jake, I'm thinkin' I should talk to him instead," Buddy offered.

"OK, yeah. You both go. It might look better."

Lobster was the unanimous dinner order. Then Buddy and Wanda walked over to the lanky red-beard on the barstool. Chuck first acted like he'd never seen them before, then like he was unnerved by their audacity. As they talked, Chuck slid off his perch, and I was afraid he was going to pick a fight with Buddy. Instead, he shook his head and left the room, just as dinner arrived.

"For sure, they think you've got something to do with their missing boat," Buddy reported. "Chuck said Bart remembered seeing you—alone in a *panga*—before they saw us with you. I was thinkin' we should try to convince Chuck we're not all traveling together. I tried to make him believe you guys are newlyweds, but it just seemed to confuse him," he said, smiling at Toey.

"Hell, he's not too bright, Jake. I think his brain's fried," Wanda added as she dug into her crustacean.

"It was worth a shot. Thanks for trying. You may have thrown them off our track a bit." I said, but didn't believe it. Bart and Chuck knew exactly what we were up to. We had repossessed their boat—how tough was *that* to figure out? And they weren't going to let us get away with it, if they could help it.

I found it difficult to eat and think at the same time, but I did the best I could, explaining my new plan. Tomorrow morning, Toey would give my dive gear to Buddy, then come to the boat with my seabag and her luggage, making sure she wasn't followed. Buddy and Wanda were to pack up their surfboards and bags and wait in the lobby for at least an hour after Toey was due to leave. Then they would take a cab and get my dive tank filled before coming to the boat. Toey and I would have everything ready when they got there.

"Your rooms are paid for, but check out anyway. If you think you're being followed, do whatever it takes to lose them." I looked at Toey. "I'm sorry, but I'm gonna have to sleep on the boat tonight. I'll take my briefcase because it's got all the trip money and documents. I'm leaving my seabag with you because I want to travel light."

"Let me come with you. I can help you get the boat ready."

"No, Toey. I want them to see you leave the hotel tomorrow morning. I'm hoping they'll think I'm still here." I patted her leg under the table. "At the very least, it should keep them guessing."

After our meal, I talked everyone into having a Mexican coffee. I remembered the ceremony, with the glasses being lit on fire, from the last time I was in Cabo with my father, just before going into the Navy. Once again, the coffee was prepared with perfect panache. Everyone applauded.

In the hallway outside our room, I kissed Toey goodnight. I knew if I followed her inside I wouldn't make it back to the boat. Besides, Pancho and Jesus were probably wondering when I would return—it had been almost three hours since we left them to finish their work.

I felt an urgency to get back so they could go home. It bothered me that I didn't know more about how these hard-working children lived. I wanted to believe they had mothers and fathers who worried about them, but I suspected they might not.

The corridors of the hotel were empty as I walked toward the rear of the building, my footsteps echoing on the hard tiles. I tried to walk more softly, tiptoeing past rooms, stepping over slivers of light with laughter escaping from under closed wood doors, and slithering past others that were dark and silent. I imagined security cameras were monitoring my slow progress, recording my movements. Every shadow contained the essence of Chuck or Bart, waiting to grab me as I moved from filtered hallway light, entered darkened stairwells, and worked my way through the building.

Soon I found what I was looking for: the hotel laundry. It had to have an outside loading dock. Three women were inside, folding sheets and towels. The hot room smelled of scorched fabric, bleach, and detergent. I got the attention of the woman working nearest to me.

"*¿Dónde está la puerta?*" I said in my best Spanish, slipping her a U.S. dollar. She motioned me to follow her past the other women and laundry carts. We turned at the end of the row of dryers, and she pointed to a door next to the loading dock's metal roll-up. I said "*Gracias,*" and opened it slowly. Sure enough, it led to an alley behind the building. Outside was an unpaved driveway with nobody in sight.

Making my way through the darkened streets, I felt like a cross between a fugitive and a kid at Halloween. Shadows cast from moonlight and street lamps made everything seem unearthly and eerie. Dogs barked and cats shrieked as I trespassed through their territory, the pungent stench of garbage overwhelming. Finally, I made it to the marina parking lot, waiting in the shadows to be sure neither Bart nor Chuck was around before stepping out of the darkness.

The gate to the dock squeaked when I opened it, startling me. Behind, a security guard coughed and cleared his throat. When I realized he was there for my own good, I stopped holding my breath, let out a sigh of relief, and laughed.

At the boat, Pancho and Juan were asleep in the cockpit. Reluctantly I woke them—they had worked hard all day.

"You guys get anything to eat?"

"*Sí, Señor* Jake. I make us a sandwich when you not come back. It is OK, no?" He was rubbing his eyes.

"You bet it's OK!" Feeling guilty, I paid them, adding a little extra. "I probably won't see you again, Pancho. We sail out of here in the morning."

"You will come back someday, yes?"

"Someday."

"Then I will wait for you, *Señor* Jake." He jumped up and hugged me.

I didn't detect tears in his eyes, though there were some in mine. After the boys left, I went below, fired up the propane stove, and made a cup of hot chocolate.

I felt fortunate my childhood had been so special. When Mother died, my father and I had become very close. Pancho's world was so different. Even so, we'd connected briefly, and I would remember him and all his "uncles" for a long, long time to come.

Looking around, Wanda and Toey had done a superb job of preparing *Shore Loser* for the voyage. All the teak woodwork had been cleaned and oiled and, even though it needed refinishing, it looked much better. Food for the trip was neatly stowed, and a provisions plan written in Wanda's hand had been posted inside a galley cupboard door. I found it while looking for the cocoa mix.

Even the heads were clean and smelled nice. It was obvious women had been on board. They had wrapped the threadbare salon cushions in sheets made up for sleeping. The two berths in the aft stateroom were also fitted with clean bedding. I selected one and tried to rest.

Sunday morning came early, I knew I needed to do some things before the others arrived. With coffee on, I sat down at the navigation station to familiarize myself with the electronics. Even though it was an old piece of equipment, the radar worked—I'd already used it.

The GPS was fairly new and menu-driven. Soon I was able to acquire a position fix and, with more tinkering, I figured out how to get the heading and distance to another waypoint. All the other instruments— wind speed and direction, boat speed and log, and depth sounder— seemed to be working. About the time I got the GPS down pat, Toey came on board.

"Good morning, Jake." She handed me her seabag.

"Morning ... coffee's hot." Kissing her on the cheek, I helped her get our bags down the companionway. "I reserved the stern stateroom for us."

"I do not think I have been followed."

"Maybe Chuck and Bart aren't up yet; they didn't strike me as early-risers," I said, relieved she had made it safely. "Or they're still waiting for me to emerge from the hotel."

I pulled the charts from my seabag and plotted our course to Cabo, recording the significant waypoints in my logbook and entering them into the GPS memory. Like magic, the GPS agreed with our present chart position.

Toey handed me a fresh cup of Norwegian starter fluid, as she looked over my shoulder. I showed her how to operate the instruments and explained how I wanted the log kept with hourly entries. Though attentive and polite, she gave the impression she already understood.

"You know how to do all this?"

"I have taken some coastal navigation classes, and I am looking forward to this trip for some good practical experience." I slid out from behind the desk so she could get a better view of everything.

"OK, smart stuff, I hereby appoint you official nav-a-guesser. If you have any questions, just ask. I'm gonna give the engine room a once-over."

By the time Buddy and Wanda arrived, we had the sail covers off, the genoa sheets led, and the engine running. It was almost noon.

"Let's get out of here!" Buddy shouted, sounding winded, as he hoisted dive gear up onto the deck. "Bart and Chuck are in the parking lot! I was thinkin' we'd given 'em the slip, but I was wrong."

"Damn! Get your stuff on board!" I turned and yelled down the hatch, "Toey, I need you topside! Right now!"

They loaded their surfboards, seabags, and my dive gear. Then Wanda leaped on board, as Buddy cast off our lines and followed.

I maneuvered away from the marina just as Bart and Chuck crashed through the gate and came barging down the dock with a security guard in hot pursuit. When they got to where we'd been moored, we were sixty yards out. Bart was waving a fist and screaming obscenities when the guard caught him. People climbed out of their boats to see what was causing all the commotion.

At about this point, Bart slugged the security officer and pushed him off the dock. Yelling like a banshee, he ran back toward the parking lot, with Chuck following close on his heels. I lost sight of them and turned all of my attention to threading fifty feet of fiberglass sailboat through the anchored steel hulks of the Mexican fishing fleet.

"I was wonderin', what do you think they'll do?" Buddy asked, climbing into the cockpit after securing the surfboards to the stanchions. Toey finished putting away the fenders and dock lines while they waited for my answer.

"Don't know. They might come after us in a faster boat. Let's get the main up." From the dark recesses of my mind came the beginning of the nightmare I'd been denying. These were my friends, they were depending on me, and *this* was definitely *not* going to be good.

Clear of the anchorage, I turned into the wind. Buddy and Toey went forward to the mast and hauled 485 square feet of six-ounce Dacron into place. When the halyard was cleated off, Buddy came back to manage the mainsheet from the cockpit, as Toey finished making up lines at the mast. I could hear Wanda in the galley, concocting lunch. Though we'd never been boating together, it was apparent my crew were all accomplished sailors and could work well as a team.

"Buddy, if they come after us, we better be ready." My mind was racing. "You got any condoms?"

"What?" he laughed. "What did you say? Are you serious?"

"Yeah, condoms. Hurry! Look in my toiletry kit. And bring the flare pistol up here. Also a plastic bucket, a funnel, and a short length of hose."

"What have you got in mind?"

"Don't talk. Just do it! Trust me! I've got an idea."

Buddy returned with the requested items, the girls trailing him, everyone wondering if I'd gone mad.

"OK, I want you guys to fill the condoms with gasoline and tie them off like water balloons."

It took some experimenting to get six filled and tied without breaking. Trojans seemed to work best. Buddy loaded the flare gun, and we were ready, not a moment too soon.

"Jake, Jake! Here they come!" Toey yelled, pointing at a *panga* speeding toward us from the marina. "Bart has a gun! I can see it!"

"OK, girls, get below. Buddy, there's no traffic in front. I'm gonna put us on autopilot. Keep low in the cockpit until they come alongside. Then throw the loaded condoms so they land around the fuel container in the stern of their boat. Give me the flare gun."

A bullet whizzed past my head, slicing a hole through the side window of the dodger, the old plastic shattering like a windowpane. Just fifteen feet of water separated us, as the *panga* came even with our cockpit. Buddy sprang up and lobbed the Mortensen cocktails with surprising accuracy, just as Bart fired a wild shot.

One of the condoms splattered all over Bart's chest. At the same instant, I fired a flare in Bart's direction, reloaded, and put a second into the stern of their boat, igniting the entire area around the gas tank and engine. The driver's clothing flashed like a blowtorch. Screaming, he abandoned the throttle and jumped overboard. The out-of-control *panga* pulled away from us, with Bart and Chuck somewhere in the blazing projectile.

I distinctly heard Bart cursing, as the fireball arced back toward the La Paz waterfront. And then it exploded, raining flaming debris in a hundred-foot circle.

Toey freaked. "Did they get out? Oh, my heavens! Did we kill them, Jake?"

"Toey, they were trying to kill us! They had guns, for gosh sake!" Disengaging the autopilot, I sighed in relief.

"Condoms," Buddy muttered, shaking his head. "Gasoline-loaded condoms."

"Yeah, condoms, honey. First time I ever seen 'em used to *get* someone 'banged-up.'" Wanda's husky laugh sounded nervous and forced.

By afternoon we had passed the cove where *Shore Loser* had been anchored the day before. Up until then, everyone had been silent, drained by the encounter with the attacking *panga*. Our engine chugged away in the background, muffled by the sound of *Shore Loser's* hull slicing through the water. It became obvious everyone's mood was a little different when we began to talk.

"Honestly, even if they were bad people, I hope we didn't kill them," Toey sighed. "I do not want to be responsible for killing anyone."

"I'm thinkin', worst case, they only got burned," Buddy answered.

"Whatever they got, they deserved, hon'; they were trying to kill us," Wanda responded and then turned to me. "You've got a strange way to use condoms. Explosive, but really bizarre."

Looking behind to make sure no one was following, winds were very light, out of the northwest, and the ocean was relatively calm. I put the autopilot on and gave the watch over to Toey, using this opportunity to acquaint Buddy and Wanda with the logbook and nav-station instruments. The rest of the afternoon, we paralleled the coast, making for San Lorenzo Point and the gap between Isla del Espíritu Santo and the mainland.

Shortly after three, we rounded Punta Diablo and were abeam Puerto Balandra. The girls put on their swimsuits to do some tanning. I pointed out mushroom-shaped "El Hongo" rock, for which the shallow cove of Puerto Balandra is famous. The fragile piece of eroded geology is on most of the postcards tourists buy in La Paz. We had escaped. Now we could relax and enjoy the trip—or could we? The nightmare still resided in the back of my mind. I hoped this was the end of it.

Time came to adjust our heading to line up with the middle of Canal de Lorenzo. To keep well clear of the large reef on the north, I steered toward the tall, cylindrical southern shoal marker. Espíritu Santo Island was visible on our port side. I wished we had time to explore its many anchorages and spectacular rock formations.

An hour later, we were able to fall off and head in a more southeasterly direction, putting the strengthening wind behind us. With Toey and Buddy eager to put up more sail, it took them just a few minutes to raise the mizzen and unfurl the genoa. I killed the engine and let the canvas carry us toward the five-mile gap between Isla Cerralvo and the peninsula. Less than three hours of daylight remained, not enough time to make it past the island before dark.

It felt good to extinguish the engine's mechanical drone and let the wind take over. Toey and Buddy had all the canvas in proper trim, and we were averaging seven knots. At this speed, we could arrive in Cabo in eighteen to twenty hours, possibly early tomorrow afternoon. Toey snuggled up to me, and I gave her the wheel. Buddy stretched out on a cushion on the starboard side of the cockpit where he could look up and check the genoa's trim, adjusting the sheet whenever necessary. Now that we had put some distance between us and La Paz, everyone could ease into a routine.

"What do you guys feel like for dinner?" Wanda asked, her head sticking up through the companionway. She and Buddy had selected the 0600 to 1200 and 1800 to 2400 watch, leaving her free to do all the cooking. It struck me funny that someone who worked long hours in a restaurant would want galley duty. "How about spaghetti with garlic bread? I wanna see if this propane oven really works."

"Don't forget salad," said Buddy, the herbivore, lifting his head from the cushion.

"You got it, honey." She tweaked his big toe and went below.

Sometime during Buddy and Wanda's watch we lost the wind—I think when we were passing Los Muertos. With the engine on and the autopilot steering, they hauled in the roller furling headsail. Through the open hatch above me, I could hear their voices on the night air, as they dropped the mizzen and struggled to fold and tie it to the aft boom.

Toey must have been exhausted. She slept in the bunk across from mine, and the noise didn't seem to bother her a bit. At 2345 I woke her in time for our watch, donned a jacket, and climbed topside. Buddy was at the helm, with clear access to the portside autopilot controls. Wanda was catnapping on the starboard side of the cockpit.

"How're things going?" I whispered.

"I was gonna say—pretty good. Pescadero Point is over there and that's Punta Arena light ahead of us. Haven't seen any running lights from other boats for a couple of hours. Ready to take over?"

"Sure. Anything on radar?"

"Nope. No wind, either. Flat as a tortilla since we left the Cerralvo Channel. So much for the windy Sea of Cortez." Sliding across the seat, Buddy touched Wanda's shoulder. "Need anything before I update the log and hit the sack?"

"Don't think so. Engine OK?"

"I'm thinkin' it seems a little hotter than normal. Could be a dirty heat exchanger or damaged raw-water impeller. I'd like to see more water coming out of the exhaust." As Wanda got up from the cushion, he gave her a pat on the rump.

"OK, I'll keep an eye on the gauges. We'll check everything out in Cabo. You guys get some sleep."

"Night, Jake." Wanda yawned, Buddy following her below.

A few minutes later, Toey emerged from the galley with two steaming mugs of coffee. I went down to check our position and read the log entries. Wanda's were comical, like a personal diary; Buddy's were just the facts, nothing more. I felt comfortable around them both.

Toward the end of my watch, I noticed the engine temperature rapidly climbing—we were losing boat speed.

"Damn!" I exclaimed, reducing RPMs. "Toey, take a flashlight to see if we're dragging kelp." She climbed out of the cockpit and headed for the stern.

"I do not think so," came back the reply after a few minutes. "But there is something white floating about fifty yards off our stern."

I took the engine out of gear so just the mainsail gave us way, made sure the autopilot was tracking, and went to look myself. Sure enough, there was an object that looked like a Styrofoam block tied like a package. We'd run over a fisherman's makeshift long-line.

Toey brought me a boathook, and I started poking the water behind our stern. The pole wasn't long enough to reach very far below the surface, and the dinghy—hanging in the davits, resting against the transom— impeded me further. I put on a safety harness, loosened the hoist lines on the dinghy, and swung it out far enough to drop the stern ladder.

I climbed down the transom—back against the rubber boat—to stab deeper in the water surrounding the rudder and hooked a twisted yellow polypropylene line. Toey handed me a knife to cut it free. The entire maneuver took half an hour—it was nearly time for Buddy and Wanda to come on watch again.

Toey swung the ladder up, while I pushed the dinghy out of the way and secured it. Shifting the transmission into forward, I ran the Perkins back up to 2400 RPM. Our boat speed improved, but the engine temperature began rising again, so I dropped the RPMs back down to 2000.

Buddy called from the companionway. "What's goin' on? Engine problem?"

"Wrapped a fishing line around the prop. I'll have to dive to free it. We'll wait for daylight." I noted the trouble in the log and checked the chart.

We were about two hours south of Los Frailes, the last really decent anchorage until Cabo. We were also three miles offshore, and I didn't want to turn back if we didn't have to. Buddy took over the watch, as Toey sat down beside me in the cockpit with fresh coffee. Together, we watched the sunrise transform the eastern horizon into radiant red and orange, while Wanda clanged breakfast pots and pans in the galley.

"Is the engine going to be all right, Jake?" Toey asked, still looking off into the distance.

"Yeah ... I think so," I replied, trying to imagine the mess I might have to deal with under water. "We'll know for sure after I get the stuff off our prop."

"I am not so sure I like the idea of your having to go in the water with us this far off shore. There could be sharks."

"Nice to have someone worry," I said, turning her head toward me and giving her a kiss.

In about an hour, it was light enough to dive. I put on my gear and strapped a sheathed knife to my leg. Buddy turned the boat into the light morning breeze, dropped the main, and shut down the motor. When I jumped in the water, it was colder than I expected. Swimming around a moment to adjust, I cleared my snorkel and dove under the hull.

Just as I thought, a ball of yellow polypropylene line was entangled in the prop, tightly wrapped around the shaft. I had to be careful not to get caught on one of the large fishhooks bristling from the mess. To cut it all away took five or six dives and about an hour.

When I removed my fins and climbed up the stern ladder, my muscles were starting to cramp. I was feeling the effects of very little exercise during the past week and vowed to get back into my workout routine, even if I had to do sit-ups on the foredeck.

We secured the stern ladder and dinghy, started the engine, and Toey and Wanda hauled the main up. Buddy put *Shore Loser* back on course and ran the engine up to 2400 RPM. Our speed seemed better, the temperature holding steady just a little above normal.

Shortly after noon, the wind picked up, and we were able to sail again. By two o'clock, we were abeam Cabeza Ballena, a minor land projection that defines the eastern portion of Bahía San Lucas. From here, we could make out the characteristic arched rock of the cape, marking the bay's western entrance about five miles ahead.

When I was a kid on my father's boat, arriving in Cabo San Lucas after the long journey down the outside of the Baja peninsula, always gave me goose bumps. Maybe it was the anticipation of being at "land's end" or, as the Mexicans say, *finisterra*. Seeing the dramatically arched pinnacle brought back the same old tingling feeling in my gut.

When my father and I had visited Cabo San Lucas eight years ago, it was being proclaimed the Baja Riviera. Many luxury hotels, condominiums, and houses were already evident, and rumors were circulating about developing the inner harbor into a marina. My father said it would never happen because of the tropical storms and hurricanes that threaten this area in the summer. It would be impossible to find investors willing to put dollars into a facility that could be reduced to a pile of rubble with the first big blow. Of course, he was wrong.

Ted had told me about staying in the new marina when he came down for recent billfish tournaments. I knew I'd now find the entire northeast side of the inner harbor filled with floating concrete docks and sportfishing boats.

For sentimental reasons, I still preferred to anchor or pick up a mooring in front of the Hotel Hacienda in the outer bay, so I chose an area clear of vessels just east of the mooring field. Toey and Buddy lowered sails, and we put down the anchor in forty feet of water. Mostly big motor yachts were on the moorings, and about a half-dozen cruising sailboats were lying to. It was 4:30 in the afternoon.

A small powerboat roared through the anchorage, lofting a parasailer, its wake causing *Shore Loser* to rock and roll. "I hope that does not continue into the evening!" Toey commented, balancing a cup of hot tea.

"Don't think they can run after dark," I said, hoping I was right. I handed her a rag to mop the spill.

"Shit! What was *that*!" Wanda joined us, decked out in her fluorescent-pink bikini. I noticed she wasn't chewing gum. "Hey, this place looks like Palm Springs with an ocean. Anybody want somethin' to drink?"

"Sure, now that we're at anchor, I think we've all earned a brew."

Wanda handed me a cold Mexican *cerveza*, specifically Pacífico, the only kind I will drink. It brought back more pleasant memories of my last voyage here.

"What's the plan, Cap?" Buddy asked, ducking under the blue canvas dodger. He'd just been forward to check the anchor after the disruptive wake.

"I'd like to take the water pump apart on the engine and inspect the impeller. How about you taking the girls and the jerry jugs into the marina for fuel. I think we need to keep at least one person on the vessel at all times."

"Yeah, that's what I was thinkin'," Buddy agreed.

"Do you anticipate we will have any more trouble from Chuck and Bart?" Toey asked, staring at the tea leaves in the bottom of her cup. "If they jumped out of the *panga* before it exploded, they will surely come after us."

"I hope not. But they've gotta know we'll stop here for fuel." I shifted subjects: "Tell you what . . . let's get our chores done, eat early, get some shuteye, and take off about four in the morning. That'll put us past Cabo Falso before the wind picks up. From here on, I'm sorry to say, we're gonna have the wind right on our nose."

"OK, that's what I was thinkin', we better get going." Buddy nodded. "Wanda, give me a hand with the jerry jugs. I've got to empty them into the ship's tank before we leave."

Toey helped me use the mizzen halyard to move the outboard motor from the stern rail to the dinghy. We lowered the rubber boat into the water and tied off the painter to a stern cleat. In a few minutes, Wanda was ready to start handing down the empty plastic containers.

The ship's tank would only take fifteen of the twenty gallons on deck. While the others were ashore, I planned to figure out our fuel consumption. Buddy climbed in the dinghy, yanked the outboard's starter cord, and they sped away.

I went below and removed the companionway ladder to access the front of the engine. When I separated the faceplate from the water pump, broken pieces of rubber came with it. I remembered there was a new impeller mixed in with the spare parts Buddy and I had collected when we cleaned the boat. By the time I had it fitted and everything back together, my crew had returned from shore. I never got to do the fuel calc.

Tying the dinghy to two stanchions amidships, Buddy hoisted the full jerry jugs up to me. The three climbed on board. Toey and Buddy walked the dinghy back to the stern, while Wanda went straight to the galley with dinner on her mind. I secured the fuel containers. Buddy and Toey raised the dinghy and stowed the outboard motor on its stern rail mount.

In short order, the boat was squared away, ready for an early departure. Buddy and I moved to the comfort of the cockpit, while Toey climbed down below to give Wanda a hand. It was almost twilight, one of my favorite times of the day.

Activity from the noisy jet skiers and speeding parachute boats had pretty much ceased. Charter fishing yachts carrying sunburned anglers were heading toward the entry to the inner harbor. The sun dipped behind the cape, its reflected rays projecting brilliant gold flashes from windows on the hillside, as the land in shadow was bathed in soothing hues of purple. The metallic yellow glow from the new marina silhouetted the palms surrounding the Hacienda Hotel. I wondered if The Giggling Marlin bar and restaurant still existed.

"What are you thinking about, Jake?" Toey asked, handing me an *Añejo* and Coke and easing her body close to mine.

"Oh, a lot of things, like . . . the first time I ever had rum and Coke was here, with my dad, eight years ago."

"You talk about your father a lot. It sounds as if you are really fond of him. I would like to meet him sometime."

"Like you to. Yes, he's a very special guy. Raised me all by himself after Mother died. I wish he were here," I said, clearing my throat and looking off into the distance. "In spite of the problems, he would have enjoyed this trip."

After sundown, Wanda served the chicken fajitas with fresh corn tortillas she'd collected in town. To do it right, you roll the tasty Mexican stir-fried mixture into a tortilla and eat it like a sandwich. We ate and talked, Wanda describing Cabo San Lucas in her own inimitable way: "It's just two paved streets of bars and restaurants, surrounding a marina filled with plastic dollar bills, at the end of a desert." I wished I'd seen it for myself. I couldn't visualize all the changes that must've occurred since my last visit.

With dinner over, Toey policed the galley, while Buddy and I reviewed the course I'd charted from Cabo San Lucas to Bahía Magdalena. I showed him how to enter the new waypoints into the GPS, then I flipped the panel switches so he could go topside and check the navigation lights. He reported they were all working properly. I'd already turned the anchor light on.

While Buddy was out on deck, he also checked the anchor chain and used the vang to move the boom over to the port side. He traveled the main sheet to starboard and tightened it. His idea was to keep the boom in one position so it wouldn't swing or make noise when the vessel rocked with the swell during the night. He did the same with the mizzen boom. By 2200 we were all tucked into our blankets and sound asleep.

Some time after midnight, I awoke, thinking I heard a thud against the hull. A few minutes later, Toey screamed. I looked up through the open hatch overhead and saw Bart's face, grotesque with festering sores from his burns. Gun in one hand, he shined a flashlight in my eyes with the other.

"Get up here, assholes! And don't try anything smart, gawd damn it! I'll blow all you fuckers away if I have to." The dim light revealed terror on Toey's face.

"OK, OK! Chill out!" I yelled, telling myself to stay calm, trying to figure out what to do next. "Let me put something on."

"Where you're going you ain't gonna need no fuckin' clothes, shithead. I'm gonna burn you like you did me. Gasoline balloons. Cute stunt. Now you're gonna hurt like I'm hurting." Pulling on my shorts, I moved forward, listening to his tirade. "Come on, asshole! Get out here! And I mean right now!"

On the way up the companionway ladder, my mind was racing, searching, trying to come up with a plan . . . Then seizing the bilge pump handle, I stuffed it in the back of my pants. Wanda and Buddy were sitting under the boom on the port side of the cockpit, Buddy closest to the mainsheet leading to the block he had secured to the starboard side earlier.

Chuck and Bart were standing on the cushions on the starboard side, Bart nearest the dodger, waving his weapon in my direction. Chuck appeared unarmed. Toey hunched down and crawled past Bart, toward the rear of the cockpit.

I sat down on the wood combing next to Wanda and inched my hand toward the winch. I nodded at Buddy, hoping he'd catch on and follow my lead. His head moved up and down, ever so slightly, signaling he understood, then he turned to face Bart.

"I think this situation calls for a gybe!" I yelled, rolling backward onto the deck and releasing the vang holding the boom to our side. Toey screamed and flattened herself on the cockpit grate.

My sudden movement startled Bart. His revolver exploded. A sharp pain seared my right shoulder. At that moment, Buddy hauled in on the main sheet. The boom swung across the cockpit to the starboard side, hitting Bart square between the eyes. Blood oozed from his forehead.

I scrambled around the dodger and clobbered Chuck on the side of his head with the hard-plastic ball end of the bilge-pump handle. All six feet of him crumpled to the deck, red gushing down the right side of his face.

Meanwhile, Buddy and Wanda were all over Bart, who had been disarmed by the boom. Buddy wrestled him down, while Wanda grabbed the weapon from the deck. I took it from her and aimed at Bart.

"OK, *now* who's the asshole?" I demanded, my own blood trickling down my back and into my pants. For a crazy split second, I hoped it wouldn't seep onto the wood deck. "Put your hands behind your head," I shouted. "Do it. Now!"

"This is for Jake and for good measure," Buddy yelled, planting a right hook across Bart's jaw.

"Don't even think about it! Next bullet's got your name on it," I barked, as Bart started for Buddy. "You make one wrong move, and I'll put you out of your misery. Buddy, don't fool around, tie him up."

"Jake, you are bleeding!" Toey cried. She hurried below and returned to place a towel against my shoulder to stem the flow. The pain was excruciating; I almost passed out.

Buddy and Wanda tied up our intruders, Wanda duct-taping each man's mouth, just for the heck of it. "I've always wanted to do that ever since I saw it in a movie," she said, proud of her handiwork.

I staggered to the starboard rail and was amazed to see a *panga* with a Mexican driver patiently waiting for our captives. They must not have paid him yet. I yelled in my broken Spanish for him to come alongside *Shore Loser,* then told him: "*Amigo, no problema para usted. Dos hombres malo. Yo pago para sus servicios.*"

I saw there were two fifty-liter containers of diesel in the *panga.* Buddy used the main halyard and winch to hoist them onto our deck—it never hurts to have extra fuel, especially when I hadn't had time to do the calculations. Then he opened the starboard lifeline gate and rolled Bart and Chuck over the side into the small boat.

"I was wonderin', Jake. Put 'em somewhere on shore?"

"Yeah, have the *panga* driver take you to Honeymooner's Beach. It's on the other side of the bay, just back from the arched rock. He'll know where it is. Leave them there and leave them tied up." I gave Buddy enough pesos to put a smile on the fisherman's face.

After they left, I followed Toey to our stateroom. My shoulder felt like it was on fire. As Toey washed the blood off my back and disinfected the wound; I almost passed out again. Fortunately, the bullet had just grazed the surface, slicing across the back of my shoulder.

"You are lucky, Jake Mortensen. You could have been killed." She kissed my cheek. "Sometimes, I think you do not need a girlfriend—you need a nurse!"

"How about both? A lover and a nurse?" I said, smiling, and kissed her back. Even though I was weak and hurting, I was still aware of how desirable she was. Pulling her to me, I kissed her again and said, "Thank you, ma'am."

"Do not even think of fooling around, Jake. You need to get some rest." She pushed away and helped me tug my shirt over the butterfly bandages. "It is one o'clock in the morning. With you in this condition, are we still leaving at four?"

"Yes. We have to, if we don't want to get beat up by the wind and sea when we go around Cabo Falso."

"Why do you think those two men are going to so much trouble to get this boat back? There must be something very valuable on board, and I think the owner does not want to lose it. It cannot just be the boat."

"Honestly, I don't know," I whispered. "We sure didn't find anything other than dirt and junk when we cleaned up. Not even the drugs I figured they were using." Suddenly, my voice became raspy, and I realized I was pretty damn weak.

Then I passed out.

CHAPTER NINE

# NORTHBOUND

I *hate* it when I oversleep. I'm always afraid I'll miss something. The muffled drone of the engine woke me—the pitching hobbyhorse-rocking of the vessel confirmed we were underway.

My shoulder blade felt like it had been raked with the claw end of a crowbar. I looked at my watch; it was after eight. Toey wasn't in her bunk, but an indentation remained where her lovely body had rested. I was upset she hadn't gotten me up when it was time to leave the anchorage.

As I swung my legs over the side of the bed and sat up, my head started spinning. I was hurting and in a lousy mood. Fortunately, at that moment, Toey entered the cabin and came over to help me.

"Jake, please, be careful!" she admonished. "Your face is so pale. How are you feeling?"

"Why didn't you get me up?"

"We all agreed you needed the rest! There was blood all over the deck this morning. You should have seen it! You lost a lot."

"Must have—I feel a little weak and dizzy."

"With the autopilot, the three of us can easily handle the boat. Buddy wants you to take it easy for a day or so. We all do." She smiled and kissed me. "I am just glad you are still with us."

"OK, OK! Promise me you'll get me up if there's any problem?" I didn't feel strong enough to argue. "Where are we?"

"We passed Cabo Falso about three and a half hours ago. The seas are a little bumpy, but not bad. There is very little wind and no boat traffic. Can I get you some orange juice?"

"Yeah, I'd like that."

I sat on the bunk's edge, my bare feet dangling above the oiled teak and holly cabin sole. *Shore Loser* lurched forward, rolling from side to side and up and down as we pounded into the lumpy ocean. Toey returned with a half glass of juice. She knew about being at sea; an inexperienced person would have brought a full glass and spilled it.

"Want some more?"

"Yes, please." I was surprised how thirsty I was. My mouth was pasty.

"Let me check your bandage."

She pushed the collar of my t-shirt back to examine the dressing, her chest at eye level as she stood over me. Too bad she was wearing that damn purple sweatshirt. Too bad I was so weak. I put my hands on her hips and pulled her closer, the roll and pitch of the boat providing an excuse to nuzzle her cleavage. She laughed, pulled back, and kissed me. The pastiness was suddenly gone.

"Jake, Jake, please, no! That is all you can have until you are better." She gave me a friendly kiss, this time on the cheek, and left the cabin. At least my mental outlook, if not my physical condition, had improved. I lay down again and conked out.

Around noon, I awoke, my rumbling stomach reminding me I had missed breakfast. The pain in my right shoulder was a bit duller, maybe I was just getting used to it. I rolled out of bed and bobbed and weaved through the cramped corridor past the engine room. Wanda was in the galley, in slacks that accentuated her figure and a baggy sweater that didn't.

"How you doin', Jake? Feeling any better?" she asked, moving out of the way to let me by. "Make you a sandwich?"

"Yes, um, thanks." My weakened state and the motion of the boat made me hang on to the wooden fiddle rails around the counter.

Continuing carefully from port to starboard past the companionway ladder, I plopped down in the seat at the navigation station. When I activated the GPS, the green LED display told we were making just under six knots over the ocean bottom. The ETA readout announced we'd be at the Punta Tosca waypoint in about twenty hours.

GPS-era electronic navigation aids are mind-boggling. Before, you had to plot it all out on a chart and do the math. Now a little black box does everything for you. Heaven help the new mariner if the computer craps out and he hasn't learned the old-fashioned way.

Given the probability of electronic failure, I still like to do it the way my father taught me, plotting the latitude and longitude on the paper chart, then making the entries in the log. The hourly positions taken from the GPS are my lone concession to the electronic age. Buddy had us running right on the rhumb line.

Punta Tosca is the southern tip of the long, barren landmass of Isla Santa Margarita, a thirty-six-mile finger protecting Bahía Magdalena. On the chart, I measured the distance from the Tosca waypoint to the entrance to Mag Bay. At our present speed, we would arrive there sometime tomorrow afternoon.

Wanda brought me a grilled ham and cheese, which I wolfed down as I read log entries. I saw where Buddy had adjusted the watch schedule into three four-hour periods and felt guilty, wondering if my injury was placing an unnecessary burden on the crew.

"Hey, Toey, your patient's up." Wanda had climbed halfway up the ladder to get Toey's attention.

"Is he ready for me to check his bandage?" Toey asked, sticking her head into the companionway opening.

"Sure," I answered, looking up. "And I want to talk to Buddy."

"He's catnapping in the cockpit. Want me to wake him?" Wanda asked.

"No. Let him sleep. I'll tell you guys, and you can fill him in later." I made the tone of my voice grumpy, for effect. I needed to feel I was regaining control of my vessel.

"Toey, why don't you come down here, and I'll take the watch while you talk to Jake," Wanda said, probably not wanting to deal with my foul mood.

Toey waited until Wanda was behind the helm. "The compass course is 290," she pointed out, then climbed down to me. Again, it was obvious both women were experienced sailors—I was fortunate to have them on board. However, I didn't let my admiration deter me from what I had to say. Feeling no longer needed, I had to let off some steam.

"I appreciate you guys taking over for me, but you must let me know when you make any changes. In spite of everything, I'm still captain and the one responsible for this boat."

"Aye, aye, sir!" Toey responded with a mocking salute.

"I mean it, Toey!"

"Lighten up, Jake. We will. How about I take another look at that wound?" Grinning, she led me to the aft portion of *Shore Loser*. So much for my imitation of Captain Bligh.

As we entered our cabin, I was still a bit wobbly but beginning to feel better. Remembering our previous encounter, she stood behind me to remove the dressings. The butterfly bandages were still holding everything together, so she left them in place. She told me there was a slight pinkness ringing the wound that could indicate infection. Otherwise, Toey thought everything was healing nicely. She replaced the gauze pad and kissed me softly, leaving me to rest.

It didn't take long to nod off. I slept fitfully. As an ex-Navy rescue swimmer and trained paramedic, I was very uncomfortable being someone else's patient. Several times I thought Toey, or someone, checked on me. But I was too tired to be sure.

Sometime during the night, I woke with a start. Over the engine noise, I heard what sounded like Buddy and Wanda arguing in the cockpit. Then Toey burst in, turning the aft cabin lights on. The resulting twelve-volt glow blinded me awake. My mind raced, trying to figure out what was wrong, imagining the worst.

"Jake, I think you should take a look at this." She helped me out of bed and we made our way to the companionway.

"What's going on?" It took all my strength to climb the ladder up to the cockpit. "Bart and Chuck find a boat to chase after us?" I asked, rubbing my eyes.

"No, but I'm thinkin' the whole damn Mexican fishing fleet decided to converge on us. Look!" Buddy shouted, his right arm tracing an arc from behind the wheel, while he steered with his left hand. "I can't figure out which way they're going."

"Shit!" Wanda added. "They have the entire ocean to fish in, and they decide to camp on us."

In the moonless darkness, we were surrounded by hundreds of white and amber lights, the boats so close I could hear their engines and generators. They were shrimpers with huge outriggers, dragging the bottom with nets, shadowy forms like amphibious aircraft taxiing on the water.

With so much illumination used for fishing, it was difficult to see navigation lights. As a boat would turn toward us, sometimes we could make out a red and, then, a green. Most of the time, we couldn't.

Gingerly, I went back down to the navigation station and punched the transmit button on the radar. An eerie green glow illuminated my face and hands as the screen came to life. The nearest vessel was less than an eighth of a mile to starboard. Fortunately, it seemed to be going in the same direction we were.

I counted fourteen boats within a six-mile radius, and others farther away. Buddy gave the helm over to Toey and came down to see if I had any ideas.

"What do you think we should do, Jake? I know they have the right-of-way and I don't want to interfere with their nets."

"The majority appear to be fishing between us and the coast on a zigzag course, sort of paralleling the land." In the darkened cabin, I had removed the daylight hood from the radar screen so we could both see. A pattern was becoming evident. "Most of them are moving at the same speed we are, or slower. I think we should work our way to seaward of them."

"Yeah. That's what I was thinkin'. Let me get back on the helm." Buddy started for the ladder.

"I'll give you the course changes. I can keep a better watch down here, using the radar. It's hard to tell how far away they are from up there."

"Tell me about it! OK, when you want to change direction, just shout it out."

Everyone was alert. Toey and Wanda stood on either side of Buddy and informed him whenever a craft seemed too close for comfort. For the next two hours, we altered our course five or ten degrees at a time until we were clear of the traffic. I don't know why lights always look closer at night, but they do. It sure makes it difficult to judge distances.

When we were out of danger in open water, Wanda was back in the galley. I looked at my watch—almost midnight. Toey had gone below to catch some winks before it was time for her watch. I made the log entry and gave Buddy the corrected course to Punta Tosca. Wanda served me a late-night snack at the nav-station—coffee and carrot cake. She must have done the baking during the afternoon.

My opinion of her had changed—I had discovered a whole new dimension to her personality. She was much deeper than the sexy-cocktail-waitress image she projected at the Busted Surfboard. She was mellow, levelheaded, and continually cheerful. Unlike so many women in my experience, there was no hidden agenda.

With Wanda, what you saw and heard was what you got. These were obviously the qualities Buddy cherished. Well, maybe the uninhibited sexy part didn't hurt either. It added spice to their relationship. And, I figured, older people in their forties needed that, didn't they?

With the excitement over, I crawled back into bed, this time sleeping soundly. Toey woke me up midmorning, wearing the swimsuit I remembered from our first day at the beach. She announced we were at the Punta Tosca waypoint, the wind was down, and the seas were pretty flat.

The pain in my shoulder had subsided, and I was feeling much stronger. My mood was better, too, so I decided to shave and clean up a bit. When I climbed up into the cockpit, Buddy was behind the wheel.

"How you doin', Jake?"

"Much better, thanks. How you holding up?" He looked tired. I suspected he'd been standing more than his share of watches. The girls were lying on the foredeck, relaxing and working on their winter tans. The head sail and mizzen sail were put away, and there was still one reef in the main. We were under power with about a five-knot headwind.

"I'm doin' OK. I was gonna say—I could use a shower, though." He sniffed his armpit, then pinched his nose.

"Just stay downwind," I laughed. "When we get to the entrance of Bahía Magdalena, you'll recognize it. The mouth of the bay is more than three miles wide. I set the waypoint right in the middle."

"I was wonderin', what's the plan when we get there?"

"Let's go inside all the way up to Puerto Magdalena and anchor for the night. It's well-protected and the bottom is good holding. It'll give us an opportunity to do our engine room checks and clean up. You can even take your shower," I chuckled. "There's also a small village, so we can dinghy ashore if we want. The girls may be ready to get off the boat by then."

"That's what I was thinkin'. Sounds good. You feel up to taking this watch for awhile?" He moved from behind the wheel. "Time for a log entry."

"Sure. Why don't you sack out and get some rest? I'm good for a couple of hours." I was eager to make myself useful again.

*Shore Loser* performed much better than I had dared to think she would. I doubted Chuck and Bart had done any maintenance while they were living aboard her. I wondered what instructions, if any, the owner had left with them when he put them in charge of the vessel.

As I ran it around in my mind, it was a strange situation. Even if the owner was a corporation, there had to be someone who cared about the boat—the president, the CEO, his wife, girlfriend, someone. Corporations don't buy yachts just for the heck of it.

I looked around the cockpit. Torn portions of the plastic cushions had been covered with gray duct tape to prevent the foam from falling out. The blue canvas dodger was in poor, barely serviceable shape, some of the stitching sun-rotted, and several seams were coming apart. The bullet holes didn't help either. I hoped it would hold together until we got to San Diego.

All the wood had been neglected—toerails, cockpit coamings, dorade boxes, and hatches needed to be stripped, sanded, and re-varnished. Painted surfaces of the aluminum masts and booms were blistered with corrosion around the stainless fittings. Elsewhere, the paint was oxidized and flaking. Wood plugs were missing in the teak decking, most of the black seam caulking needed replacement.

It would take a lot of elbow grease to make this old girl a yacht again, but in good shape, she would be comfortable to live on, and she sailed reasonably well. I wondered about the bank's plans for her. Put her up for auction, sell her to the highest bidder? Did they already have a buyer? Or would they go with a yacht broker? Is there such a thing as a wholesale market?

I didn't have a clue about how these things worked. Even though I was becoming attached to the vessel, I knew I could never afford her. A love affair with a boat is more damaging to a man's pocketbook than one with a woman. In my present financial condition, I had best forget it.

Toey took over the noon watch. Feeling almost normal, I decided to keep her company, but soon fell asleep stretched out on the long starboard cockpit cushion.

Unlike most entrances to the other lagoons along the Baja California Peninsula, the entrance to Bahía Magdalena is clear, deep, and wide. We arrived about one-thirty in the afternoon, along with a pod of California gray whales.

"Jake, Jake, look! Two huge whales . . . and they are right next to us!" Toey's yelling woke me up. She was as frightened as she was excited. "What happens if they hit us?" The gray hulks had surfaced for air, their barnacle-encrusted backs barely breaking the surface of the water. Just twenty-five feet off our port, the rush of air and waterspouts gave away their location.

"No problem," I said, drowsy and trying to be funny. "They've got the right-of-way. I think its called tonnage."

Mag Bay is one of the larger coastal lagoons visited by several species of these huge marine mammals during their annual migration from Alaska south to warmer waters. Traveling about twenty hours and 100 or more miles a day, a 6,000-mile trip takes them six to eight weeks. Each year, Bahía Magdalena, with its many miles of protected waterways, is the winter calving grounds for California grays—one of the biggest nurseries in the world.

The gracefulness of such titanic creatures has always been a mystery to me. I love to watch them gliding through water, as if swimming in slow motion. As a child, I heard stories of sailboats colliding with these gentle giants but was never afraid when they came close to my father's boat, *Danish Mermaid*.

And I wasn't concerned now, as they surfaced near *Shore Loser*. I figured the engine noise would keep them safely distant. At the wheel, Toey didn't share my confidence. She was sure they were going to run right into us.

"Jake, what do I do if they come closer?"

"Don't worry. We're all going in the same direction." We'd entered the bay and were headed toward a low sandy point off Belchers. The main was flogging from the boat being pointed directly into the wind. I snubbed up the mainsheet and traveled it to port. "Just steer a steady course. We're lucky they haven't calved yet."

"What do you mean?"

"Cetaceans are real protective of their babies." I couldn't resist displaying my knowledge. "The calves weigh about a ton and a half and are fifteen feet long when they're born. Every day, they consume as much as fifty gallons of milk and put on nearly seventy pounds. They fatten up for several months before they head north to their summer feeding grounds in the Arctic."

"Wow! Where did you learn all that, Professor Mortensen?" She leaned over and kissed me. The motion of her breasts against her sweatshirt revealed she wasn't wearing a bra.

"I read a lot." I laughed.

"What is so funny, Jake?"

"Nothing."

By three in the afternoon, we'd traveled the eight miles from the entrance of Mag Bay to Man of War Cove. Three other sailboats were anchored in the sheltered water in front of the village. They were part of the thousand or more "snowbird" cruisers that, like the California grays, travel down from Canada and the U.S., seeking the warmer Mexican climate.

Some stay. Others go back home before the hurricane season or continue on to the Panama Canal or South Pacific. Usually, they're loaded down with tons of unnecessary gear. These three were no exception: Underwear and other assorted apparel hung from the lifelines, drying in the afternoon sun.

We dropped the hook in twenty feet of water, backed down to set it, and killed the engine. The small fishing village of Puerto Magdalena had grown somewhat since my father and I visited. One-story concrete buildings snuggled against the barren hillside circling the anchorage. I remembered the unpaved streets and identified the small fish-packing facility and desalinization plant.

A dusty, dirty place, Puerto Magdalena reminded me of old mining towns in the Mojave Desert. Behind the settlement, a desolate yellow-brown mountain extended upward 600 feet to form the backside of Cabo Corso. At the water's edge, deteriorated pilings from an old pier jutted from a partially submerged rock groin. Uphill from the abandoned wharf, a wooden framework was the beacon tower—on the face of the whitewashed building next to it, a sign proclaimed "Harbormaster" in faded blue letters.

"I think we have to dinghy over there to check in," I said, noticing a *panga* approaching from the harbormaster's direction as I spoke. "On second thought, maybe not."

A stocky Mexican in blue jeans rolled up to his calves and a red-and-black checkered flannel shirt edged a fiberglass fishing boat alongside us and tied up. He introduced himself as *Delagado de Capitania del Puerto* and requested our ship's documents. I gave him the papers Mary had processed for me in La Paz, hoping they were all in order.

Toey seized the opportunity to exercise her Spanish and found out his name was Gregorio. He seemed friendly enough. He asked where we were from, where we were going, and how long we would be in the anchorage. She answered, and he said he'd return our papers in an hour.

Toey also learned from him there were two small *tiendas* in the village where she and Wanda could buy fresh vegetables. They decided to hitch a ride ashore, while Buddy and I cleaned up the boat.

When they returned two hours later, we'd pretty well finished our chores and washed up. The main and mizzen sails were covered, the deck was saltwater-scrubbed and squared away, engine room checks were completed, and everything was properly stowed.

Buddy even moved his and Wanda's sleeping gear up into the bow "to make room so we can have a nice dinner." But I knew what he really had in mind: The forepeak bunk was a lot cozier and considerably more private.

I paid Gregorio his fifty-peso fee, plus a *propina* for running the girls ashore, and signed his log book. We waved goodbye as the *panga* sped away; Buddy carried the groceries down below.

"Wow, looks like we're getting ready for a formal, sit-down meal!" Wanda remarked, noticing the main salon had been cleared. "Guess I better whip up something really special. First thing I'm gonna do, though, is clean up. OK to take a shower, Captain?"

"Sure, just go easy on the water," I replied. "It's better if you use the shower in the stern. Since you're cooking, why don't you go first and, then, Toey. Buddy and I already washed." Deciding it was better to stay out of the way, Buddy and I grabbed a couple of *cervezas* and headed to the cockpit.

As the sun set behind Cabo Corso, my friend and I stretched out on opposite sides of the wheel, caught up in our own thoughts. My shoulder was much better: no pain, just soreness. Things were healing. In the distance, I heard a generator start. The smell of wood cooking fires drifted over the water from land, as yellow incandescent lights, glowing dimly at first, flared up at various locations ashore.

On board *Shore Loser,* the aroma of whatever Wanda was whipping up wafted into the cockpit. I couldn't identify it, but it smelled wonderful. I hadn't realized I was so famished.

Toey poked her head up through the companionway. "The dinner is ready, you guys." Buddy and I collided at the hatchway trying to be first.

Wanda dazzled us with Swedish meatballs, my favorite. For dessert we had a special "choc-o-loco" ice cream. The girls had found chocolate Popsicles on shore, cut them up, and added rum. Our dinner conversation was carefree and happy. Now that we'd shown our pursuers, once and for all, who was boss, we all felt the worst of the trip was over. It was time to mellow out and enjoy one another and the voyage.

After dinner, Toey and I cleaned up the galley and retired to check how my injury was healing. Once in our cabin, she peeled back the bandages and said softly, "Everything looks fine." She was so close, I simply couldn't resist, I pulled her to my chest as we kissed. Our lovemaking was just heating up when we were interrupted.

"Ah, ah, ah! Aaaa … aaawgh … aawghh!"

"What the heck is that?" I whispered, as my imagination went crazy. Bart and Chuck attacking us again? Toey and I froze, hanging on to each other. The scream was high pitched and sounded like someone in pain.

"Aaaawagh … aaaawagh … oh, gawd! Oh, gawd!" It was coming from the forward portion of the boat. "Buddy!! Oh, gawd, yes! Oh, gawd! Aawh, aw, aw, aw! A, a, a, a, a … aaaah!" You don't realize how small a fifty-foot boat really is until moments like this. All Toey and I could do was laugh.

As moonlight filtered through the overhead hatch, I thought back to *our* first time. Now, the look in Toey's eyes was more familiar, more loving yet the impishness remained. I knew this trip had become dangerous and uncomfortable for her, and yet she was dealing with it, for the sake of a new relationship—our relationship. I was a pretty lucky guy.

"Shall we *quietly* make some noise of our own, Jake? Can you handle some physical therapy?" Toey discarded her top, a devilish look on her face. Soon, wearing just white cotton panties, her back slightly arched, she was sitting up on her bunk. My aroused anatomy made doffing my shorts difficult, but Toey was eager to assist.

Groping and fondling, she was all over me. I wanted so much to please her—to make her forget the noisy bikers, Chuck and Bart, Miles' drug problem, my injury, and all the other ugliness of the world we had experienced together. I'm sure we made a lot more noise than Buddy and Wanda. After all, we were younger and had considerably more stamina, and we couldn't let ourselves be outdone by the two seniors in the forward cabin.

Finally exhausted, we lay in my cramped bunk, our skin glistening. The anchorage was peaceful and quiet now. I lovingly stroked her jet-black hair. She murmured something in Chinese. Modestly, I pulled a light blanket over us. A protective reflex, I guess.

Outside, the water lapped at the hull, making a crackling sound like cellophane being wadded up and pulled apart. I figured it was anchovies, water termites, or some other minute microscopic marine creature nibbling at the underside of the vessel. From the forward portion of *Shore Loser* came muffled conversation and laughter. Otherwise, all was tranquil. Even the distant village sounds of children and chickens had stopped.

CHAPTER TEN

# DRUG RUNNERS

Warm tentacles of morning sunlight penetrated *Shore Loser*, spreading brightness everywhere. All four of us were laughing, smiling, and in good spirits. No one mentioned what went on the night before—it was a secret we all shared.

"You guys ready for breakfast?" Wanda asked, bubbly as always.

"Nothing heavy for me," I replied, climbing around the end of the main boom.

Toey and I took the canvas covers off the sails. I had taken for granted—unfairly maybe, because she was with me—that she would help with the mundane running and maintenance of the vessel and always pitch in, without my having to tell her what to do. Many times she made it clear that this voyage wasn't a chore but a way to increase her knowledge of how to be comfortable at sea.

I reminded myself I had a long way to go to understand what she was all about. Exceptionally bright, sometimes her mind conjured up unreasonable fears, which irritated me to no end. Like dynamite, she was a tightly compressed package, full of surprises—I needed to put as much energy into our relationship as she was.

We unhooked the canvas fasteners and shook off the moisture accumulated during the night. In the engine room, Buddy checked fluid levels and made sure everything was ready for the next part of the trip. Wiping motor oil from his hands, he emerged after topping off the generator and engine.

"How about a fruit plate, yogurt, and granola?" Wanda suggested from the top of the ladder, securing her hair with an elastic band and giving her Doublemint a workout. "It needs to be eaten." I was struck with the realization that this was the first time I'd noticed a wad in her mouth for several days. I wondered if there was any connection with the previous night's activities.

"Sounds good to me." I was anxious to get underway before the wind came up. I knew it was about 250 nautical miles to Turtle Bay. At six knots, it was going to take us about forty-two hours, roughly a two-day run.

When we had all the sail covers put away, I went down below and turned on the single-side-band marine radio. I wanted to catch one of the morning ham nets. I remember my father listening to these for onsite weather and sea observations. I'm not a licensed amateur, so I can't transmit. But I can listen. Entering the frequency numbers, I tuned up.

"Hey, guys, come here!" The warm-up session of the Sonrisa Net was all about two guys getting beat up in Cabo and left to die on a beach. There was also chatter about an increase in drug trafficking and speculation this mugging might be somehow related.

"Wow! Chuck and Bart must've really made up a bitchin' story." Wanda was the first to comment. "Shit! I wonder how long it took someone to find them?"

"They were probably discovered by the first tourists of the day, who thought they would find the beach deserted," Toey giggled. "I bet those vacationers were surprised! Except for Bart's burns, I did not think they were injured that badly. But, if they were, it is OK with me, after what they did to Jake." She rested her hand on my good shoulder. The other one, though still sore, was healing nicely.

Soon a net controller cut off the radio party-line, and a call went out for "any emergency or medical traffic." Next came the call for vessels underway to check in. We heard transmissions from three boats on the route between us and Turtle Bay reporting three- to four-foot seas and winds ten knots out of the north-northwest, pretty normal for this time of year.

"Enough eavesdropping. Conditions sound reasonable, so let's finish breakfast and get the heck out of here." Switching the radio off, I attacked the bowl of mushy fruit and yogurt Wanda had put in front of me on the chart table.

"We need to pick up some fresh stuff when we get to Turtle Bay, Jake. This is the best I can do with what we've got."

Underway, we observed more whale spouts at the mouth of Mag Bay. White plumes of air and water broke the sparkling surface like mini geysers. The pod seemed to be traveling in pairs, maybe fifty yards away, majestically in total command of their environment. Toey was apprehensive they would ram us. Sitting with her back against the companionway bulkhead, she pulled her knees to her chest and watched, fearful of a blubber-and-fiberglass collision.

Wanda, fascinated, clicked off two rolls of film. Her childlike excitement was a pleasure to see. In snug blue-jean cutoffs and a yellow sweatshirt, she knelt on the cockpit seat cushions, elbows on the elevated teak combing to steady the camera.

The result was her fanny sticking up in the air, exposing a portion of cheeks and a hint of something more, wiggling with each foamy geyser. Buddy and I were delighted with the view. Otherwise, the twenty-five-mile voyage from Bahía Magdalena to Cabo San Lazaro would have been dull as the doldrums.

When we neared Bahía Santa Maria, two cruising sailboats passed us heading south. They'd probably spent the night in the barren, wind-swept anchorage opposite Cabo Corso and tucked behind Cabo Lazaro. Since I figured they had just made the crossing from Turtle Bay, I called to them over the VHF. They said their voyage had been uneventful and confirmed the winds to be northwest ten to fifteen knots, depending on the time of day.

Like the boats we saw anchored in Puerto Magdalena, their decks were cluttered with the usual assortment of fuel jugs, spare anchors, storage chests, solar panels, inflated dinghy, outboard motor, and other miscellaneous "necessities" for their vagabond lifestyle. Dacron sails, which had probably been white when they left their home ports, were now dirty and stained. The hulls were also discolored, encrusted with ocean salt, marine growth, and engine exhaust soot.

Once past Cabo San Lazaro, I set a northeasterly course that would close with the mainland around Punta Abreojos. *Abreojos* means "open your eyes" in Spanish—the area gets its name because of the many offshore rocks and reefs surrounding the low sandy point.

I really didn't want to investigate too closely. However, from listening to Ted and remembering the voyage with my father, I knew the seas and winds would probably increase during the long crossing. Even though we were under power and a reefed main, because of the heading it was going to be more comfortable to crack off a bit.

The next day, when we were around thirty miles from the mainland, I adjusted course to a more northerly direction that put us on a direct line to Bahía Tortuga. The wind had died down, and the seas flattened out to a long swell out of the northwest.

By sunup the following morning, we could clearly make out Cabo Tortola and Punta Sargasso, the landmasses marking the two-mile-wide entrance to our refueling and provisioning destination. Entering the bay around 9 A.M., we found several other sailboats at anchor. A large sportfishing boat was tied stern-first to the dilapidated old cannery pier, taking on fuel. My log book reminded me it was Christmas Day. I was surprised fuel was being sold. I had thought it was a much more important holiday in Mexico than in the United States and expected everyone to be home with their families.

"Go ahead and drop the anchor," I yelled to Buddy, as we pulled into the anchorage near the refueling wharf. Toey and Wanda had already lowered the sails and were tying them to the booms. I selected an open area in the vicinity of the anchored sailboats, opposite the pier. One of the boats was *Just Us II*, which had reported the weather on the Sonrisa Net before we left Mag Bay.

"We're in twenty feet," I yelled, giving Buddy a thumbs-down.

"OK, here goes the hook!"

Buddy released the windlass gypsy, dropped the forty-five-pound plow anchor, and let out 100 feet of chain as I bumped the throttle lever into reverse. The anchor grabbed and held well enough to tug on the chain. I pulled the fuel shut-off and twisted the ignition key.

As I did, I noticed a red and white *panga* speeding our way. Its driver had taken the cover off the big 45-hp Yamaha on the stern and was adroitly managing the throttle and shifting the motor by hand. He was obviously used to operating his boat in this fashion. I saw Toey grab some fenders and tie them off to protect *Shore Loser*. As the Mexican banked his vessel at full speed and careened to a stop against our hull, she reacted just in time.

"*¡Feliz Navidad!*" Toey yelled, without smiling.

"*¡Feliz Navidad!*" the handsome young fisherman responded, a red, white, and blue bandanna tied around his head, his skin weathered and dark. Even though it was midmorning, a dozen spent beer cans littered his boat, and he was opening another.

"*¿Basura y diesel?*" By way of greeting, he offered to pick up our garbage and take our fuel containers to the dock to be filled. Toey talked to him, while Wanda scrounged through *Shore Loser* for trash, and Buddy and I untied our empty jerry jugs and handed them down to him.

"*Mi nombre es Jorge. ¿Tiene usted una cerveza? Por favor.*"

"He wants to know if we have any beer to give him." Toey was looking at me as though uncertain about asking the question.

"Sure. Go ahead and give him a couple. Maybe he can help you guys find the fruit and vegetables we need for the rest of the trip." Wanda handed him three bags of trash.

"Where'd all that stuff come from?" I asked.

"Mostly from changing your bandages," she replied, ducking under the dodger and going back down for Jorge's beer. Disappointed, I noted that Wanda had changed from her tight shorts into sweats. Toey had on her only clean pair of slacks and an Alameda Yacht Club shirt. Both women were eager to go ashore.

It took them and Buddy almost two hours to find what they needed, while Jorge refilled our fuel containers. When they returned, Jorge hoisted the containers over the lifelines and climbed on board. Surprised and then glad to have his assistance lifting the heavy jugs, I removed the deck fill cap.

"*¿Por favor, señor?*" Jorge took the clear plastic hose from me and began siphoning diesel into the ship's tank. Buddy and I didn't have to do anything, except make sure Jorge didn't overfill things. It doesn't take much to create a huge, oily slick, and I didn't want us to contribute to screwing up the environment.

When our main tank was full, I sent Jorge back to top off our plastic containers again. He returned in about half an hour and hoisted them on board. Buddy lashed them to the lifelines, while I paid Jorge and gave him two more beers. The ones Wanda had given him were already gone, and he looked thirsty.

"Jake, Jorge told us there has been a lot of illegal traffic through here in the last few days," Toey said, wrapping her arm around me as we watched Jorge untie from *Shore Loser.* "The last suspicious boat to fuel up took on more than 2,000 gallons. It was a big Hatteras Sportfisher, seventy or eighty feet long. Two of the men on board sound just like Bart and Chuck. I am worried."

"Don't be, Toey. If it's them, they're now somewhere ahead of us. If they're mixed in with drug running, I don't think they're going to want to stop and wait for us. We're moving too slowly." My tone was condescending, and I knew it, but I was irritated.

I understood her fear—fear was good, if it didn't cloud our thinking. Otherwise, fear can get you killed. I was also concerned for our safety, just as much as she was—I just wished there was a way to make her feel more comfortable.

"Well, Jorge says the Mexican Navy has been alerted. He thinks they may try to intercept the smugglers somewhere off of Cedros Island. The fishermen monitor VHF Channel 14. We can contact them and find out more about what is going on if we need to."

Brushing her hair out of her eyes, Toey persisted. "I do not want to get in the middle of a conflict. Our escape from La Paz and Cabo San Lucas was frightening enough. Jorge cautioned us to be careful, and he was serious, Jake."

"Toey, it's highly doubtful the Mexicans will catch them. Hatteras Sportfishers are very fast," I said, gritting my teeth. "I just wish I could remember why this one seemed so familiar. I'm sure I've seen it, or a similar one, in San Diego recently. Did Jorge remember the vessel's name?"

"He told me, but I cannot remember. I think it was a vulgar name. Maybe that is why I put it out of my mind. I am sorry."

All our fuel-stop chores had been completed; the wind in the anchorage was increasing: It was time to finish preparations, if we were going to leave tonight. I decided to call *Just Us II* on the VHF. I suspected they had been monitoring the weather up ahead much better than I had. I was right, they had been on the amateur radio ham nets throughout the day and also had recent WeatherFax printouts.

From Marina Del Rey, California, George and Vicki had been cruising the Sea of Cortez and Mexican mainland for the last two years and were now returning home. It was time to rebuild the cruising kitty so they could come back and do it again in a few years.

From what they'd pieced together, they were convinced the crossing north of Cedros Island did not look good for the next two or three days. We could expect twenty-five knots of wind out of the north-northwest in the afternoons and six- to eight-foot seas. Also bound for San Diego, George and Vicki had decided to sit and wait at anchor for a few more days. I couldn't afford the same luxury. My crew was running out of vacation time, and I needed to get the delivery done.

Hoping to learn more, I punched in Channel 14. There was confusing chatter in Spanish spoken faster than I could hope to understand. "Toey, help me. I can't figure out what they're saying." I moved out of the navigation station seat and let Toey slide in. She held up a hand, signaling for silence, as she strained to listen and adjusted the volume on the radio.

"They're talking about the Mexican Navy trying to intercept a big sportfishing yacht near Punta Morro at the south end of Cedros Island," she interpreted. Then she paused for a moment. "You were right. The Hatteras was too fast and got away. The Navy has alerted all commercial fishermen to report any sightings." She paused again, as several Mexicans tried to talk on the radio at the same time. "Also, wind and sea conditions are deteriorating. Most of the fishing boats are headed for anchorage at San Benito Island or along the lee shore of Cedros."

Now we knew with certainty, the next part of the trip was going to be rough. The possibility of encountering Chuck and Bart, in addition to bad weather, was not something I wanted to think about. With Buddy looking over my shoulder, I studied the chart and plotted a course inside Isla Natividad and up the leeward side of Cedros. My calculations showed that, if we left Turtle Bay right after dinner, we would exit the north end of Cedros about dawn. Buddy agreed with my plan. We both felt the winds would be at their lowest velocity in the early morning hours.

We had an early dinner. Then Buddy and I hauled anchor, while Toey and Wanda cleaned up the galley. Under reefed main, we worked our way along the rocky section of coastline extending north from Turtle Bay to Punta Eugenia.

The night smothered us; there were no lights along this section of coast but for the two navigation beacons at the entrance to Bahía Tortuga and the one on Punta Eugenia. As we started across the Dewey Canal, we could see the lights of the small village on Natividad off to our port side. Up ahead in the distance, a sulfurous glow illuminated the salt-loading port at the south end of Cedros Island.

Wind velocity increased from fifteen to twenty knots out of the west-northwest, and the seas became nasty and confused. *Shore Loser's* fifty-foot-long hull pounded onward against the wind, slamming into wave after relentless wave. The angry sea flying across the bow drenched our vessel's tired canvas dodger. I hoped it would hold up to the punishment.

Then, as quickly as it had come, the wind subsided. We had crossed the channel and entered the lee of the big island's eastern shore, opposite the deep-water salt-loading depot at Morro Redondo. As the wind disappeared, the sea flattened out to a long, comfortable rolling swell. Large oceangoing merchant vessels from all over the world halt in this protected open roadstead anchorage, awaiting turns to pick up salt.

Much to the aggravation of environmentalists concerned with preserving whale breeding grounds, salt is mined and loaded on barges at Scammons and other coastal lagoons on the mainland. The barges are then towed across to this huge, six-million-ton storage facility on Cedros. Tonight, no vessels were anchored, but a freighter was tied up to the wharf adjacent to the mountain of white crystals. Conveyor belts on cranes were transferring salt from the giant stockpile into the vessel's cargo holds.

"Jake, I was wonderin', what have I got crossing in front of us? See the lights?" On watch, Buddy had turned off the autopilot and was gripping the wheel with both hands, trying to peer around the dodger at the same time.

"Looks to me like a tug towing a barge! Head for a point five degrees aft of the last light."

Sure enough, it was a tugboat with a load of salt completing its crossing from the mainland. The vessel's running lights seemed correct; however, there was just one white light on the barge that was more or less 100 yards behind the towing boat. It would have been disastrous if Buddy had not been alert and tried to cross between the two boats, for the steel towing cable would have seriously damaged our hull, if not sunk us.

The remaining night transit of the twenty-one-mile-long island was pleasant and calm. Using radar, we kept about two miles offshore. Our timing was perfect. As we approached Cabo Norte, the north end of the island, we caught the sun rising, its warmth filtered through a patchy layer of puffy low-level clouds. Now for the moment of truth. This is where wind velocity, sea conditions, fog, and other weather patterns often combine to make the crossing to the mainland a challenging test of vessel and crew. We were prepared for the worst.

But the worst didn't happen—not then. Seas were a bit confused and lumpy, but tolerable. Clearing free of the lee of the island, we encountered fifteen knots of wind on the nose. But after about an hour, the winds started dropping, and we were able to stay on a course plotted to San Diego, 330 degrees magnetic.

During the morning, the ocean swell continued to build from four, to six, to eight feet, out of the west. By mid-afternoon, the wind increased to twenty-five knots out of the northwest. I made everyone put on lifejackets and harnesses, before I headed the boat up directly into the wind and tried to hold her there, while my crew struggled to put the second reef in the mainsail. Heavy six-ounce white Dacron flailed violently, the fabric snapping like shotgun reports.

Again and again, *Shore Loser's* bow climbed up a foam-spattered wave, only to crash and shudder down the back side. Winds continued to build to thirty knots, gusting to forty. Our speed over the ocean floor had reduced to one or two knots. Something didn't feel right.

Dad and I had been through some pretty terrible stuff on *Danish Mermaid*, much rougher than this, and I always felt safe. But I knew dad's boat was in good shape, well-cared-for. I wasn't so sure about *Shore Loser*, and I began to have misgivings about our repossessed vessel's ability to withstand this magnitude of brutal sea conditions.

Giving the helm over to Buddy, I went below to plot a new course. The girls had done such a good job of securing things earlier that only a handful of books and charts littered the cabin floor.

*Shore Loser* trembled as she slammed down off crest after crest. I had to find an anchorage we could run to and get out of this weather. The hull lifted off another wave and came down with a tooth-jarring crash. The whole vessel vibrated.

Sitting at the navigation station, I felt nauseous. I couldn't believe it. I have never been seasick in my life. Ex-Navy guys don't get seasick. Clenching my teeth in determination, I completed what I was doing, then headed back up the companionway ladder to the cockpit and fresh air.

"Fall off to a bearing of 350 degrees! We're heading for San Carlos anchorage!" I had to shout to be heard over the roar of the wind and sea. "That course will keep us well south of Sacramento Reef. We should get there early tomorrow morning."

I moved to the back of the cockpit and sat down. My face felt hot and I was dizzy. The salt spray felt good.

"I'm thinkin' I like this better, Skipper." Buddy had made the course correction, and the boat was taking the crests of the waves at more of a forty-five-degree angle.

"Jake, you are white as a sheet! Are you OK?" Over the noise of the crashing sea, Toey also had to yell. She and Wanda were on each side of the companionway, under the protection of the dodger. Salt spray was coming around both sides, soaking the aft part of the cockpit.

"Yeah, just a little woozy is all. It's not nice down there," I yelled back. I felt sick and embarrassed. But I didn't throw up.

Whipped into a turbulent frenzy by the high wind velocity, salt spray flew off the top of each monstrous breaker, frothy foam streaming down the front side in lacy rivulets. Only the black frigate and brown booby birds benefited, as they glided on the air currents generated by the undulating surface of the sea. We were still more than thirty-eight miles from the nearest point of land. I couldn't begin to imagine the horror of being in a vessel of this size during gale- or hurricane-force winds.

With the vicious conditions continuing throughout the night, none of us could sleep. We went down below only when absolutely necessary. About four in the morning, I made out the outline of land among the sea scatter on the radar screen.

We entered the protection of San Carlos Anchorage, such as it was, about dawn. Two rusty steel Mexican shrimp boats, a U.S. thirty-two-foot Grand Banks trawler, and one Canadian sailboat were at anchor. The wind was still blowing twenty knots when we dropped our big plow in twenty-seven feet of water. It held, and Buddy let out 250 feet of chain for peace of mind. He rigged a bridle to keep the pressure off the windlass and locked everything down tight.

I surveyed my crew. They were cold, wet, disheveled, and exhausted. Toey's hair hung over her face, she used both hands to push it aside so she could see. Wanda's ponytail had gone AWOL hours ago, her only fashion statement totally out of control. Her sweats were soaked, and so was her jacket. Both women still had on their lifejackets and safety harnesses. Buddy looked much better than I felt. He had managed to stay relatively dry by wearing the red foul-weather gear he used for offshore races in Southern California. Everyone was silent.

"The Baja chart book says this place is always windy, so it's one of the best locations in North America for windsurfing," I said, trying to make light of what we'd just been through. My crew was not impressed with this piece of trivia.

In spite of the wind and the chop it created, the anchorage was moderately flat and calm. Once secure, we all needed to crash for some much-deserved rest; cleaning up the boat could wait. Buddy and I stretched out in the cockpit so we could maintain some sort of anchor watch. The girls went down below.

Four hours later, I woke to screaming and yelling on the VHF radio. I'd purposely left it on, and when my head cleared, I realized someone was desperately trying to get our attention. The trawler that had been anchored between us and the shore had somehow broken free. Propelled by twenty-knot winds, she was dragging down on top of *Shore Loser*.

I shook Buddy awake. It was too late to hoist anchor. The powerboat was over the top of it and less than seventy feet from our bow. I started *Shore Loser*'s engine and slowly powered off to port. Realizing what I was trying to do, Buddy rigged fenders and lines along our starboard side.

Fenders already lined the port side of the powerboat. As the trawler drifted by, Buddy threw lines to the older man and woman standing on deck. They made the bowline fast just as their hull slammed alongside *Shore Loser*'s fendered side with a dull thud.

Toey and Wanda almost hurt each other scrambling up through the companionway at the same time. "Jake! What in heaven's name is going on?" Toey was first into the cockpit. She had grabbed a jacket and was wearing nothing but her white cotton panties underneath.

"Toey! Wanda! Quick, toss them a stern line!"

A second, younger, couple was standing in the aft cockpit. They were scared and didn't know what to do.

"Here," Toey shouted. "Catch this line and make it fast to a stern cleat."

The combined weight of both vessels jerked our anchor chain taut with tremendous force. Buddy checked his bridle and was satisfied it was holding.

Fortunately, the trawler was just thirty-two feet long to our fifty, so it was easy to secure her alongside. Our anchor tackle was big and strong enough to handle the added load of the second vessel. Buddy and I adjusted the mooring lines and fenders so the two boats worked together properly. With things under control, Buddy whistled at Toey. Embarrassed, she went below to put on some clothes.

The rafted powerboat was *Our Kids Inheritance,* out of San Diego, California. The owners were Robert and Pat Samuelson, a pleasant couple in their seventies. Bob was a retired fast-food exec; he and Pat were making their way home from the Panama Canal. They had spent three years cruising Costa Rica and Mexico and two years in the Caribbean. Their crew was Jack—Bob's son from a previous marriage—and Jack's wife, Beth. They were all shaken.

"Thank you, thank you," cried Pat. "We were trying so hard to get you on the radio to warn you. Thank you, again."

"I knew we were dragging, and the engines wouldn't start, and now the main battery banks are dead," said Bob, holding his wife's hand.

Buddy and I climbed on board and determined the engine fuel filters were clogged. Buddy changed them, while I checked their generator and got it running. The ship's batteries did not have enough power to turn over the twin Ford Lehmans, but, fortunately, the Onan generator had a separate starting battery.

"Let's run the generator long enough to bring up your main battery banks. You can try to restart the engines when the batteries register thirteen volts."

"Again, I don't know how to thank you guys," Bob said. He was tall and lean, with a receding hairline—his hand shook as he extended it to me. In every other way, he looked physically fit.

"I really don't know what happened to our anchor," exclaimed his wife, Pat, short and trim, with beautiful silver hair. "We were hooked in tight. We've been anchored for more than twenty-four hours. It's been windy but, otherwise, everything's been fine."

"Let's check it out, Bob," I suggested, as we headed for the bow.

What we found was not pleasant. The port side of their nylon anchor bridle had parted. As a result, the chain had pulled off to starboard, doing considerable damage to the bow pulpit, platform, and bow roller. The pressure had snapped a link in the chain—the anchor was lost. All that remained was a short length of chain and the starboard portion of the anchor bridle.

"You folks have any more ground tackle?" I asked.

"Sure. Gosh damn, will you look at that?" He held the broken chain in one hand and scratched his head with the other. "I think you guys saved us from a lot of grief. My wife and I have a lot of experience boating and know what we're doing, but I think we're getting too old for this." His tone was contemplative and sad.

"Hey, stuff happens." A stupid statement, but all I could think of under the circumstances. Their retirement lifestyle, which I'm sure Bob had worked for all his life, was becoming dangerous. Mortality was staring him in the face, and he was scared.

It was two hours before we could restart the engines. Bob and his son replaced the ground tackle on the bow with a spare anchor, chain, and rode, which Bob had stored in the stern. Buddy and I released the mooring lines, and Bob and Pat motored away from us to re-anchor. The boat would be fine for the rest of the trip to San Diego. The same couldn't be said for its owners.

"Bet they sell the boat and buy a motor home." I had my arm around Toey's shoulder.

"It is sad," Toey said. She'd changed into warm clothes and smelled of fresh perfume.

"Yeah. I think people should do their most challenging cruising when they are young and strong. They can still be active in boating when they get older, they just have to be honest about how much they're prepared to endure," I said, waving at *Our Kids Inheritance*, now safely at anchor. Still wearing my foul-weather gear, my hair felt damp with saltwater, and my scalp itched.

"I am just glad they are safe."

"A good first mate and good crew always helps." I smiled at Toey.

"Unfortunately, Bob selected poorly when he put his inexperienced son and daughter-in-law on board. I'm just glad I didn't make a similar mistake."

I think Toey was agreeing with me when she poked me in the ribs. But I wasn't quite sure.

CHAPTER ELEVEN

# HOME AGAIN

"Jake! Jake! Look! Out there, on the horizon. I think I see the Point Loma light!"

It was December 30, the morning of the fourth day out of San Carlos Anchorage, and Toey had just spotted the famous lighthouse. The flashing sequence of the powerful beacon was unmistakable. But to be absolutely certain, I went below and checked the navigation instruments. On the radar screen, I saw the characteristic "male genitalia" shape of Point Loma, drooping south from the coastline ridge.

With our location confirmed, I plotted our GPS position. We were fifteen nautical miles from the entrance to San Diego Bay, the Coronado Islands on our port side and the lights of Rosarito Beach behind us to starboard. Toey had us right on course to the outer whistle buoy, SD-1.

Sadly, I realized our voyage was almost over. We were homing in on the very spot where this whole adventure had begun. I climbed back up into the cockpit and moved behind the wheel.

"Think of it, Toey. If Ted and I hadn't rescued Monty's wife and his boat, we wouldn't have made this trip. Funny how things happen."

In the pre-dawn hours, the Pacific Ocean was placid, shimmering in reflected light from the moon and the city. I altered our course slightly, to align with Point Loma. SD-1 buoy was flashing white off to our port, SD-6 flashing red dead ahead; Point Loma Light was also ahead. And, in the distance off to starboard, I could see the distinctive arch created by the procession of yellow lights across Coronado Bridge.

Out of the darkness, the calm was shattered by the unnerving sound of a vessel speeding toward us—invisible, I couldn't pick it up on radar. Within seconds, it was alongside, red, white, and blue lights flashing. Silhouetted against the many lights of the city, I recognized a James Bond-like military inflatable, with six heavily armed men in helmets and dark clothing. Two of them had night-vision binoculars in their headgear, another had heat-sensing goggles.

"United States Coast Guard. How many people on board?" a young male voice boomed from a handheld loud hailer.

"Four." I was pretty sure he already knew the answer to his question.

"What's the name of your vessel, where you coming from, and where you headed?"

"*Shore Loser*. We're arriving from Mexico and are proceeding to the police dock to check in."

The rigid-bottom inflatable continued alongside us for several minutes. Then it sped off, into the darkness from which it had come. U.S. tax dollars at work, fighting the war on drugs?

An hour later, the sky turned lemony and the horizon crimson, as the sun rose, reflecting off San Diego's tall buildings. We took red channel buoy number six to starboard and turned toward Shelter Island. The cylindrical base bore four large, shiny-brown harbor seals, oblivious to our return. Vigorous barking repelled a smaller seal trying to climb aboard their already-crowded resting platform.

Toey woke Buddy and Wanda. Now that our Mexican holiday was over, it was time to check back into the United States. Toey lowered the Mexican courtesy flag and replaced it with the yellow quarantine signal.

We headed toward the San Diego Harbor Police facility located at the entrance to the yacht basin on the southwest end of Shelter Island. This is the clearance point for all small craft arriving from foreign ports. Here, U.S. customs, agriculture, and immigration officials can board vessels; while, across the channel, three yellow quarantine mooring buoys are used by yachts arriving after hours or when the dock is full. Above, on a grassy knoll, the Harbor Police office is staffed twenty-four hours a day. Three or four police vessels are usually moored at the seaward end of the dock.

As we approached, I noticed *Our Kids Inheritance* was already tied up and under inspection by two customs officers and a dog. Bob and Pat were off their boat, talking to one of the uniformed men. The other officer had just completed an interior tour, with a big German shepherd, and was leading the animal back along the cabin toward the transom. We waved, turned *Shore Loser* into the wind, and dropped our mainsail. I guided her into the dock, and Wanda and Buddy cleated us off. Then I went below to get the ship's papers and crew list.

When I climbed back up the companionway ladder, we were surrounded by three husky, heavily armed harbor cops, one at the bow, one amidships, and the other at the stern. The officer who'd been talking to the Samuelsons approached us, weapon drawn and tilted upward, while his partner restrained the dog.

"Don't anyone move! All of you remain on board!"

"What's wrong, officer? We're just returning from Mexico," I replied, thinking, *What kind of a homecoming is this?*

"Is this the vessel *Shore Loser*, U.S. Documentation number 987345, belonging to Bayview Development Company?"

"That's what the ship's papers say. But I have a court order to repossess this vessel on behalf of First Interstate Bank and return it to the United States. We picked her up in La Paz."

"How many of you on board?"

"Four."

"All U.S. citizens?"

"Yes."

"You the captain?"

"Yes, sir. Name's Jake Mortensen."

I handed the papers and our passports across the lifelines to the customs officer, who holstered his pistol, while the Harbor Police kept their guns trained on us. This was looking serious, if not downright dangerous. The canine controller tied up his dog and walked over to help his partner review our documents. My friends remained seated in the cockpit, while I stood at the lifelines waiting.

"OK, everyone, just hold tight while we check this out." The second officer took my papers and started walking up the ramp toward the Harbor Police building. The three remaining cops didn't move. Neither did we.

In about twenty minutes, the customs officer returned to converse with his partner, then he came over to me, his manner more relaxed. The Harbor Police were dismissed, and both customs officers boarded our vessel.

"Your story seems to check out regarding the repo job. I talked to the court judge and Mr. Banks at First Interstate. However, we still have a lot of questions. Do you know this vessel was reported stolen to the San Diego Harbor Police about two years ago by its previous owner, a Mr. Peter Hammer? On top of that, DEA has reports from the Mexican government of drugs being dealt from a vessel called *Shore Loser* by two men in La Paz, Baja California. This vessel fits that description. Do you know anything about that?"

I was dumbfounded. What did Peter Hammer have to do with this boat? I couldn't make the connection.

The second officer returned my documents. He was the younger of the two, tall and blond, his smile revealing crooked teeth. The first officer was kind of grumpy-looking, a brown-haired bureaucrat with a paunch. Both wore navy-blue Treasury Department uniforms.

We sat in the cockpit for what seemed like an hour, while they asked questions and filled out forms. They were particularly interested in Wanda's vivid descriptions of Chuck and Bart. Or maybe they were just interested in her; she was pretty animated.

We told them we thought Chuck and Bart had arrived ahead of us, delivering a load of drugs on a big Hatteras Sportfisher. I noticed them exchange a significant glance. We didn't know whether we were suspects or not.

When they wanted to go below and open everything up, I didn't object—I probably didn't have a choice, anyway. They brought the dog aboard, and all he did was shed hair all over. We'd searched the vessel before leaving La Paz, so I felt pretty certain they wouldn't find anything incriminating.

They'd just taken the dog down into the saloon when a huge commotion broke loose on the docks. Half a dozen uniforms came running down the ramp, jumped into two Harbor Police vessels, and started the engines. The customs officer's cell phone rang, and he climbed back up into the cockpit to answer, the canine controller right behind him, trying to pull the big German shepherd up the steep companionway ladder. The dog got the hint and bounded up into the cockpit, knocking his master flat on his butt.

Then, great news: "OK, you folks are cleared to go. If we have any more questions, we'll call you."

They dragged the dog off the boat and up the ramp toward the parking lot, as both Harbor Patrol boats pulled away from the dock, lights and sirens operating. I started *Shore Loser's* engine.

"Whee-oo-ee! I'm thinkin' something big must be going down somewhere!" Buddy whistled. "Wonder where?"

"Don't know, but our next stop is the Knight and Carver shipyard in Quivira Basin," I said, jumping off, releasing dock lines, and climbing back on board. In spite of the hostile reception, it felt good to be back home.

"I was gonna ask, what do you think was going on back there?"

"Here, take the wheel, while I go down and listen in on the VHF." I gave the helm over to Buddy and went below.

Channels 16 and 22A were alive with traffic regarding a mayday from a vessel called *Broad Jumper*. The Coast Guard, YachtTow, Vessel Assist, and the Harbor Police were responding. The name of the boat tugged at my memory; I was sure I knew it from somewhere. Maybe I'd cleaned its bottom.

I went back up to the cockpit. "You guys know a boat named *Broad Jumper?*"

"That is it! Jake, that is the name of the Hatteras Sportfisher that was in Turtle Bay!" Toey could hardly contain her excitement. "That is the name Jorge gave me. I have been having an awful time trying to remember."

"You've got to be kidding!"

Suddenly, it came back to me: *Broad Jumper* was Peter Hammer's boat. I remembered Ted and Bill discussing it at the shipyard over a month ago. Also, the customs officer's comment about Hammer reporting *Shore Loser* stolen two years ago had been rolling around in my mind.

I was shocked. Surely, Mr. Hammer wasn't involved in narcotics trafficking. He was a wealthy businessman, a member of several prestigious yacht clubs, and a promoter trying to save the Russians' America's Cup effort. He was too visible. Surely, he wouldn't be stupid enough to let his vessels be used for illegal activities. It was too risky; his boats were too well-known. It just didn't figure.

Toey and I put up the mainsail and, with Buddy at the helm, motored back out the channel toward Point Loma. Once clear of the kelp beds, we turned north and started up the coast toward Mission Bay. Suddenly, a Harbor Police vessel, siren screaming, sped by, doing twenty knots.

On the horizon several miles ahead of us, there was a tremendous white mushroom burst of water swelling up from beneath the ocean's surface. At first it looked like a miniature atomic blast, then it turned bright red with black smoke, followed by the deafening sound of an explosion.

I could see two small vessels, probably Harbor Patrol or YachtTow, dangerously close to the blast area; they had to have been damaged by it. I thought about Ted and hoped he wasn't there.

"What the heck was that, man?" Buddy asked, straining to see around the dodger.

"Don't know. I'm going to go check the radio again. Keep heading that way, but stay outside the kelp."

My feet barely touched the companionway, as I swung below. Various public agencies were jamming the VHF with frantic exchanges. A police vessel had been damaged by the blast and was sinking. Officers had been blown into the water, and rescue attempts were underway. The exploded vessel, *Broad Jumper*, had showered debris everywhere and sunk immediately. A search was being organized for any survivors. As we got closer to the disaster scene, everything looked chaotic. Recognizing Ted's voice on the VHF, I followed him to the YachtTow working channel.

"*YachtTow I. YachtTow I.* Ops Center on Channel 18-alpha."

"Ops Center. This is *YachtTow I.*"

"Roger, Ted. What's going on out there?" Betty sounded worried.

"Not good, Betty. We've got three injured in the water and no sign of survivors from the exploded boat—junk everywhere. We're OK on my boat."

"What's next, Ted?"

"I'm going to stay out here and help search for survivors. Don't know how long it'll be. I'll keep our working channel on the second VHF. I've got to monitor 16 and 22A on my primary radio. Call if you need me."

"Contact! Contact! Hey, Ted, this is Jake Mortensen on *Shore Loser.* We're the sailboat coming your way from Point Loma. Can we help?"

"Jake? Welcome back! It's great to hear your voice, man." Ted hesitated for a moment. "Can't use your help right now. The Coast Guard and other agencies have it under control. Where you taking the boat?"

"Knight and Carver Shipyard."

"Good, I'll catch you later. Dinner somewhere?"

"You bet! Red Sails Inn?" My crew nodded their heads in agreement. "Seven o'clock. My treat."

"Sounds good. OK if I bring Jill along?"

"Sure."

"OK, Jake, you got a deal. Seven o'clock, Red Sails Inn. Coast Guard's calling me on 16; we better get off the radio." Ted was all business again.

"OK, *Shore Loser* out."

"*YachtTow I*, clear to Channel one-six."

*Broad Jumper* had exploded about two miles north of New Hope Rock and half a mile off the rugged Point Loma shoreline. She was well inside the kelp beds and had sunk in five fathoms. The dense marine vegetation was hindering rescue efforts.

Fortunately, within minutes of the blast, the three San Diego Harbor policemen were pulled from the water. All had major injuries and were rushed to a waiting ambulance in Quivira Basin. After a thorough search of the area, nothing was found of *Broad Jumper's* crew, not a single body part or piece of clothing. It was as though they had vanished or were trapped inside when the vessel went down.

We continued north toward the entrance to Mission Bay, staying well outside the notorious kelp beds and the accident zone. As we passed, we saw the Coast Guard RIB, Harbor Police, YachtTow, Vessel Assist, and SeaTow teams setting out fluorescent-orange buoys to mark the area, while the Coast Guard installed a floating ring to contain spilled fuel, some of which was still aflame in patches on the surface.

The search would probably continue until nightfall and then resume in the morning with professional divers. The whole episode brought back sickening memories: the Navy, San Clemente Island, Wally's mutilated body in the aircraft wreckage.

Even though they had tried to kill us, the thought of Bart and Chuck dying this way was gruesome. I visualized their faces, twisted in grotesque death masks as they fought for air, ensnared in debris under a bed of kelp.

If any of the crew were conscious when the vessel went down, they would have been confronted with the horror of trying not to breathe. No matter how desperate the drowning person is, he won't inhale until almost ready to black out. We'd learned about it in Navy SAR school.

There is a point when the concentration of carbon dioxide in the blood is so high, and the oxygen so low, that sensors in the brain trigger an involuntary gasp for air. This phenomenon occurs after about ninety seconds of holding one's breath.

When that first desperate gulp drags in water, spasmodic gasping automatically takes over, flooding the lungs. If the person is conscious, terrifying thoughts must sear the mind.

Suddenly, I was fighting back nausea. Even if Ted had asked, I didn't think I could search for dead bodies. I hadn't had the stomach for it in the Navy, and I still didn't.

"You all right, Jake? You look strange." Toey put her arm around my waist.

"Yeah, just thinking."

"About your friend Wally?"

"Yeah, about Wally."

Forcing the gruesome stuff back into my subconscious, I guided *Shore Loser* up the coast, past the Y-shaped fishing pier at Ocean Beach, and into the channel entrance to Mission Bay. A moderate swell rolled out of the west and broke on the south jetty. Having previously encountered this potentially dangerous condition, I lined up with the left quarter of the channel toward the north jetty. Surfing with the swell, we entered between the two rock structures. Inside, the water flattened out, and we lined up with the channel markers to avoid the shoal areas.

A mile down the channel, we jogged to port, then turned immediately starboard into Quivira Basin. The trip was over. We were home. I steered into the wind so Buddy and Wanda could drop the mainsail.

While I'd been lost in my mental torture, Toey and Wanda had cleaned up and changed into white shorts and their favorite sweatshirts, Toey's purple and Wanda's lime green. Considering everything we'd been through, it was remarkable—they were acting as if we were finishing a pleasant afternoon sail.

With the helm given over to Buddy, I went below to call the shipyard. "Knight and Carver Yacht Center, *Shore Loser* on Channel 9."

It took several minutes for a response. "Shipyard here. Switch to 72?"

"*Shore Loser*, switching to 72."

"That you, Jake?" It was Bill Sweetwater. "Monty Banks said you'd be arriving around now. How was the trip?"

"Tell you when we see you on the dock. We're in the basin now, headed toward the yard. Where do you want us to put her?"

"Pull alongside where you and Ted Blithe tied up *Papa's Toy*. I'll be there in a minute to give you a hand."

"Thanks, Bill. *Shore Loser* out."

"Welcome back to San Diego, Jake. Shipyard out."

I relieved Buddy of the helm. Wanda and Toey already had the fenders and lines ready; I directed them to set for docking on starboard. We maneuvered past the bait barges on our right and the Islandia Hotel Marina to our left. Turning around the anchored barges, we proceeded toward the shipyard, where the huge travel lift and towering cranes were visible landmarks rising above the masts of docked vessels.

We homed in on them and made our way toward the long dock where Bill waited. Toey handed him the bowline, as Buddy jumped off with the stern. I pulled the fuel tee and shut the engine down. Bill was ogling the girls.

"Like your selection of crew, Jake."

"Meet Toey and Wanda. Don't be fooled by their good looks; they can probably handle a sailboat better than you. I think you know Buddy. He teaches sailing at some of the hotels here in Mission Bay."

We shook hands all around, then my crew got right to work cleaning up, while Bill and I headed up the ramp toward the office. I was anxious to call Monty and eager to find out what would happen next with *Shore Loser*; I'd grown attached to her. I was also anxious to get paid. I had a $1,000 bonus coming.

"Good morning, First Interstate Bank," announced a very young switchboard operator. "This is Julia. How can I help you?"

"Good morning, Julia. My name is Jake Mortensen, and I would like to speak to Monty Banks."

I'm sorry, sir, but Mr. Banks is in a meeting. Can I put you through to his message service?"

"No, Julia. I would like to speak to a real person. Can you get a message to him?"

"I'm sorry, sir. I can only put you through to his message service."

"How about his assistant."

"I'm sorry, sir. She's in the same meeting."

I had to be rude to three secretaries to reach his assistant and was so angry I almost blew it. Fortunately, I remembered Grace's name or I don't think I would've gotten through at all. Grace got Monty to the phone, and he sounded sincerely relieved to hear my voice. He wanted the vessel hauled out as soon as possible. We agreed to meet at the yard at ten the next morning to go over expenses and discuss final payment. He wanted to hear the whole story later at the yacht club, congratulated me several times, and said the police had told him we were followed. He wanted to know if it was true, but he sounded rushed.

"My client is one intense dude," I said, after hanging up.

"You got that right," Bill nodded. "Now that you've repossessed the boat, he's afraid someone might try to vandalize it. Wants us to keep it under guard—extra security, that kind of stuff. What gives?"

"Don't really know. The guys who were living on board followed us from La Paz to Cabo, and we think they even followed us here. A couple of real thugs, they tried to do us in—twice."

"You're kidding."

"Nope. I'll tell you the whole thing over a drink sometime. You hear about *Broad Jumper* blowing up?

"No! I hadn't heard that."

"It just happened. We saw it on the way in."

"Well, I'll be damned. I did hear that Peter Hammer reported the boat stolen a couple of weeks ago, big reward and all that. Posters are in all the marine businesses around town." He pointed to one on his bulletin board. "Strange stuff. You know, Hammer used to own this boat, too."

"Yeah. The customs guy told us."

"Well, he also reported *Shore Loser* stolen about two years ago. Understand he sold it to one of his clients, some land developer, about a year ago, after it was recovered anchored at Catalina Island."

"Bayview Development Company?"

"Sounds right, but I'm not sure."

"This gets stranger and stranger by the minute. What's happening with the Russian boat? Hammer's involved with that one, too."

"Yeah, I understand he's raised a lot of money for them, but hard to say where it's all going. Since Hammer's initial payment, the yard hasn't gotten a cent more—we'll probably end up donating our services. The Russians don't even have enough to buy food. I've seen women from some of the yacht clubs coming in here with home baked stuff so the sailors have something to eat."

"Really, that bad?"

"Yeah. In spite of everything, the crew's still working hard to prepare the boat, but they're way behind. The Challenger Series starts on January 14; that's just two weeks away."

"Well, what can I say? Hope they make it. I'd better get back to my own crew, 'cause I owe them a good dinner and a night on the town."

"See you in the morning?"

"Yeah. Ten o'clock."

Back at the dock, things were pretty well squared away on *Shore Loser*. I suggested Buddy and I grab a cab and go get our cars. The girls agreed to stay and finish cleaning the interior. By early afternoon, all our gear was off the boat, and I turned the keys over to Bill Sweetwater. Our job was done.

We drove over to the house in Pacific Beach where, to my surprise, things were reasonably tidy and I wasn't embarrassed to let the girls use the bathrooms. Miles' absence was conspicuous; Ted wasn't home yet. We had the place to ourselves.

Toey wanted to go to her apartment to change before dinner. Wanda didn't care. She said she was just as happy to use our iron and make do with something from her seabag. The two women were so different—the trip had made that apparent. Maybe the age difference had something to do with it, but what did I know about women?

Toey insisted on calling a taxi and wouldn't let me take her home. She said she wasn't trying to be difficult, she just wanted to be alone for a while. I hugged her and told her I'd pick her up around six-thirty. With a kiss, she smiled and left.

"That's one classy lady, even if her boobs *are* bigger than mine." Finished with her shower, Wanda was stuffing her mouth with Chiclets. "You damn sure better treat her nice, Jake Mortensen, or you're gonna lose her."

"I've got to figure her out, first."

"Shit, that's never gonna happen, honey. Accept the mystery or forget it."

"What do you mean?"

"Me, you know, everything's on the surface. But Toey, she keeps everything bottled up. She's a deep thinker—thinks too much, sometimes. She's special. Don't mess it up, Jake. She loves you. But she don't understand it, either. You're both idiots. Lovable idiots, but idiots just the same."

"Well, she needs to *talk* to me then, damn it! I can't read her mind."

"Give her time, Jake. She's worth it."

Thank heavens, Buddy walked in just then. I don't handle advice well, and I wasn't really sure where Wanda was coming from. I hadn't figured her out, either. Buddy's presence gave me the chance to duck out of the conversation.

I needed a shower. The thought of water pounding my tired body was a pleasant alternative to Wanda's lessons for the lovelorn. I felt physically and mentally exhausted. The trip had taken more out of me than I wanted to admit. Now that it was over, I felt the letdown, or was it because I was back on land again?

That's it, I've never thought about it before. When I was out on the boat, my world was defined by the limits of the hull—everything was in its place, practical and orderly, just the sea and me. Back on land, everything was chaotic, and crazy, and without limits. I was no longer captain, I had lost control, and I didn't need an over-the-hill babe telling me how to proceed with my love life, either.

As I entered the bedroom, I peeled off my shirt and pants and tossed them on a pile of dirty clothes from the trip. On top of the dresser, stacked and bound with a rubber band, was all the mail that had accumulated: final discharge papers and check from the Navy, two letters from my father, lots of junk advertising, and a letter from Minnesota. Ted must have put it there.

Setting the Midwest letter aside, I sat on my bed, tossed the junk mail into the wastebasket, and scanned my father's letters. His were basically reminiscing about the trip we'd taken together on *Danish Mermaid*—lots of good memories floated off the handwritten pages. I'd read them thoroughly later and give him a call. Last time we talked was when I'd decided to go after *Shore Loser*. He had encouraged me to do it. Said it "vould be good for da soul." I wasn't sure yet whether that was true or not.

The return address on the Minnesota letter said Mrs. Wally Oleson. A baby-blue envelope with a bouquet of spring flowers on the bottom left-hand corner, its perfume was familiar. My hands trembled as I tore it open, the postmark indicating it had arrived five days after Christmas.

*27 December 1994*

*Dearest Jake,*

*Words cannot express the wonderful feelings I have for you and all the guys at HS-451. I know Wally's death touched all of his Navy friends more than I will ever know, but I think it touched you most. The way you consoled me is proof of that. Thank you! Thank you! I was alone, and in your grief you still cared enough to help. I will never forget us standing in the doorway and crying like children. Jake, that meant a lot to me. I know it was difficult for you and I thank you for just being there.*

*Minnesota is cold and white this time of year, but it is one of the ways I know it is really truly Christmas. It is part and parcel of my childhood memories, Wally's too. It is a prelude to spring—everything covered and getting ready for the rebirth. It is a holy time—a good time to be back here with my family and high school friends.*

*That Wally's baby should be born on Christmas is a special gift, and I thank Wally for that. Six pounds, 15 ounces, and 21 inches long. Strong and healthy. I've named him Walter Jacob, after you, Jake—and Wally. I will teach him that his name comes from two men who were good friends, both special, gentle, and caring. I am sure he will be proud of it one day.*

*I am fine, just a bit sore. Having a baby is not something I would want to do every day even though the delivery went well with no complications. When I leave the hospital I will be staying with my parents at the address on this letter. They have been just wonderful. Wally's parents live close by and they have also been great. If it were not for both sets of parents helping with expenses, I do not know how I would have managed. I don't get much money from the Navy. I plan to get a job as soon as I am able. The grandparents have offered to baby-sit. I do not know what the future holds, but I am sure everything will turn out all right.*

*Well, that's it for now. Please stay in touch, Jake. I care about you very much. Wally's son and you are all that I have left to remind me of the man I loved. I will be forever grateful for your kindness.*

*Fondly,*

*Anna*

I must have held Anna's letter for over half an hour. Maybe real men don't cry, but I couldn't hold back the tears. I covered the letter protectively, hoping my weeping wouldn't damage it, holding it like something sacred and fragile. I was devastated by emotions I didn't understand—happy that she and the baby were OK and depressed that they were so far away that I couldn't see them.

This whole thing was stupid. I was out of control again, all thoughts banished except the desire to hold Anna in my arms. I wished she were my wife, not Wally's, so I could protect her. Our last embrace seemed so long ago, but I vividly remembered her prettiness and vulnerability, her blond hair, her ripe belly, and her tears. Come on, Mortensen, get a grip!

What would it be like to have a son? To be a father? Damn it, Wally, you were too young to die. You had it all—a loving wife and a future—and some stupid bureaucrat, shuffling paper and sitting safe behind a desk, issued an order that took it all away. Damn the Navy! Damn the "War on Drugs"! Damn governments and politicians! Damn other people's decisions made without regard for the sanctity of life. *Damn it all!*

I vowed never to let anyone play games with my life. Not this kid. No, sir. No way. Not then, not now, or in the future.

I tucked the letter away beneath my folded shirts in the back of a dresser drawer, where no one would ever find it but me.

Wiping the tears from my eyes, I endorsed the back of my Navy check and put it into an envelope addressed to Anna.

CHAPTER TWELVE

# BAD GUYS

By six-thirty I had cleaned up my act and felt composed, sitting in Van Gogh in Toey's driveway. A new, dark-green Ford Escort was parked in front of the garage next door. I climbed the stairs and rang Toey's doorbell. She greeted me in an apron over casual clothes.

Feeling uneasy, I searched for something brilliant to say. "Got new neighbors?"

"I do not know yet, Jake. The car was there when I arrived home. I have been cleaning ever since I got back. My place is a mess with two weeks' worth of dirt." Wiping her hands on her apron, she added, "At least it is not a motorcycle parked down there."

"No, it's an old folks' car," I quipped. "You going to dinner dressed like that?" Irritated she wasn't ready, my conversation deteriorated from witty to rude.

"Jake! Certainly not! Please, make yourself comfortable and give me a minute." Pulling off the apron, she threw it at me. "I am sorry. I did not realize the hour was so late."

In twenty minutes, she reappeared, wearing a light-blue silk sheath with delicate silver embroidery on the shoulders and down one side. It had a mandarin collar and a tight bodice, barely containing her ample bust, defined by protesting nipples straining against the shimmering fabric. The embroidered side of her skirt accented a slit rising more than halfway above her knee.

I was surprised she'd chosen to wear something so "Suzy Wong" after my clumsy opening remarks. Maybe she wanted to feel seductive again, now that she was off the boat. My earlier irritation was replaced with mild embarrassment. Now I felt underdressed in a surfer shirt and white cotton trousers. Once again, she'd caught me off guard, and I didn't know what to do about it.

We walked to the waterfront restaurant and, after our long voyage, the sidewalk seemed to move with us. I could tell Toey was having difficulty navigating normally. Land sickness: a drunken feeling, minus the booze. Mine had all but worn off during the afternoon, while hers had not. She held tightly on to my arm; a chill in the damp night air encouraged us to hurry.

We were the first of our group to arrive at the Red Sails Inn. Shina, the seemingly always-sunshiny waitress, welcomed us, standing in front of the 1950s-style, pleated upholstered bar just inside the carved-wood entry.

"Boy, are you guys gussied up! Two for dinner? Haven't seen you in a while."

"Right. We've been in Mexico."

"Vacation?"

"Yes and no, partly work. Got a table for six inside, Shina? We'd like to be by the fire."

"You bet. It's kinda quiet tonight. I guess people are holding back until tomorrow, New Year's Eve. Follow me."

Grabbing some menus, she led us past the bar into the main dining room. We followed her ample posterior to a table near the stone fireplace. Deciding she wasn't overweight, just chunky, I marveled at the stress her shorts were under and tried not to stare.

Toey's tightly sheathed figure was a dramatic contrast to Shina's plump casualness. I pulled a chair away from the slab-wood table; Toey smoothed the silk over her firm little bottom and sat down. As she did so, her garment opened, exposing her right leg.

To get a better view, I leaned over her shoulder and kissed her neck. She covered up by crossing her legs. I gently pushed the chair forward, and she gave me the first smile of the evening.

What was it with this woman? I couldn't tell if she was teasing or trying to get my goat. I bet Anna never played these games with Wally, or Wanda with Buddy, or Jill with Ted.

"Get you folks something from the bar?"

I ordered a fruit juice for Toey, a rum and Coke for me, and sat down next to her. Gazing into the fire, we said nothing. Neither one of us felt very talkative.

Then our friends and drinks arrived. Wanda was dressed very casually; Jill wore a flowery Polynesian number. The guys were in laid-back Ocean Pacific beach togs like me. We ordered crab hors d'oeuvres, cocktails all around, and dinner.

Wanda was exploding with enthusiasm and couldn't wait to share the details of our trip. In light of the discomfort between Toey and me, it was painful having Wanda around. She was so effervescent, telling the story embellished with her own offbeat perceptions.

Buddy tried correcting her "facts" several times, finally giving up and letting Wanda narrate in her own unique way. Forty-five minutes passed before she reached the end of the tale and the climactic explosion of the *Broad Jumper.*

"Like, wow! Tubular! I can't believe you guys did all that stuff in just two weeks!" Jill exclaimed. "That was totally awesome!"

"Speaking of *Broad Jumper*, Ted, what really happened?" I asked, edging in before Wanda resumed.

Just then, Shina brought dinner. Buddy was having a large Caesar salad, while the rest of us were presented with huge portions of fish.

"I probably don't know any more about *Broad Jumper* than you do," Ted answered. "Rumor is the Hatteras had been used to make a drug drop at Mariner's Cove. YachtTow was responding to their mayday call when you guys arrived. I really don't know much more."

"What caused the blast? Any survivors?" I had succeeded in wrestling control of the conversation away from Wanda. She had turned from talking to eating.

"None. The Coast Guard is sending divers down in the morning to examine the wreckage. The boat was returning from Mexico, but it hadn't checked in with customs. We don't even know how many people were on board. We think there was a fire before the explosion."

"Bill Sweetwater told me Peter Hammer reported the boat stolen several weeks ago."

"That's right! It's the big flap all over the waterfront. Boat turns up missing; the next thing anyone knows, it explodes off Point Loma. It's going to be a challenge for the insurance companies and law enforcement to resolve this one."

"You think it really *was* carrying drugs?" I asked.

"Yeah, I do—even more so after hearing about your trip."

"Think the explosion was just a cover-up?"

"Maybe."

We continued to talk about the substance-abuse problem around Mariner's Cove and Dog Beach. I found the whole discussion disturbing. I'll never understand why people ruin their lives with cocaine and heroin. No one mentioned him, but I'm sure we were all thinking about Miles. He kept promising to quit but never did. Drugs were so much a part of his music scene that they had become a way of life—or death.

"Like, it's such a waste when drugs destroy famous and talented people like John Belushi," Jill said, pushing her empty plate away.

"But lots of unknowns die, too," I interjected, figuring someday Miles might be one of them.

"Well, I think less people would use drugs if they weren't so available," commented Ted. "Law enforcement should do a better job of stopping the flow across the border."

"Get real, dude. The cops and border patrol are doin' the best they can with the resources they've got." Buddy weighed in. "More police is not the answer. Maybe only the users have the answer."

"Hey, remember, people also die from alcohol abuse," I said, holding up my empty glass to the waitress. "And big Mama Cass, of the Mamas and the Papas, died of overeating. I think my father told me she choked on a turkey sandwich, in bed."

When dessert came, I brought up the America's Cup Race. I seriously wanted to shift our conversation to something positive. I was also anxious to find out if there were any employment opportunities for an out-of-work repo captain.

"We saw the Russian America's Cup race boat at Quivira Basin. How's all that going?"

"Don't know much about them, either. Just what I read in the *San Diego Log*," Ted answered. "Seems Peter Hammer raised a lot of money, and they still intend to compete in the Challenger Series. It starts January 14. The Russian team's been working pretty hard to get their boat ready, but I understand they still don't have any sails, and they're missing some winches and other hardware—problem with customs or shipping, or something."

"How about spectator boats? Anyone you know need a captain?"

"Check with Monty Banks when you see him tomorrow. Maybe some private yachts will. All the charter companies I know of already have crew."

We talked about what to do the next day, since it would be New Year's Eve, but no one was overly enthusiastic. Wanda suggested that anyone who felt like it could show up at the Busted Surfboard; she'd be on duty, filling in for those who had worked in her absence.

Ted knew he'd be on call for YachtTow throughout the holiday, since drunken boaters were at their worst then. I thought I might keep him company on night patrol, just for something to do. It would depend on how things went tomorrow at the shipyard.

Thankfully, Toey didn't get on her soapbox about the chances of the all-women team in the upcoming Defender Series. I couldn't have handled that. What started as a celebration of our return turned into a real downer. Everyone was just plain worn out, in spite of the coziness of fireside dining.

I was anxious to get the evening over with, so I paid the bill out of money left from the trip. When Ted and Buddy tried to chip in, I refused, saying, "The bank can afford it," and stuffed the receipt in my pocket.

I walked Toey back to her apartment and, on purpose, kissed her goodnight at the bottom of the stairs. I couldn't seem to shake my depressed mood, and as desirable as she was, I didn't feel like making love. She kissed me back but didn't ask me up. For a few minutes, we hugged, warming each other against the night chill. Two intense weeks together, day and night, had taken a toll on our relationship. Maybe it was time to be apart for a while.

It was a relief that she seemed satisfied just kissing me on the cheek. Watching her climb the stairs, I wondered why she had dressed so seductively. Silk clung to her every curve. I was suddenly sorry she hadn't tried to change my mind, but knew it was too late when I heard her slam the door and throw the bolt.

Got to the shipyard early the next morning, I'd been up since five, finishing the accounting and preparing for my meeting with Monty. When I arrived, *Shore Loser* was hanging in the fabric slings of the travel lift, being moved to a back portion of the yard, not far from the Russian boat. The bottom and the keel were badly in need of new antifouling paint. In some areas the paint was totally gone. Other than that, I was pleased the hull was clean. The Mexican diver had done a good job of scraping the barnacles before we left La Paz.

To me, *Shore Loser* looked attractive, a strong sailboat with lots of potential. Some hard work, and she could become a beautiful yacht again. Without realizing it, I had become attached to this hunk of fiberglass. In my mind, I pictured her all fixed up.

Then it became obvious to me, I was in love—true love, not just an attraction. Maybe that's what was wrong with my relationship with Toey: *Shore Loser* was competing for my attention. I wondered if Toey could understand, but at this point, I wasn't sure I even cared. I decided, right then and there, having the boat was important. If Toey couldn't settle for a share of my affections, then too bad!

"Morning, Jake." Bill Sweetwater interrupted my reverie, his hand extended in greeting. Monty Banks was close behind. "Looks like you got her here in pretty good shape."

"Yes, you did a good job," Monty agreed. He had someone with him I didn't recognize. "Jake, this is Lester Jabber. He's a marine surveyor, a professional boat-poker, if you will. The bank has hired him to appraise *Shore Loser* so we can establish a value."

The metal stands were in place, supporting the hull; the travel lift was out of the way. Les went right to work. He had gray-brown muttonchops and a gray-streaked yellow-brown moustache, his round wire-frame glasses giving him a nerdy look. He was probably trained as a marine engineer or naval architect, but looked more like a deck hand, his skin dark and leathery. His shirt pocket burst with pens and pencils, his blue jeans were threadbare at the knees, and his tennis shoes were scuffed and ragged. I liked him immediately.

Using a phenolic hammer, Les sounded the hull. He checked the strut, cutlass bearing, and propeller for electrolysis and wear. Scratching his head and pulling on his moustache, he scribbled notes on a pad of paper. Then he got a ladder and climbed all over the boat. Sensing we were in the way, we retreated to Bill's office and let Les do his thing.

"Les a good surveyor?" My mind was hatching a crazy plan.

"Yes. He's also a pretty good appraiser. That's why we use him. He'll tell us exactly what the boat is worth in its present condition."

"Then what happens?" I didn't want to sound too curious. My palms were sweating. I tried not to give myself away.

"We list it with a couple of brokers and try to sell. If we can't move it within six months, we auction it. Why all the questions, Jake?"

"What if I decide to purchase *Shore Loser* from you at its present market value, less a broker's commission?" I blurted. "Would the bank go for it?" I hoped I didn't sound too anxious.

"Yes, we might even finance it if you had a good co-signer." Monty said, smiling. "I'd like to get the bad debt off our books as quickly as possible." I couldn't tell if he really believed I was capable of buying the boat. I thought I saw him wink at Bill.

Once Monty concluded his shipyard business, we walked back to *Shore Loser* and talked to Les. Based on what he had seen so far, Les felt the boat would probably survey out around $75,000, as is.

I expressed interest in purchasing it to fix up. Les consulted the books in his briefcase and said a Gulfstar 50 ketch of this vintage would be worth $160,000 to $175,000 in good condition. But he cautioned this was just a guess that should be confirmed by yacht brokers in the area. Because of the holiday, the survey report would not be completed until sometime next week.

After thanking Les, Monty suggested we go get some coffee and discuss the trip finances and how to proceed if I really wanted *Shore Loser*. We drove around the marina to the coffee shop at the sportfishing landing adjacent to the Islandia Hotel.

I picked a booth next to the window overlooking the fuel dock. Several boats were tied up, taking on their fill of diesel for the holiday weekend. Monty ordered a huge chili and cheese omelet, and I asked for a coffee.

I figured it was probably his second meal of the morning. The big guy had definitely added pounds since the last time I saw him. The booth, too small to comfortably accommodate his girth, squished his belly against the table. At his request, we moved to more ample captain's chairs at a freestanding table in the middle of the room.

"I've got to go on a diet," he admitted, doing up a popped button on his shirt. "You have the trip accounting and a bill ready?"

"Yep." I pushed the papers and an envelope of receipts across the table.

"How about an invoice?"

"It's all there, Monty, including the ship's papers. I'm sorry my stuff's handwritten. I didn't have time to get it typed. The bank owes me an additional $1,687, plus the $1,000.00 bonus."

"Good. Here's the bonus check." He handed me an envelope. "I'm going to need a typed invoice. Include your social security number and the bonus amount I've just given you. I'll make sure you can pick up the check for the remainder from Grace on Tuesday."

I watched as he dumped generous amounts of Tabasco sauce on his omelet and started shoveling calories into his mouth. The only "health food" in front of him was the orange slice and parsley garnish. Temporarily satiated, Monty talked about my purchase of *Shore Loser*, burping several times without embarrassment.

I would have to make an offer in writing, accompanied by a good faith non-refundable deposit of 10 percent. He thought the bank would accept $75,000, no less, for a quick sale. He said he couldn't remember, but thought that number was close to the amount remaining on the existing loan. The bank would need a co-signed, completed credit application.

With the credit committee's approval, he thought he could push everything through in a couple of weeks. Grace would have a loan package ready when I came by on Tuesday. With a final gastric outburst, he concluded our conversation: "I think you just may have bought yourself a boat, Jake Mortensen. Congratulations, and Happy New Year. See you next week?"

What had I just done? I began to have misgivings. How was I ever going to afford it? I didn't even have a steady job. Of course, Monty knew that—he knew I was self-employed. Was he just stringing me along? The idea was crazy.

I used the payphone in the corner of the restaurant to call my father. It seemed like the thing to do. After all, my whole plan hinged on my father's good credit rating and his helping me with the deposit money.

"Hello, Dad."

"Dat you, Jake?"

"Yep. How's your love life?"

"Good, Son. How's yours?"

"Guess what! I think you and I just bought a boat."

"You crazy, Jake? Vat do I need anodder boat for? I haff already got a very good vun, *Danish Mermaid*."

"I know that. I'm talking about a boat for me to live on, Dad, but I need a financial partner. We can better than double our money."

As quickly as I could get it out, I explained the whole scheme. I'd live on the boat while I was fixing it up to save expenses. He could come down and give me a hand with the carpentry when he had time. It all seemed to make sense. My father became interested, then wanted to know what the interest rate on the loan and the payment schedule would be. I had to admit I hadn't even asked. My father was always practical; I was the dreamer.

Nevertheless, he was encouraging; I can't remember his ever being anything but. I told him I appreciated his vote of confidence and said I'd fill him in on the details Tuesday, after I picked up the documents. I thanked him and hung up, feeling much better. I hadn't told him we needed to come up with $7,500 cash for the deposit. I'd get to that later.

Outside the coffee shop, I hopped into Van Gogh and drove back to the shipyard for another look at *Shore Loser*. Les was still surveying.

"Well, Jake, did you decide to buy her?" He was in the cockpit, writing.

"Yeah, I did." I sat down opposite him. "What do you think? She a good boat?"

"She's actually in pretty good shape. Most of the problems are cosmetic, from lack of maintenance. She doesn't meet some USCG compliance and ABYC recommendations. But it's only money."

"Is it possible to get a copy of your report and recommendations?"

"Sure, but it has to come from Mr. Banks. Sorry, he's paying for it. Funny you should ask, though; another guy just came by with a lot of questions about the boat. I told him the same thing."

Hearing that someone else was interested bothered me, but I didn't say anything. When Les left, I went into the main salon and sat at the navigation station, as I had done so many times during the past two weeks. It felt comfortable. I closed my eyes and imagined I was underway, sailing to some exotic port.

After spending what must have been hours looking around the vessel that would soon be mine, I went to find Bill Sweetwater. He was standing by the Russian boat, talking with three of the crew. A big blond sailor was complaining about the yard's lax security. He seemed very upset, his arms windmilling in every direction as Bill tried to calm him down. Behind them, a bright-red hull glistened in the afternoon sun, white plastic still covering the keel, bow, and rudder. When Bill saw me, I became his excuse to get away.

"Don't know what's gotten into these guys. They claim two men were sneaking around the yard early this morning, although security people didn't see anything unusual. Regardless, they've doubled their patrol for the holiday. The Russians suspect one of the other teams is spying on them. God knows who would be interested— possibly the press."

"What's going to happen?"

"I told them that, if they want better security, they better get the KGB on it. Just joking, of course, but they didn't find me amusing." Bill shook my hand. "You buying *Shore Loser*?"

"Yeah, I think so."

"Good. She's a fine vessel. Let the bank put bottom paint on her first, though. They have to do it, whether you buy the boat or not, and it'll save you some money." He smiled. "Besides, they've already contracted with us."

"Thanks for the tip."

"And I almost forgot: Peter Hammer was asking about your boat when he was here today. It used to be his, you know."

"Yeah, I know." I pointed behind him at the hull of the Russian boat. "They going to be ready to compete?"

"Can't say. They've been scrounging used winches and hardware from the Australian and Japanese teams. Lack of competitive sails is the latest problem. Peter told me he and his friends have been working on it. The ones coming from Russia won't get here in time, so they got some of the other syndicates to donate from their training programs, and North and Ullman have offered to re-cut them. I just don't know—lots of rumors flying around. The boat hasn't even been in the water yet."

"Guess we'll just have to wait and see if they show up at the start line. I wish them luck."

"Yeah. They have bigger problems with the America's Cup Organizing Committee over whether or not they're a proper entry. Looks like a friggin' mess to me."

"How late you open today?"

"Until four. It's New Year's Eve, you know."

"Yeah, I know. I'll be back before then."

"Hey, Jake, it's almost four now," he said, looking at his watch. "If you are really coming back, I'll tell the guard it's OK to let you in later."

I wasn't sure what to do next. I really wanted to go get Toey and bring her back to the shipyard. Because we were being so chilly with one another, I was apprehensive. But, regardless of what was or wasn't going on between us, I was anxious to share my plans and dreams. That's what a relationship is all about, isn't it? I needed to know how Toey would react to my living on a boat and fixing it up. It was suddenly very important to me. I don't know why, it just was. I'd gotten my father's approval; now it was important to get hers.

When I turned the ignition key, I still wasn't sure what I was going to say. I was deep in thought the entire trip, Van Gogh auto-negotiating the familiar route, seemingly without my guidance. Pulling up to Toey's apartment, I snapped out of it. Her garage door was wide open, and I heard the vacuum going. She was working on her car.

"Need some help?" I said, approaching her yellow Toyota.

"Jake! You startled me! I did not expect you today." She held the vacuum wand in her right hand like a weapon, her other hand holding a paper bag. "I thought you were working with Ted, so I decided to clean my car. Here, can you put this in the dumpster for me?"

Taking the trash like an obedient puppy, I walked out to the utility receptacle beside the apartment. I still didn't know how to tell Toey about my purchase plan. When I came back, she was standing behind the car, lifting the vacuum. I took it and followed her upstairs. Looking at her in short shorts and a halter top, I almost forgot why I came.

"Toey, I've got to talk to you!"

"So talk. I am listening." Sounding aloof, she walked toward the kitchen, and I followed.

"I'm going to buy *Shore Loser*. I'm going to fix her up and live on her." It tumbled out so fast my knees got weak and I sat down at the kitchen table, amazed.

"Why am I not surprised, Captain Jake Mortensen?" She turned to look at me with a frown. "I was beginning to think there was another woman, or you were mad at me. I am glad to hear it is only a boat. *That* I can live with."

"Oh, really. Do you think you could live *on* the boat?"

"Well, I do not know about that," she said, pursing her lips and putting the vacuum in the pantry. "I do not think there would be enough storage for me. But I am glad for you, if that is what you want."

She came over and sat in my lap, looking up at me roguishly. She smoothed her hair behind her ears, her eyes sparkling as I put my hands under the back of her loose top. To my delight, she wasn't wearing anything underneath. As usual, things were quickly becoming sexual and getting out of control. She was overwhelmingly desirable, but I had come to talk.

"Let's continue this on the boat. Please, Toey," I whispered hoarsely.

"In the shipyard? It will be cold," she whispered back, nibbling on my ear.

"In the shipyard. We'll take jackets and watch the fireworks." Regaining my composure, I added, "And maybe we'll make some of our own."

"OK!" She wriggled in my lap one last time and jumped off. "I think I have some wine and snacks. Give me a few minutes. I know I can put something together."

We piled her bag and picnic basket into the back of my Volkswagen shortly after the sun had gone down. Heading toward the shipyard, I realized it was a good thing we were both dressed warmly. Van Gogh, open on the sides, offered little protection against the damp night.

When we got there, the gate was locked, so we had to wait for the guard to let us in. He warned us the Russians were still working on their boat and were pretty jumpy. He suggested we introduce ourselves to them before going aboard *Shore Loser*; I told him we would. Spotting the picnic basket behind the seat, he smiled, saying, "Happy New Year, Mr. Mortensen," as he let us drive past.

The entire area around the Russian vessel was brightly illuminated. Most of the mercury-vapor industrial lighting was focused on the flat deck, casting a yellow glow on the ground beyond. Several crewmembers worked on the winches and other equipment. The white-painted aluminum mast had been stepped, the stainless steel rod rigging was in place for support.

I recognized the crewman who had argued with Bill Sweetwater earlier. His eyes squinted into the glare of my headlights as we approached. Turning toward *Shore Loser,* I parked beneath her bow. The Russian hurried over as we were getting out. When he saw it was me, his eyebrows raised.

"Vat you do here? Yard is closed." His English was strongly accented, but understandable.

"Name's Jake Mortensen. This is Toey Wong." I extended my hand in greeting. "What's your name?"

"Boris, Boris Ivanovich."

He explained he was captain of the Russian team and asked us why we were in the yard after hours. I told him we had permission. I was the new owner of *Shore Loser,* and we had come to celebrate New Year's Eve.

I suggested the Russians consider us extra security. He didn't seem convinced. He told me about the recent intruders and let me know that he and all his men were staying on the race boat overnight as an extra precaution. Toey and I wished his team good luck and said we hoped they would get a chance to compete in the America's Cup Challengers Series. He thanked us and went back to work.

I raised the wooden ladder and placed it against *Shore Loser's* hull. Toey and I climbed up to the darkened deck. From there, we could clearly see the men working on the illuminated deck. Her mysterious keel and rudder were in the shadow cast by the vessel's competition hull. Toey took the picnic basket into the cockpit. In the glow of the work lights, I saw her familiar smile and knew everything was going to be all right.

Unpacking the basket, she extracted two small crystal glasses and a white ceramic urn with a red wax plug. I opened the wooden cockpit table and secured it. While she set things up, I took her bag below, then brought up the cockpit cushions so we'd have something comfortable to sit on.

"OK, my little Chinese flower, what do we have here?"

She had set a romantic table and lit a votive candle next to the binnacle. Before me were peanuts still in their shells, chestnuts in syrup, and other nutmeats arranged on placemats decorated with Chinese symbols.

"Something very special," she said, pouring a clear liquid from the urn. "This is called *Mao-Tai,* which means "Thatched Terrace." It is not really a wine. It is a spirit my grandmother used to serve for the New Year's festival. Be very careful."

"Wow! This is potent stuff." The taste I took burned all the way down. "Great drink for a cold night."

"I warned you," she laughed. "It is 110-proof and is made from sorghum grain. It is stronger than pure Russian vodka. Maybe we should share it with the guys on the Russian boat."

"Sharing with them is not exactly what I had in mind for this evening." I moved next to her and put my arm around her shoulder. "You know why they're staying on the boat, don't you?"

"They are afraid of something?"

"No. Rumor has it they can't afford lodging. They don't even have enough money to eat. Bill told me various groups have been donating food."

"That is so sad."

Off in the distance, fireworks lit up the northern sky over Pacific Beach pier. I looked at my watch. It was only eleven. Someone must have jumped the gun. Toey nestled against me for warmth. We sipped our drinks, while I rambled on about my plans for restoring *Shore Loser.* I told her how the whole thing had come about, including my father's involvement.

When we were on our second drink and getting ready to count down to midnight, a commotion started over by the Russian boat. A blood-curdling yell came from somewhere under the vessel. Suddenly, the metallic snap of a gunshot ricocheted through the shipyard, just as fireworks erupted over the Islandia Hotel.

I pushed Toey to the cockpit floor and eased my way out on deck for a better view. More shots, screams, and yelling came from below; more pyrotechnics exploded in the sky above. I slowly moved across the aft deck and looked over the edge of the teak caprail. Beneath me, near the Russian vessel, three men were struggling, but I couldn't make out who they were.

"Jake! Look out! On the ladder!" Toey screamed.

In a split second, I saw the dark hulk of a man rise above the edge of the deck, just three feet away. Silhouetted against the detonating sky, he had a pistol in his right hand.

Without conscious thought, I rolled onto my back, pulled my knees tight to my chest, and kicked the ladder away from the boat with all my strength. Fortunately, I'd forgotten to secure it to the lifelines—fifteen feet of wooden ladder swung away from *Shore Loser's* hull, with the climber still attached.

The man fired twice in desperation, clinging to the ladder as it smashed to the ground. Immediately, the Russians and one of the security guards were on top of him. He was screaming in pain; I guessed his back was broken.

The danger over, Boris repositioned the ladder so Toey and I could climb down. Flashing lights and sirens blazed at the shipyard entry gate. We ran over to the Russian vessel, where the two intruders were being held for the police. One man, the short stocky one, was still crying out in pain. The second, tall and bearded, was silent and subdued.

Clutching my arm in terror, Toey recognized them immediately. I did, too. Chuck and Bart had not perished in the explosion of *Broad Jumper*!

CHAPTER THIRTEEN

# DEATH AND MONEY

What a bizarre way to celebrate New Year's Eve! Four policemen arrived in two black-and-whites. Chuck was handcuffed and placed in the rear of one of them, without putting up any noticeable resistance. Bart, on the other hand, was violent, foul-mouthed, crazy, and difficult to control. Having sustained multiple injuries from the fall, he was carted off in a police ambulance, the screeching siren mimicking his protestations.

"Can't imagine what those two were trying to do," I grumbled, unable to make sense out of why Chuck and Bart were still bothering us. It was like a rerun of a bad movie.

"I said it before, and you will not listen to me," Toey insisted. "I think there is something very important hidden somewhere on this boat. Something they are trying to recover before you find it."

The Russians were surprised to learn the intruders weren't spying for competitors. Boris said he thought he recognized one of the men as someone he'd seen during a meeting with Peter Hammer the day before. But he wasn't sure. Toey and I were just relieved that finally Chuck and Bart would be behind bars.

With what remained of the *Mao-Tai*, we toasted Boris and his crew. Then we toasted the St. Petersburg Yacht Club, which they were sailing for. When the Chinese booze was exhausted, the Russian sailors toasted us with sturdy Russian vodka. We toasted the New Year; and their boat, *The Age of Russia*; and glasnost; and . . . Two security guards from the yard joined us, and we all got terribly drunk. Around three in the morning, Toey and I somehow made it back to *Shore Loser*.

The sun found us both asleep in the cockpit, not at all the way I had planned to welcome in 1995. Morning New Year's Day in a boatyard is as quiet as any place on this earth can get, until..."Anybody alive up there?" a voice reverberated from somewhere down below. My head was thick and throbbing. The inconsiderate person doing the yelling sounded like Bill Sweetwater.

"Yeah, give me a minute." I looked at my watch. It was ten in the morning, New Year's Day, January 1, 1995. Toey was sprawled on the opposite side of the cockpit. She groaned and rolled over, turning her back to me. I groped for my Ray-Bans and made my way down the ladder. Bill, who looked like he hadn't had a drop to drink on New Year's Eve, greeted me cheerfully.

"Understand you had some excitement around here last night. You guys OK? You look a little peaked."

"Yeah, just a tad hung over is all. The two guys that chased us up the Baja tried to board *Shore Loser* around midnight. Still don't know what they were after."

"You going to file charges?"

"You bet. Boris and I have to go to the station to do it. First, though, I've got to deal with this headache. There's a good reason why the Chinese and the Russians will never get along—their booze isn't compatible. I just hope the Russians are suffering like Toey and I are."

"Well, I'm glad you guys are OK. I understand they tried to shoot up the place. Any damage to your boat?"

"None that I know of."

"OK, but be sure to check her really good for bullet holes below the waterline. I'd hate to see her sink when we re-launch her," he laughed. "Hah, gotcha!"

Bill left, and I went to check on Toey. She was trying to gather up her things—she looked terrible.

"I need to go home, Jake," she pleaded. "Please." Her brow was wrinkled in a frown. "But, first, we need to talk."

"OK, go ahead." I didn't like the tone of her voice.

"Jake, I love you. I love you, but I am afraid of continuing with our relationship. You scare me!"

"What . . . what do you mean?" It didn't take a rocket scientist to realize she was upset over the events of the past couple of weeks and last night, but why with me? I really hadn't done anything wrong.

"Every time I am with you, something terrible happens: a fight, you get shot, someone tries to kill us. You are a magnet for trouble. I am sorry, Jake, but I am not used to dealing with this kind of stuff." Her voice began to rise. "I am a schoolteacher, for heaven's sake! I think being an old maid is a lot safer."

"I don't know what to say, Toey," and I didn't. "Stuff happens. It's just part of life."

"No, Jake! *Stuff* does not *just happen!* And I do not want this kind of *stuff* to be part of my life anymore," she was almost screaming. "My life was serene before I met you. Even the noisy bikers didn't move in next door until after I met you."

"Oh, come on, Toey. How can you hold me responsible for other people's actions? That's just not fair." I felt like she was attacking me. Her rage was out of control, voicing what I thought were old unfounded fears. I was exasperated, tired, and hung over, too. My life in the Navy had been pretty predictable up until Wally got killed; and then I met Toey, now it seemed like nothing made any sense.

"Please, take me home, Jake. I need time to think about all this."

A sullen silence developed between us as we carried stuff down to Van Gogh, maybe it was a way of attempting to keep things civil. I drove her home and left her to deal with whatever was going on in her head, besides the headache.

When I got to my house, Miles and Ted's cars were gone. I parked and went through the back patio, where Buddy was repairing dings on one of his surfboards, his portable tape player pulsating with music from the *Yellow Submarine.*

"I was wonderin', you and Toey have a good New Year's Eve?"

"Yes and no. Can you turn that noise down?" I said, holding my head. "How about you?"

"Wanda had to work, so I hung out with her at the Busted Surfboard. At midnight, even the help was allowed to drink. She's upstairs in my room, sleeping it off."

"At least you guys are still speaking to each other," I mumbled.

"Wow, are you in a bad mood. Toey's mad at you? Why?"

Buddy was shocked when I told him there had been yet another incident with Bart and Chuck.

"I can't believe those two dorks are still alive! I was thinkin' they went down with *Broad Jumper.*"

"If they did, they had dive tanks on. My guess is they set a timer on the explosives and used scuba gear to escape before the boat went up. The kelp beds make good cover."

"Hey, while Wanda's recuperating, I was gonna go catch some waves. Interested?"

"I don't know. I'm pretty hung over."

"Yeah, that's what I figured. Come on. I'll leave her a note. Surf's up. Not great, but it's up. Longboard stuff, and it sounds like you need to get physical."

"OK. You talked me into it," I mumbled.

We racked up our boards on top of Van Gogh. Buddy loaded the ice chest with beer and soft drinks. I changed, got my wetsuit and other beach stuff, and we were off. The middle-of-the-day California sun had started warming things up; cruising in my open Baja Bug, with the wind blowing in my face, started the attitude adjustment.

We passed Quivira Basin and negotiated the cloverleaf onto Sunset Cliffs Drive, then paralleled the San Diego River flood control channel past Dog Beach and into Ocean Beach.

"I was gonna say—wasn't that Miles' car over there in the parking lot we just passed?" I saw it, too, and heard the worry in Buddy's voice.

"Hope he isn't buying again. That's where he got busted last time," I said, remembering our Thanksgiving outing. "I'll never forget that night. I was just about to score with Toey when you called."

"Sorry about that. But I was thinkin' I'd really like to check it out if his car is still there when we leave."

"OK," I agreed.

I parked as close as possible to the Ocean Beach pier, and we unpacked. For a holiday, the place was not as crowded as I had expected it to be. Maybe most of the world was hung over. We moved our stuff onto the sand near friends, who were heckling some non-locals trying to surf a rather crappy beach break.

Buddy and I pulled on our wetsuits, waxed up, paddled out beyond the shore breakers into the moderate swell, and then we sat—waiting. The rest of the bunch could stay near the beach in the spotlight, trashing the small stuff with their shortboards. Doing spinning aerials was not what he or I had in mind.

Buddy was patient and wanted to wait for the big one. I just wanted to get rid of my hangover. During the afternoon, our patience paid off— we caught a bunch of mediocre waves and three good gnarly ones. It was just the therapy I needed.

When we headed back for shore, I wasn't tired, just cold. We'd been in the water over two hours; it was past quitting time. Meanwhile, our friends were still heckling the show-offs squirreling around in the shore break. Grabbing a beer, I joined in dishing out the verbal abuse.

"So, I was wonderin', what're you going to do about Toey?" Buddy asked, sipping a Diet Coke.

"I just don't know." He'd popped the one question I didn't want to deal with. "Maybe I'll let her work it out by herself."

"Hoping she'll come crawling back? Come on, Jake, get real! I'm thinkin' you're gonna lose her if you play it that way."

"You sound just like Wanda."

"Well, if you're lookin' for more than a one-night stand, listen to her then, man. She knows about these things."

"I don't know. You guys have a different kind of relationship." I was grasping here, still not knowing what I was searching for. "Number one, you're older; number two, you let each other do their thing without getting in each other's face."

"Nah, we're just doin' what's right for us. Neither one of us wants to get married; we don't want to be tied down like that, don't want that kind of commitment. But we sure like being with each other, sharing each other's company. We like it a lot—enough to not want to change each other."

"It seems Toey wants something more," I said, my headache coming back. "Something I'm not willing to give up: my freedom."

"Like the unwise surgeon once said, 'Suture self.'"

We packed up, said goodbye to our friends, and lugged everything back to the car. Buddy emptied the ice chest and secured it behind the seats, while I bungeed our two surfboards on top of the padded roll bars.

We drove past the surf shops, snack bars, and other beachfront businesses to Dog Beach, where Miles' beat-up convertible was now the only vehicle on the asphalt lot. I pulled in on the passenger side. The tattered canvas top was up, and the windows down.

Climbing out of my car, I saw Miles slumped low in the driver's seat. He was still wearing the clothes he had on New Year's Eve. It looked like he'd passed out.

"Hey, Miles, too much celebrating?" I didn't like the look of things.

Buddy beat me to the door and jerked it open. Miles fell toward him, and Buddy tried to prop him up to keep him from rolling out onto the ground. Miles' face was pasty white, his lips a deathly black, his eyes open and staring.

"Miles, Miles! Talk to me! It's Buddy. Oh, God! Miles!"

I checked for a pulse. There was nothing. He looked dead, and he was. Had been for a while. "Buddy! Go call the police."

"Miles saved my life in Nam! I can't let him die! I just can't . . . " His voice trailed off.

"Go! *Go*, man! Make the call, Buddy! He's dead. There's nothing you can do." I wanted to get him away from the ghastly scene as quickly as possible.

"Miles, Miles! Oh, God, why?" he pleaded, his face pale, eyes staring.

"Go, Buddy. Now! There's a payphone over by that light standard. Call 911. Go! Now!"

I gently pushed him out of the way and stuffed Miles' semi-rigid corpse back into the car. He looked like a wax dummy. He smelled . . . like death. I guessed he had overdosed. There was no evidence of foul play. Holding his head upright through the open window, I slammed the door, and he slumped into his former position.

I walked over to my car and waited for Buddy, hoping to steer him away from seeing his dead friend again. It wasn't a pretty sight. Buddy returned. The police and coroner were on their way.

We all deal with death differently. Of course, I had empathy for Buddy losing his friend in such a terrible way but, at the same time, I had no warm and fuzzy feelings for Miles. My concern was Buddy. I assumed he and Miles had been friends a long time. They were about the same age. Whenever Miles had been a pain-in-the-butt at the house, Buddy always defended him or made excuses. Now I knew why.

It wasn't long before a couple of patrol cars arrived, soon followed by the coroner's van. Within minutes, a crowd of onlookers had formed— ghoulish people materializing out of thin air.

The coroner did his crime scene once-over and zipped Miles into a plastic bag. Buddy and I waited around long enough to find out how to claim the remains from the morgue. Apparently, there was no next of kin, and Buddy wanted to make sure Miles got a proper funeral, even if he had to pay for it himself.

The first week of the New Year whizzed by; all of us were having trouble dealing with Miles' death. In addition, I had the business arrangement to conclude with my father so I could purchase *Shore Loser*. Then I had to get her back in the water and over to the Islandia Marina.

Buddy and Wanda made all the funeral arrangements. Wanda was amazing. She found a reasonably priced mortuary to handle the cremation and got the owner of Dizzy's Office jazz club and some of Miles' fellow musicians to chip in. For the most part, Ted and I just tried to be there for Buddy, doing whatever he needed.

*Pearly Gate's* in Pacific Beach did an almost believable job of pretending to care about the deceased and the mourners. The place was located in a neighborhood of converted one-story, stucco and wood-sided California bungalows built in the early forties. Two rather unkempt palm trees marked either side of the wood and stained-glass entry, and whitewashed stones filled the street frontage.

A short ceremony of remembrance was to be held in the mortuary's bland, velvet-curtained parlor at three o'clock Friday afternoon. Miles' urn was placed on a white marble table at the front, flower arrangements behind and on either side of it.

The white ceramic jar containing what was left of his incinerated body looked insignificant amid the bright foliage. Its whiteness suggested virginal purity, totally at odds with how Miles had really lived. The irony was that Miles was the reason Buddy never drank after the war.

The hardwood pews were crammed with people I didn't recognize, most around Miles' age. Some could have been Vietnam vets, I wasn't sure. Even though Toey attended with me, I couldn't decide whether it was because I'd asked her to or because she really wanted to pay her respects. We sat silently in the front row with Ted and Jill and Wanda and Buddy.

John and Louie and some other musicians performed with music appropriate to the occasion—slow mellow jazz, the kind Miles used to play on his piano. He would have liked it. Except for the undertaker, there wasn't a dry eye in the place.

Afterward, even though we had a lot to talk about, Toey and I didn't speak as I took her home. Memories of Wally's death and Anna's sorrow kept swimming around in my head. Miles' funeral and Toey's silent treatment, adding more negative energy, were dragging me down.

I had to get my mind on something positive, so I decided to call my father to see if he'd spend the rest of the weekend working with me on *Shore Loser.* I don't know what I would have done if he'd said no—I really needed some cheering up, someone to talk to, someone to listen. He said yes.

The slip Monty Banks had arranged for me at the Islandia was on the same dock as the Ocean Alexander, *Papa's Toy.* I had met the captain, Larry Klienschmidt, just briefly when Ted and I helped move the yacht to the shipyard. Now neighbors, we quickly became friends.

Larry was about my age, blond and muscular, with a southern accent. He had been caring for and driving big powerboats most of his life. Born and raised in Florida, he had gotten the majority of his sea time in the waters between Fort Lauderdale and the Keys as a private-yacht and sportfishing charter captain. An accomplished boat handler and mechanic, he did all of his own maintenance on the vessels he ran. He'd moved to San Diego less than two years ago, his police training in the military helping him land a job with the Harbor Police. That's how he ended up captaining the police commissioner's yacht.

Early Saturday morning, my father came down from Long Beach to see the boat he now half-owned and to give me a hand. He brought his favorite woodworking tools. Most were Japanese and razor-sharp, and he knew how to use them expertly.

After breakfast, I went to work cleaning up the engine compartment, while my father started tearing the dry-rotted wood out of the shower in the aft head. The shower stall on a Gulfstar 50 is sandwiched between the toilet compartment and the machinery space on the starboard side. Around the perimeter, where the Formica side paneling meets the fiberglass pan, the plywood backing was soft and punky. He worked all morning, removing the panels carefully so he could use them as patterns.

It was nearing lunchtime when my father removed the forward panel of the enclosure. Light came flooding through a large hole in the fiberglass bulkhead separating the shower from the engine compartment, illuminating the space behind the generator. I was removing the generator's metal sound shielding and had just managed to release the back panel, which had corroded to the base pan.

There, sealed in heavy plastic, were five packages hidden in the space between the fiberglass stringers supporting the generator and *Shore Loser's* outer fiberglass hull.

"Boy, oh, boy! Jake, vhat da you tink ve've found here?"

Four of the parcels were approximately twelve by six inches square. The fifth was about the size of a large briefcase. They had strips of plastic foam wedged in around them and were secured in place with three-inch gray duct tape.

Because they were secured in the dark recess behind the generator, Buddy and I had overlooked them when we inspected things in La Paz.

"Dad, wait a minute. Don't touch anything." My father was reaching for the briefcase-shaped package. "This has got to be the reason Bart and Chuck were chasing us."

"Vhat are you talking about?"

"The two thugs who were living on the boat in La Paz—Bart and Chuck! Well, they chased us all the way back to California. Their last attempt to board the boat was New Year's Eve, when it was still in the Knight and Carver yard. They're both in jail now. Toey kept saying they were trying to recover something other than the boat. I should have listened to her. These packages have got to contain money or narcotics."

"Uf-da! Ve better call da cops. Right now."

"Not yet, Dad. Before we do anything, we should think about this. Let's go get some lunch first." I locked up and yelled over to Klienschmidt. "Hey, Larry, we're going to get something to eat. If you see anyone come near the boat, kick 'em off the dock. We've left a lot of special woodworking tools out, and we don't want to lose them."

"Sure, Jake. Don't worry."

We walked to one of the restaurants in the hotel. I picked the one with a great view of the swimming pool so my father and I could check out the bathing suits while we were dining and lighten up a bit. I was afraid that what we had just found could have some pretty serious repercussions, if not handled properly.

How would I explain this to the police? What if they thought my crew and I were involved? The customs official at the police dock had mentioned that a boat fitting *Shore Loser's* description had been used for selling drugs to cruisers in Mexico. Obviously, it was my boat they were talking about. Yet the drug-sniffing dog hadn't found anything. Maybe it was because the stuff was in the engine compartment, completely sealed off from the living spaces.

I needed a diversion to give me time to think before I presented all this to my father, maybe girl-watching would help.

"Wow, Dad, look at the babe on the diving board." She had long flaxen hair and was wearing a tiny, iridescent-blue bikini.

He had other things on his mind. "Son, I tink ve should call da cops, right avay. Ve haf not touched anyting. Ve do not know vhat is really in da packages, do ve?" Dad was worried.

"No, but I've got a pretty good idea."

"If dere is money, or narcotics, you are not going to keep it. I did not raise you dat vay. So, vhat is da problem? Call da cops."

My father was right. Keeping the money, even if there was a lot of it, had not even crossed my mind. But I'd been panicked about my friends and me getting blamed for something we didn't do. An adolescent reaction, I realized now.

I remembered back to my younger days at Long Beach Yacht Club. Some of the older, spoiled-rotten teenagers would vandalize a Coronado 15 or Lido 14 in the dry-storage yard—probably to get even with someone who had beaten them on the racecourse. Invariably, one of my group would get accused because we were always seen there working on our Sabots. I remember my father was on the board of directors and continually defending us. He kept saying, "Yust tell da trudt and it vill be OK." And it usually was. The youthful offenders had always gotten caught.

"You're right, Dad. You're always right. But first I'm going to give my banker friend a call—the one who got me into all this. Order me a BLT and a Pepsi, OK?" The blond chick was getting ready to dive again. I noticed my father now looking in her direction with a little more enthusiasm.

I walked out into the reception area to use the payphone. Monty Banks wasn't at home, so I tried him at the San Diego Yacht Club. It was Saturday; the beginning of the America's Cup Challengers series was just a week away. The place had to be a madhouse. Of course, he was there.

"Monty? Jake Mortensen."

"Jake, how can I help you? But make it quick. We're really busy here." He was in control, as usual.

"I'm sorry to bother you at the club, but I've got a problem. I think we've discovered narcotics on *Shore Loser.*"

"What? Oh, my God, you must be kidding!" He sounded shocked.

"No, I'm *not* kidding. We haven't opened or touched anything, but I'm convinced some packages we've found are what Bart and Chuck have been looking for."

"Where are you?"

"Hyatt Islandia Hotel, next to the marina."

"Damn! I wonder if that's why a rep from Bayview Investment Company has been pestering the hell out of me. They tried to buy back the boat, you know. Even threatened to sue the bank. Said they would pay off the loan. We finally told them we'd already sold it to someone else, but they keep wanting to know who bought it and where it is."

"You haven't told them, have you?"

"Nope. It's none of their business." Monty was reassuring. "Look, Jake, hang tight. I have a good friend on the narcotics squad with the San Diego Police Department. His name is Richard Tracey. I'll call him right now and explain. Is there a phone where you can be reached?"

Holding the receiver with my chin, I signaled the receptionist. She brought me the necessary information so I could give it to Monty—he said he'd get back to me in a few minutes. I let the receptionist know I was expecting an important call. When I returned to my father, he was watching the blonde towel herself off. She was going through all sorts of delightful gyrations.

We enjoyed food for the eyes, as well as the stomach, as I related my conversation with Monty. We had just finished lunch, and the blonde had stretched out on a chaise lounge, when a phone was brought to our table and plugged in.

"Hello, Mr. Jake Mortensen?"

"Yes."

"This is Inspector Tracey. Monty Banks says you found something that may be of interest to us."

"Think so. But I don't know what, for sure. Haven't opened it yet."

"Good. I understand the boat is at Islandia Marina in Quivira Basin. Slip G-18?"

"Yes, G-18."

"OK, go back to the boat and wait for us. My partner and I will be there in twenty minutes. Don't let anyone on board and don't touch anything. Leave everything just as you found it. And, please, don't discuss this with anyone."

My father paid the check, and we walked by the pool for one last lingering view of the blonde, now on her stomach with her skimpy top unhooked. Neither of us wanted to leave; the scenery was too good.

On the way back to the boat, I paid particular attention to the marina laid out before us with its 190 slips. It had all the amenities you could ever want: good security, restaurants, bars, coffee shop, fuel dock, laundry, blonde in the pool—everything. The only problem is you can't live on your boat. You can stay on board for short periods, you just can't use it as your principal residence. What a bummer.

When I finished getting *Shore Loser* ready, I'd probably have to move her to one of the marinas on Shelter Island. Unfortunately, that meant I'd be farther from the good surfing spots. On the other hand, I'd be closer to work if I continued with YachtTow. Decisions, decisions: just another one to have to make down the road.

It didn't take long for the narcotics officers to arrive. I was surprised they weren't in uniform. In fact, when they came to the boat dressed in street clothes, I was concerned they might be from Bayview Development.

"You Jake Mortensen?" The two guys flipped open leather wallets with I.D. and badges.

"Yes."

"Inspector Tracey, here; and this is my partner, Joe." In his Hawaiian shirt, blue jeans, and tennies, Richard Tracey reminded me of a cop on the Hawaii-Five-O television series—he was definitely Hollywood. Joe, his partner, was a short muscular guy, dressed just as casually and carrying a leather valise that looked like a gym bag.

I'd seen enough movies to know they were both wearing guns, but I couldn't detect where. I introduced them to my father and invited them down into the main cabin.

"OK, where's the stash?" Richard seemed to be the one in charge.

"In the engine compartment. But it may be easier to look at it from the aft shower." I led them to the rear cabin and pointed toward the head. "Through there."

Joe pulled a high-powered flashlight, a stethoscope, and a pair of latex gloves out of his bag. Stretching the gloves over his bulky hands, he went in to take a look. It took him just a few minutes to remove one of the brick-like packages. Using a razor-sharp knife, he slit one end and exposed the white powder inside. Satisfied about what he was looking at, he taped the package back together.

Next, he pulled the larger parcel out and examined it thoroughly with the stethoscope plugged in his ears. Seeing how cautious he was, Father and I looked at each other. Could this be a bomb?

Once Joe was convinced it wasn't, he went back to the main salon and placed the parcel on the table. We watched in silence as he used his gloved hands and knife, like a skillful surgeon, to strip away the layers of plastic. He was being careful not to destroy any fingerprints that might be on the wrapping.

The uncovered object was, in fact, a very expensive-looking leather briefcase. Using another tool, Joe picked the locks. When he opened the case, my father and I gasped. Before us were stacks of U.S. currency, banded with white paper marked with the amounts in each bundle. Doing some quick math in his head, Richard whistled out loud.

"Well, I would say you guys made quite a find here. If my guess is right, there's over a million bucks in this case, and—depending on the quality of the cocaine—maybe a street value of another two million. No wonder those two goons were following you."

"Yeah," I said, drawing in a quick breath and looking at my father. "This stuff is worth a fortune. They weren't after the boat at all."

"Son, you vas lucky you und your friends don't get killed." My father gave me a worried expression.

"Monty tells me they're using a development company as a cover, but we can't prove anything." Richard looked at me with steely eyes that didn't miss or divulge a thing.

"Yeah, Bayview Development Company!" I said. "After what my crew and I have been through, I'd sure like to see them all put away where the sun don't shine. You guys are the experts. Tell me what I can do to help nail them."

Ghostly visions of Wally and Miles flashed through my mind. "I'd like to see all drug peddlers rot in hell." Out of the corner of my eye, I could see my father shaking his head in disapproval.

"You would?" Tracey laughed. "So would we. But first I need to get some crime lab people out here, in plain clothes, to dust for fingerprints. Next, I need fingerprints from you and your crew. Who knows, we may get lucky and at least be able to identify some of the characters we're dealing with."

"I've got an idea. What if I contact Bayview Development and offer to sell them *Shore Loser*? The next move would be up to them," I said, caught up in the heat of the moment. "My guess, based on how aggressively they've been bugging Monty Banks, is they'll move quickly to get the boat back."

"Is dis safe, Jake? Vhat if da crooks try to play rough?"

"We might be able to do what Jake is suggesting. We could have someone tailing him at all times. When he goes to a meeting, he'd be wearing a wire." Tracy scratched his chin.

"If we do this, we'd be coaching and watching him all the way." He looked at my father. "I don't think there is anything to worry about, Mr. Mortensen," Richard said, talking himself into it.

"They want the boat back. They don't know we've found the money and drugs, and still won't, if we're careful. The key is to keep a lid on the whole thing." He was punching buttons on his cell phone to call the crime lab.

When the technician arrived, it took two hours to dust the boat. While that was being done, the narcotics packages and money were marked as evidence and taken away. Father and I were fingerprinted, and I promised I'd get the rest of my crew to submit their prints the first of the week.

Using a tape recorder, Richard had me describe how I had repossessed the boat and the circumstances leading up to our arrival in San Diego. He was particularly interested in Chuck and Bart's involvement, asking me to clarify details whenever he thought it necessary.

Richard made another call to verify Chuck and Bart were still in custody. He assured me they were isolated and wouldn't be talking to anyone but his staff for a very long time.

We established a time on Monday when Richard would meet me. He needed the rest of the weekend to get a phone line installed to *Shore*

*Loser*, because he felt it was important that I make the initial call to Bayview, and all other calls, from the boat. Electronic equipment would have to be installed so everything could be recorded.

In spite of my father's apprehension, he said nothing, but decided to stick around until the sting operation was over. He knew I was hooked. This was going to be another adventure—I was choosing to put myself in danger again.

CHAPTER FOURTEEN

# JAKE AS BAIT

"Bayview Development Company. How may I help you?" a sexy feminine voice gushed in my ear.

"Good morning. I'd like to speak to the president of the company, please." I was having trouble holding the receiver, my hand was shaking so much.

"I'm sorry, sir, Mr. Sleak is in a meeting. May I help you?"

"Don't think you can, miss," I said, sucking in air, then speaking in a measured tone. "You see, it's very important I talk directly to Mr. Sleak. I'm the new owner of *Shore Loser*. Sleak's been trying to contact me." I looked at Tracey and then at my father. I was uneasy, wanting to impress them both.

"Well, lucky you. I have my instructions, honey. No calls and no interruptions until the meeting is over," she replied in a syrupy tone.

"Go interrupt him anyway—honey." I held the receiver with both hands to steady it; my voice sounded tougher, like someone I didn't know. "He's gonna want to talk to me. And if he misses this call, he's gonna be really upset with you. I'll hold." This was turning out to be much more difficult than I thought it would be.

"Well, if you insist."

"I insist."

Richard Tracey sat at *Shore Loser*'s salon table, recording the conversation. We used the marina telephone line wired into the dock box next to my boat. A plain, brown, residential slim-line receiver had been installed at the navigation station. It amazed me how the cops got it activated so quickly. It would have taken a civilian several weeks just to wade through the paperwork.

My father sat quietly across the table from Richard and listened. In a few minutes, I had an irritated Leonard Sleak on the line. I tried to stay cool.

"Sleak here. Who am I talking to?"

"Jake . . . Jake Mortensen, new owner of *Shore Loser*."

"Last I heard, the boat was in Mexico, leased to two guys cruising the Baja. Who the hell are you?"

That did it. My anger ratcheted up to a new level, and my hand stopped shaking. This guy wasn't so slick; he was just a jerk, a drug-peddling scumbag. I took a deep breath and verbalized what I was thinking.

"Let's cut the baloney, Sleak," I said, with renewed confidence. "The boat was repossessed because you didn't make the payments. You know it, and I know it. I understand you've been trying to find me."

"Where'd you hear all that?"

"From a Mr. Monty Banks at First Interstate Bank. He says you want to purchase the boat back. That true?"

"Might be. You selling?"

"Maybe, if I can turn a quick profit." I looked at Richard to see how I was doing. He smiled encouragingly. My father just shook his head, unable to hear both sides of the conversation. I knew he was thinking hard when his thumbs tucked themselves into the straps of his bib overalls.

"OK, Mr. Mortensen, you've got my attention." Sleak's speech became calmer, more controlled. "How about us getting together for dinner tonight at the Cliff House in La Jolla?" Then, a long pause. "Seven o'clock?"

"I'll be there." I took a deep breath, again. "Seven o'clock . . . tonight."

Hanging up, I turned toward Richard, who was removing his headset and grinning like a guy with a winning hand in a high-stakes poker game. The main salon of *Shore Loser* had suddenly become very confining. I felt claustrophobic and headed up the ladder behind my father, who had just climbed up into the cockpit to get some air.

"Good job, Jake," Richard applauded, following me. "You set the hook. Looks like the next step is to fit you with a wire. You still up for this?"

"Sure," I said as convincingly as I could, but I wasn't, really. I sat down next to my father.

"Jake, you don haf to go troo vit dis, you know." Dad was still having trouble with the concept of his son putting himself in danger.

"What did you think I was doing, Dad, when I was in the Navy jumping out of airplanes? I don't see this as being any different," I said, bothered by his concern—I'd never thought of him as a worrier. And besides, I told myself, I'm doing it for Wally and Miles. Maybe if there were no drug dealers like Sleak, Miles and Wally would still be alive.

Richard and I went over the plan again. My job was to lure Sleak back to the boat after dinner. I would be wearing a recording device; Richard and his partner would listen to everything. The more I could get Sleak to talk, the better. The police promised they'd get it all on tape; if something started to go wrong, they'd be close by. The whole thing sounded incredibly easy. I hoped they were right.

My father decided to stay on the boat and continue working, as though nothing was happening. Maybe he was in denial, maybe he just wanted to stick around for the outcome. I really couldn't be sure how he felt, but I sensed he was convinced the whole thing would turn into a disaster.

Mid-afternoon, I went home and picked up clothes to change into for dinner. The agents were at the boat when I returned. Father was still working, getting rid of the rest of the dry-rotted wood in the aft head.

He tried to stay out of the way, while observing my introduction to the covert world of narcotics investigation. The two agents demonstrated the voice-activated recorder and microphone and showed me how to conceal it. Again, they assured me they'd be watching and listening to my every move.

By six I had showered and changed into white pants and my best Hawaiian shirt. What the heck, it was as dressy as I got. My father had helped me tape the small microphone to my chest. The recorder and miniature battery pack fit comfortably in my pants pocket.

I was nervous, but also ready to get on with it; I wanted to see these guys get caught. Father uttered words of encouragement, but I could tell his heart wasn't in it. Then he told me I had just put my socks on inside out.

The Cliff House Restaurant hangs over the Pacific Ocean on a prominent rocky bluff in La Jolla. It's been there a long time and advertises one of the most spectacular views of the ocean in this quaint seaside village. The male waiters all wear 1940s-style black tuxedoes.

The architecture is 1950s modern—you enter from the top, at street level. From the high-ceilinged dining room, the floor steps down the hill in three levels, the entire side facing the ocean enclosed in glass. Crashing surf climbs the rocky edifice, only to explode with tremendous force underneath the concrete terrace.

By the time I arrived, the sun had disappeared, and the view was lost. Even though it was Monday, the place looked full. I asked to be shown to Leonard Sleak's table. A waiter led down through the platforms of tables filled with laughter and conversation to where Sleak was seated with two men in a corner of the great room. All three stood as I approached.

Sleak was tall and skinny, with a pencil-thin moustache. He wore a sport coat and no tie. The others looked like professional linebackers. Mafia hit-men types, I imagined. One had his blond hair slicked back into a stubby ponytail. The other guy reminded me of a biker I'd seen in front of Toey's apartment.

"Mr. Mortensen? Leonard Sleak." He extended his right hand. "Are you alone?" he said, pumping my arm up and down like a bilge pump handle.

"Yes, I'm alone," I said. "Why do you ask?"

"No reason. Meet my associates, Mr. Calabrazzi and Mr. Krause." Reluctantly, but firmly, I shook their hands, and the four of us sat down. Without asking, Sleak had already ordered dinner, which the waiter was beginning to serve. "What would you like to drink, Mr. Mortensen?"

"Nothing, right now." I could have used a Meyers and Coke, but decided against it. "I understand you want to buy the Gulfstar 50 back."

"You like to get right to the point, don't you, son? I like that." Talking calmly, he looked right through me. "A silly bookkeeping error caused us to lose that boat, you know. With all our construction projects, the accountants overlooked it. My wife is very upset. She was really attached to *Shore Loser*. Lots of sentimental value, you understand."

"If your wife was so attached to the boat, why did you lease it to some others in the first place?"

"Stupid thing to do for my marriage, but my wife and I weren't using it that much, and you know how the bean counters have tunnel vision," he laughed.

"Then why'd you stop making the payments?" Playing the game, I pushed a bit.

"The men we leased it to were supposed to keep the payments up. When accounting found out otherwise, it was already too late. Regrettable mistake."

"Who were the two men?" For the sake of the wiretap, I thought I'd play hero and try to trap him. "Why'd you lease the boat to them?"

"I thought we were here to talk business. Why all the questions?"

"Just curious." I backed off for a moment, then plowed ahead in my clumsy Mortensen way. "The two guys you leased the boat to tried to board my vessel New Year's Eve. Now they're in jail."

"How much is it going to cost me to get *Shore Loser* back?" he asked with a poker face, ignoring my comments.

"$180,000." I tried not to stutter or blink.

"That what you paid for it?"

"None of your business. Take it or leave it." I was trying real hard to sound tough.

"Can we see it first? I understand she's back in San Diego. Where's she berthed? What condition is she in?"

"Whoa, now *you're* asking too many questions." I smiled.

"Just anxious to see her. Now, where is she?"

"Islandia Marina in Quivira Basin. Slip G-18. Right now, I'm living on board. When do you want to come by?"

"Tomorrow. What time?"

"How about in the morning?"

"Then 10 o'clock tomorrow morning. OK?"

"Yep, I'll be there."

Without really tasting it, I hurriedly finished my dinner. Sleak made small talk, but we both knew our discussion was over. His goons didn't say a word, they just kept eating and staring, their silent scrutiny making me increasingly uncomfortable.

I was concerned I had gotten nothing on tape that would help the police, but at the moment that was the least of my worries. I just wanted to get the heck out of there. The instant it seemed appropriate, I excused myself.

Anxious to get home to *Shore Loser*, it took me just twenty minutes to race back. I don't think Van Gogh had ever been driven so fast. When I arrived, my father was sitting in the main salon, drinking black coffee sucked through a sugar cube tucked in his cheek, one of his Norwegian habits I will never get used to.

"Vhat happened? Dey suspect anyting?" he asked.

"I don't know, Dad. Sleak said he'd be here at ten tomorrow morning. We ought to turn in and get some rest."

I removed the wire and placed the recorder on the navigation table. On purpose, I left it switched on, hoping Richard or one of his men would keep listening. There was always a chance Sleak and his goons might try something during the night.

My father took the bunk in the forward stateroom, and I took one in the stern. I put the companionway boards in place, but didn't slide the Lexan hatch all the way shut. I told my father to lock his cabin door, I'd do the same. In spite of any apprehension, my body was numb and exhausted.

Tossing and turning, I couldn't get comfortable. About an hour later—I guessed it was around eleven or midnight—I heard something moving out on deck. Then I heard the companionway hatch slide open. I froze. The Mafia guys were here.

I heard them enter the cockpit, then climb down the ladder into the main salon. How many? Did they have guns? Oh, my gosh, my father was sleeping in the forward cabin. First, Toey; and, now, my father; why was I being so reckless with those I loved. Had he locked his door as I'd told him to?

I eased the stern deck hatch open above my head. With both feet firmly planted on each bunk, I gradually raised my head and torso through the hatch and looked around. I didn't see a soul. With both arms I hoisted myself upward through the hatch and rotated my body so I was sitting on the edge of the opening. All I could hear were muffled sounds in the main salon.

I looked across the cockpit through the open dodger, toward the bow. Thank goodness, my father had done the same thing. He had climbed out the forward hatch and was quietly closing it. Together, we moved toward the cockpit. I got there first and, with one rapid motion, silently drew the companionway hatch closed and locked it—but not quietly enough.

From below, two gunshots blasted through the forward corners, sending shattered Lexan in all directions. I heard my father cry out in agony. He was hurt.

"Goddamn it! Get out of the way!" It was Richard, weapon in hand, pulling my father out of the cockpit, across the deck, and toward the starboard side. At the same time, his partner, Joe, jumped over the lifelines on the port side toward me. He wanted me off the boat, too.

More shots exploded from within the salon, destroying what remained of a once perfectly good hatch.

"Get the hell away from the boat!" Richard sounded like he meant it. He and Joe were both wearing bulletproof vests.

Joe lobbed a teargas canister through the shattered hatch into the salon. My father had retreated across the dock toward *Papa's Toy* and had propped himself up against the dock box.

Larry Kleinschmidt was on the flybridge, watching the whole thing. His vessel's huge spotlight illuminated all of *Shore Loser's* deck. I'd forgotten Larry also worked for the Harbor Police; Richard must have alerted him that something was coming down.

Within minutes, he was at my side with a first-aid kit, helping me make my father comfortable. I had unbuttoned dad's coveralls, sticky with blood and plastic fragments, then, pulled off his shirt and used it, wadded up, as a compress against his chest.

"I called for an ambulance. He get hit by a bullet or pieces from the hatch?"

"Lexan shards I think. I've got the bleeding stopped," I said, talking over my father, not wanting to look down.

In my gut, I knew he was going to be all right, but he was in pain, pain as a result of being around me, as a result of my recklessness. I was sure this was the reason my relationship with Toey had gone sour; now I might lose my father.

I swallowed back the acid welling up in my throat; my hand shook. Larry was thinking quicker than me, less distracted. He removed the compress to inspect the wound, clean it, and make sure I'd removed all the plastic splinters. Dad continued to groan from the pain.

More cops arrived with the ambulance, the number of armed personnel surrounding my besieged boat multiplying dramatically within minutes. In addition to Larry's spotlight, my hull and cockpit were bathed in the light from two portable floods.

Several times, Richard commanded the men to come out without their weapons. Finally, they emerged one at a time through the companionway hatch. I recognized them as Sleak's two associates. Their hands furiously rubbing their irritated eyes, they were rendered harmless. I was surprised

Sleak wasn't with them. Quickly checking for other arms, Richard took them into custody, reading their rights off a Miranda card, as the handcuffs clicked into place.

My father rested his hand in mine and gave it a squeeze, as the paramedics re-dressed his wound and gave him a shot to make him more comfortable and fight infection. He had only a flesh wound. Uniformed officers muscled the two thugs away to a waiting patrol car.

My boat was trashed, messed up big time, but the ordeal was over. I was fortunate the gunmen hadn't put up more of a struggle. I was fortunate my father was going to be OK.

"Well, thanks to you, Jake, and your father, we got at least two of them," said Richard, walking toward us. "It's a start. Is Mr. Mortensen going to be OK?"

"Yes, thank you," I said, squeezing dad's hand again. "The paramedics released him, but he's going to feel it for a while."

"Good, you had us worried for a moment. I hate collateral damage. Gives the police a bad name." I'm sure Richard was trying to be funny, but it didn't come across that way.

"To get Sleak, we'll have to make these two jerks talk, and we're good at that sort of thing," Joe grunted, gathering up his gear. "The other two jailbirds, Bart and company, are already singing, but so far it ain't the right tune—mostly about Mexico, and nothing we can verify."

"Without some really concrete evidence, it's still gonna be tough to get a warrant for Sleak's arrest. In the meantime, either Joe or I will be keeping a tail on him, just in case he tries something. As you've probably already figured out, Larry is in on this, too. Don't be surprised if you see him hanging around a lot more. Another thing, now that we know your dad's injury is minor: I need you to assess the damage to your boat and give me an estimate as soon as possible. I think the commissioner has got a way to make sure you get reimbursed."

"I sure hope so. They ruined the hatch."

"Trust me."

With all the excitement over and everyone gone, Larry served my father and me a drink, and offered to let us spend the night on *Papa's Toy*. We took him up on it. My father needed some rest, and I needed to calm down. Neither of us was in any hurry to go back on board *Shore Loser*. We knew it would reek of teargas and be a terrible mess.

"I meant to ask you, Jake. How would you feel about running *Papa's Toy* for a couple of days next week?" Larry asked, after dad went to bed, something else was obviously on his mind.

"Sure, if I get a chance to have you check me out ahead of time. What's up?"

"Well, the boss wants the boat to go out every day of the America's Cup Challengers Series. He's got a ton of people signed up. Thing's fully catered. I'm sure there'll be a lot of drinking. All you've got to do is stay sober, run the boat, and keep everybody safe."

"Piece of cake. When you want me to do it?"

"How about Sunday and Monday? I've got a hot date flying in from Lauderdale for the weekend. Haven't seen her since I left Florida."

"Why not take her with you? She'd probably enjoy it."

"Not a chance, Jake. She gets seasick and hates boats."

"OK," I laughed, "but can I crew for you on Saturday, to learn the boat?"

"You've got it. Thanks. I'll talk to you more about it as we get closer to the event."

Larry continued to ply me with liquor, while we spent another hour talking about what had just happened, drug dealers, boats, and anything else that came to mind. I was still recovering from the police action that had just hurt my father and thoroughly messed up our new boat, when a really harebrained thought popped into my head.

Fortunately, my father had checked out of the conversation and was fast asleep in a cabin down below, so he didn't hear what came out of my mouth next.

"Larry . . . do you remember when Ted and I towed you over to the shipyard?" I asked, jogging our memories. " . . . the guy that was mixed up with the Russian team?"

Yeah, Hammer, Peter Hammer. He's been in the news a lot recently. Lost his boat in a freak explosion. So?"

"Well, in my gut I just know Hammer and Sleak are somehow mixed up in this drug and money laundering thing together. There are way too many coincidences."

"So? Go on," Larry said.

"They're both collecting money for the Russian team, money the team's never seen. They both owned *Shore Loser* at one time. Sleak's goons, living on *Shore Loser* in La Paz, must've known about the stash, because they chased us all the way back to San Diego on Hammer's power boat, then blew it up."

"Be tough to prove."

"Maybe not, if your boss, the police commissioner, could put them in a situation where they might accuse one another to save their own skins." Now the booze was talking, and I continued with enthusiasm. "I bet Boris Ivanovich, the Russian team captain, would help set it up. After all the garbage he's been through, hampered by lack of money, I'm sure Boris would be interested in learning what Hammer has done with the Russian funds."

"Interesting talk coming from a drunk," laughed Larry, picking up empty glasses. "I'll suggest it to the commissioner, if I can remember. I don't know about you, but I need to get some sleep. It's three o'clock in the morning."

My father stayed a few more days, recovering, and helping me put *Shore Loser* back in shape when he could. We had some long father-and-son skull sessions, sitting in the cockpit in the evenings. Involving him in the sting operation was really stupid and irresponsible on my part. If something happened to him, I would be devastated. I was truly sorry when he had to return to Long Beach.

CHAPTER FIFTEEN

# SPRINGING THE TRAP

It was early Saturday morning, January 14, 1995, when I met Larry at *Papa's Toy*. A day I will never forget. I was glad I'd spent the time with him on Thursday going over the ship's systems, because this morning he seemed totally focused on getting ready for his guests. People started arriving well before noon.

Today, the first day of the Louis Vuitton Challengers Series, I couldn't help but be excited and was sure we were going to have a full boat. I concerned myself with securing the colorful banners and flags that would identify *Papa's Toy* as an official spectator vessel, then started preparations to leave the dock.

Larry and his uniformed crew formally greeted the arriving group of his boss's business associates. We really looked like a party boat. Once certain everyone was on board, Larry joined me at the bridge.

"You ready to take her out?"

"Just give the word," I replied.

"I should warn you, Hammer is here, with Boris and the Russian team. Sleak is also on board. We made sure of that."

"What are you talking about?"

"Your idea, remember?" Larry said, with a troubled look. "The Russians couldn't qualify their yacht, so my boss insisted that Hammer and Sleak bring them out so they could at least watch the races. Virgil used all his yacht club political clout to put them in a position where they couldn't refuse. That's the set-up. Most of the guests are undercover cops. I just don't like using *Papa's Toy*. Too dangerous, in my opinion."

Wow!" I exclaimed. "Pretty elaborate, I sure hope it works."

"So do I. We want you to stay up here, out of the way. Just help me run the boat. OK? Your job and mine is to keep *Papa's Toy* safe. Richard Tracey and his people are in charge of managing the bad guys. OK?"

"Whatever you say," I agreed, hesitantly. It was all coming together too fast. After the arrests and my father getting injured, I wasn't prepared for this. "I know Boris and his crew are really bummed out that they won't be competing—you know they blame it all on Hammer," I commented, starting the engines. "If anything, that's going to help stir the pot."

"Yeah, and Virgil insisting some of *The Age of Russia* investors come along seemed like a stroke of genius. Now, I'm not so sure. We're gonna have our hands full if something goes wrong." Larry was grimacing as he turned to go down to the deck below.

As soon as he was sure his vessel was secured, Larry and his crew released the dock lines. When he gave me the signal, I eased the big Ocean Alexander out of her slip and into the fairway. Under normal conditions, a boat this size is simple to maneuver—twin screws and a bow thruster make it all too easy. Soon Larry was beside me on the bridge and ready to take over.

"Good job, Cap. You make it look like you've been driving *Papa's Toy* all along."

"Like I said, piece of cake. What's next?"

"Well, first, we got to go find our position in the spectator fleet."

Once out of the channel and past the breakwater, Larry guided *Papa's Toy* toward a cluster of vessels just beyond the kelp beds, between Point Loma and Ocean Beach.

"Kind of foggy out here, with a long swell, and light, shifty winds," Larry remarked, disturbed by the conditions.

"If we don't like it, the racers aren't going to like it either," I agreed. Then I asked what was really on my mind. "Did someone coach Boris on how to confront Hammer and Sleak?"

"You bet we did. He's to accuse Hammer, the fundraiser, and Sleak, the fund trustee, in front of the investors. From what I understand, he is supposed to loudly threaten to go to the press and expose them. Boris was very angry when one of our men explained the whole thing to him. I hope he'll do precisely what he was told to, not take things in his own hands and try something foolish."

"Me, too," I mumbled. This was *not* going to be good. I liked Boris and didn't want anything to happen to him. I also found it strange the police commissioner would let his boat be used in this way. It was like it was a *yachting thing,* and he was trying to keep it under wraps.

Once in position, Larry held *Papa's Toy* in place, using the shift levers with the big engines at idle. Because of the depth of the water, it was impractical to anchor. We were assigned a place in the spectator fleet on the right side of the course. It was our responsibility to stay well clear of the racers.

Through the haze, I could barely make out the race committee boats that defined the start line. Two America's Cup yachts were sparring in the area downwind of them. Small Coast Guard vessels, white and red Vessel Assist, and yellow YachtTow boats were policing the area, keeping other vessels clear of the competition. Today's first race was Australia versus Japan.

For the last few America's Cup competitions, the racecourse has differed a little bit each time. This year was no exception. In match racing, the start is one of the most exciting parts. Probably in order to appeal to ESPN and other media coverage, the race committee chose to shorten the line and make the start even more dramatic. They also shortened the time the two competing boats had to engage each other, from ten minutes to five.

"There goes the starting cannon. Wow! Look! *OneAustralia* was trying to force *Nippon Challenge* over the line early!" Forgetting what might be going on with our passengers, I could hardly contain myself. Match racing is the best, and I had a ringside seat for the series start. The winner would receive the Louis Vuitton Cup and go on to challenge the Americans for yachting's greatest prize.

Everyone figured John Bertrand's well-funded *OneAustralia* as the favorite to win, especially with Cup veteran Rod Davis at the helm. In addition, quite a bit of controversy surrounded the *Nippon Challenge*. I had heard complaints from the Russian team and other rumors around Quivira Basin about late-night grinding noises and lengthy periods of around-the-clock activity in the Japanese compound. There was also grumbling from the Australians and other competitors, questioning whether team Nippon's extensive changes were making it a new boat.

Over the last few weeks I'd read everything about the event I could get my hands on. I learned the new IACC boats are built of space-age materials with the latest technology. They are 30 percent lighter than the twelve-meter boats that were used from 1958 to 1987. They're also bigger and have 40 percent more sail area. Boats and crews have to orchestrate their efforts so they work together like a well-oiled machine. There was just too much at stake. One screw-up or equipment failure, and you lose.

Then, as the two boats beat toward us, their bows rising up and down as they sliced through the water, things on *Papa's Toy* suddenly got crazy.

"Larry, down there on our bow. Is that Hammer and Sleak shoving each other around? Boris is there, too," I said, pointing over the windscreen. "Looks like things are going down! Where are the police?"

"Damn! I can't leave the bridge. The racers are headed this way. I've got to stay clear of their path!"

"Do what you have to, Larry," I called back, as I hurried away. "You steer the boat. I'll go and see what's going on," I yelled, caught up in the excitement. Then I mumbled to myself, "I hope Richard's close by."

"No, Jake! I'm supposed to keep you up here! That's my orders."

With Larry's voice ringing in my ears, I scrambled down the ladder from the bridge to the pilothouse. Through the helm station windows,

I could see Hammer on the foredeck. Silhouetted against the two large Kevlar sails bearing down on us, he was yelling at Sleak and Ivanovich. All three were gesturing wildly. As I moved through the pilothouse door, Boris hurried over to intercept me. He grabbed me by the shoulders and wouldn't step out of the way.

"Do not come out here, Jake! Zis men devils!" His face was red, his eyes filled with hate and anger.

"What do you mean? Who's the devil?" I grabbed Boris's wrists, pushed his hands away, and squirmed free.

"Hammer. And zat man talking to Hammer. He has gun. Hammer is crook. Let him kill Hammer. Zis not happen in Russia."

"Well, it ain't gonna happen in the U.S. of A. either!" I said to myself, with renewed courage, as I moved along the side of the pilothouse.

Most of the guests, or cops, or whatever they were, were in the main salon or on the stern and upper deck, watching the two hi-tech racing machines swoop toward our boat with incredible speed. *Nippon Challenge* and *OneAustralia* were hard on the wind, side by side, their exotic plastic sails sheeted in as close as their crews could manage. Neither yacht was about to fall off or give an inch. I knew Larry had his hands full, trying to stay clear and downwind of them. It was becoming apparent both yachts intended to use the cover of the spectator boats to break free of each other. *OneAuatralia* was going to pass on our port side, less than two meters away.

"You're an asshole, Hammer! You and your fucking organization have ruined me. I'm going to make sure people know the truth about you, like I do—you and your dirty money. You're not going to make me the fall guy anymore! It's over."

Sleak was facing me, his back against the port bow rail. I saw something flash in his right hand as it rose. Without warning, Hammer lowered his shoulder, plunged forward, and hit Sleak with the force of an NFL tackle playing for the golden ring in the Super Bowl. Sleak jerked backward and tumbled over the teak railing, falling into the water ten feet below.

In the same instant, the Australian boat, doing twelve knots, shot the gap between *Papa's Toy* and the next nearest spectator boat. I ran to the rail and stood by Hammer. Lines creaked as the sheet trimmers on the sailing machine ground away, the hi-tech fabric tightening into the shape of perfect airfoils. Rod Davis and the Australians, intent on sailing their vessel to its maximum potential, never saw Sleak enter the water.

*OneAuatralia's* bow missed *Papa's Toy* by less than a meter. It didn't miss Sleak. A pool of crimson was churned up in the wake generated by the passing race machine, the only evidence marking where Sleak had entered the water. Hammer turned toward Boris and me, his face hard and ashen. My star witness was overboard, probably dead.

"You saw it! He tried to kill me!"

"Save it, Hammer." I yelled, still looking at the water for any sign of Sleak.

"You're under arrest, Peter Hammer." The voice from behind was Richard's.

"What? What for? You saw it. He was drunk, he had a gun, he tried to kill me. I was just defending myself." Hammer struggled as Richard and Joe wrestled the short, stocky man's arms behind his back and cuffed him. Several gold chains burst loose from around his neck. "This is embarrassing! You won't get away with it. I have important friends on this boat!"

"Yeah? So do we," Richard laughed, as he hustled the man below decks.

I learned later that Richard had pre-selected a stateroom for use as a holding area. What I didn't know at the time was that half the undercover cops had moved the investor guests to the stern and upper deck as the confrontation ensued. Surprise, surprise. The whole thing was well-planned and would have worked, if we hadn't lost Sleak overboard. Without his testimony, it would be harder to convict Hammer. He was just too clever.

"Jake, over zere. I see body."

Boris had just picked up one of Hammer's broken chains and stuffed it into his pocket. His other hand was pointing at a lump of clothing floating off our port side.

My instincts as a Sea-Air Search-and-Rescue guy took over. I stripped off my shirt, shoes, and pants, grabbed a life ring, and jumped in. It was freezing. My muscles tightened up immediately. I'd forgotten how cold the Pacific was this time of year without a wetsuit.

Within seconds, I managed to get Sleak's body over to *Papa's Toy* and up against the swim step. Multiple eager hands helped me lift my bloody burden back onto the boat.

Incredible as it may seem, Sleak was alive. His impact with the racing boat had only crushed his right arm and shoulder. One of Larry's crew handed me a blanket to wrap myself in, while Richard and his men administered CPR and first aid. He was in pretty bad shape, but he'd live to implicate Hammer in the whole filthy narcotics and money laundering business.

Larry pulled *Papa's Toy* out of the spectator fleet and motored back toward the marina. Now that it was over, his boss wanted the cops and their captives off his boat as soon as possible. All I could do was stand in the aft cockpit, hugging the blanket for warmth.

Beside me, Boris looked dejected and miserable. With the capture of Hammer, his world had just collapsed even more. He didn't understand what had just happened, and I wasn't sure if I did either.

I could only guess how Hammer was tied in with Sleak and the drug running stuff with *Shore Loser*. For all I knew, he might even be the mastermind. After all, both the boats involved had belonged to him at one time. Though I was freezing, the thought that Wally and Miles' deaths might finally be avenged warmed my insides.

"Iz all rong, Jake. Hammer is bad guy. He say he try to help Russian team. He say he raise money. Where it is?"

"Yeah, you're right. He's one bad dude. He probably *is* the reason why you guys aren't sailing today."

"No money come. None from Petersburg. None from friends of Hammer." His eyes looked down and away. "Our boat not pay bills. Shipyard locks up *The Age of Russia* to sell her. My comrades and I have deportation to Russia. It is nightmare!"

"Damn it!" I mumbled to myself. There must be something I can do for my newfound Russian friend and his team. His country was struggling to achieve order from chaos. His hopes as an international yachtsman had evaporated because of world politics and greedy people like Sleak and Hammer. There was no way I could ask him to hand over the gold chain he had pocketed.

As Larry guided *Papa's Toy* into her slip, I vowed to spend tonight with Boris and his men, perhaps the last time I'd get the chance before they had to leave.

"Why don't we meet at the yacht club and congratulate today's winning racers?" I suggested.

"Iz not good idea," he refused, feeling he and the other Russians would be too embarrassed. When I suggested we have dinner at the Busted Surfboard, my non-yachting hangout, he brightened up, saying he would like that. I gave him directions and taxi fare, and made him promise to be there by eight. He said he would, and I believed his word was good.

As Larry's crew cleated the dock lines, I prepared to go across to my boat. I needed to change into some warm, dry clothes.

"Jake, don't leave yet!" It was Richard, yelling at me from the bridge. He was standing next to Larry. Uniformed police and ambulance attendants on the dock received his prisoners—almost a repeat of earlier in the week.

"Hang on a minute. I've got to get out of this wet stuff and clean up."

When I returned to *Papa's Toy*, Richard Tracey and Larry Klienschmidt were in the main salon, having a drink. A rotund older man I'd not seen before had joined them. Larry and Richard both stood up as I entered the cabin—the other guy remained seated. Wire-rimmed Coke-bottle glasses rested on top of his wavy, white hair; his rosebud mouth was almost lost in the folds of a double chin. Yet I think I detected a smile.

"Jake, I want you to meet my boss, Police Commissioner Virgil Lee Klean," Larry said, heading for the bar. "Can I fix you a rum and Coke? Meyers, right?"

"Yeah, thanks." I shook Commissioner Klean's pudgy hand. "Pleased to meet you, sir."

Pale and swollen, with liver spots on his hands and face, he reminded me of an older, inflated version of Monty Banks. His huge shirt had loud, hand-painted flowers all over it.

"And I am very pleased to meet you, Mr. Mortensen. Richard tells me you were the key to busting up a pretty big narcotics and money laundering organization."

He wheezed, as he continued, "We've been after Hammer for years, but neither the Feds nor our people could get more than circumstantial evidence. With Sleak's arrest, we've now got someone substantial willing to testify against Hammer and give us all the evidence we need, thanks to you. Congratulations, son. The Feds pay pretty well for this kind of thing. How much actual money did we recover, Richard?"

"Over a million in cash—one point four to be exact."

"Well, now, since we did all the work, D.E.A. can afford to let loose of most of that and keep the dope. We'll take a percentage for the department and give Jake here something for his efforts and property damage.

"Let's see, around 10 percent, $150,000? I'm sure the other commissioners will go along with it. Some of the money may have to go back to the investors in the Russian effort, if we can establish a link. At least three of the investors are good friends of mine—otherwise, I wouldn't have let *Papa's Toy* be used in this way. Sound OK to you, Mr. Mortensen?"

"That's more than generous, sir," I sputtered. The numbers racing around in my mind meant I was going to be able to pay off the loan on *Shore Loser* and have money left over.

"Normally, any reward is for arrest and conviction. But we're more than halfway there, so I'll get them to waive that."

I could hear his chest rumble, like he was having trouble breathing or trying to laugh. "You'll have to pay taxes on it, you know. The Feds giveth and taketh away. And the State'll want its cut, too. Doesn't seem right, but that's the way it works. Richard here'll stay in touch with you."

That was it. The audience was over. Larry led me out of the ship's saloon and winked as he shook my hand. I thanked him profusely. I was ready to thank *everyone*.

Wow! A $150,000 reward! Up 'til then, I'd been flat-on-my-butt broke. I couldn't wait to call someone and tell them my good fortune. My father, Toey, anyone—maybe even Anna.

It was late Friday afternoon, so Toey should be home. I decided to call her first, using the phone I now had on *Shore Loser*, a fringe benefit of the sting operation. "Toey! You sitting down?" My voice must have been two octaves higher than normal.

"Are you OK, Jake? You sound strange. Are you calling to apologize?"

"What?" She had just taken the steam out of my announcement. "Apologize for *what*?"

"For not believing the women's team was any good . . . they beat *Stars and Stripes* in the first round robin. Did you not hear? They won by sixty-nine seconds!"

"The girls won by sixty-nine, huh? You've got to be kidding," I said, laughing. "Bet there are a lot of jokes running around about that."

"That is *not* funny, Jake!"

"I'm sorry, I apologize," I said, realizing I'd gone and stuck my foot in my mouth again. "Honestly, that's *not* why I called."

"What can be more important than *America3* beating Team Dennis Connors?"

"I just made one hundred and fifty thousand dollars!"

"$150,000? You are kidding me. What did you do? Rob a bank?" she asked, sounding more Chinese than ever.

"No. It's reward money for helping capture two bad guys. We've got to get everybody together tonight at the Busted Surfboard to celebrate. I'll tell you the whole story then." My head was spinning. "I need a great big favor."

"OK, Jake, if I can."

"The Russians, Boris and his crew, are going home, being deported. I'd like to give them a friendly send-off, something good to remember us by. Got any ideas?"

"No. But let me work on it. Why are they being deported?"

"Well, maybe not deported, just having their visas revoked. Same thing. Don't know the whole story. Apparently, the crew was barred from racing and had to abandon the boat. Their vessel is being held for payment of overdue bills. They never saw any of the money Hammer raised for them. It was a scam. Right now, they don't even have enough to fly back to St. Petersburg."

"Oh, Jake, after they have tried so hard to get into the competition, it sounds so cruel."

"Yeah, you're right. I'm going to see what can be done to help them. You do your thing, and I'll do mine." There I went again, asking her to do something for me, and I still wasn't sure about our relationship. Mortensen, you're on a roll.

Then I called Monty, telling him the whole story about Sleak and Hammer. He didn't seem too surprised; his friend Richard Tracey had already filled him in. I explained the situation about the Russian sailors and told him I was treating them to dinner at the Busted Surfboard tonight in Pacific Beach. He said he'd see what he could do to help them, and sounded like he meant it.

Then I made calls to Ted and Buddy. Ted said he'd call Jill. When I phoned the saloon to make reservations, Wanda was already on duty. She said she'd have tables set up on the outside deck when we got there.

"I don't have time to get to the bank for enough cash. Can I put it on my credit card?" Even though I was about to be $150,000 richer, I didn't want to tell Wanda that. At the moment, I was broke.

"Shit, Jake. Your limit big enough to handle this group?" she laughed. "Hell's bells! Make everyone pay their own way! Since when do you have to be the big spender?"

"I'll tell you the whole story tonight, Wanda. You won't believe it."

"I can't wait to hear. You sound excited enough to be a teenager who just discovered girls are different from boys," she laughed. "I'll talk to my boss about the tab; I'm sure we can work something out. He owes me."

The flurry of excitement over, my hand shook, resting on the phone. I was overcome with thoughts about Anna. I don't know from where or why, but they were there. I looked at my watch, concerned about the two-hour time difference between California and Minnesota; it wasn't too late to call.

"Hello."

"Hi, Anna. It's Jake Mortensen."

"Jake! I can't believe it's you! Oh, my goodness—how are you?" she asked, excited. I could hear my namesake crying in the background.

"I'm so good, I can't believe it!" And I told her the story.

She said she was doing well, but didn't elaborate. As we talked, she became distant and cautious, maybe because we hadn't communicated in so long, or maybe because of my good fortune. Understanding women is something I continue to have difficulty with. I think it's genetic.

"I'd like to use some of the money I'm getting to set up a savings account for little Jake's college education."

"No, Jake, no!" She started crying and protested, "I can't let you do that." When I kept on in my clumsy Mortensen kind of way, she gave up and thanked me.

In spite of all my spontaneous exuberance, the call to Anna ended up being kind of a bummer. She acted like a woman does when she wants to break off a relationship—the conversation was so weird. When I hung up, I decided I wasn't going to let it get me down. Not tonight.

The gang was already waiting for me when I got to the saloon around seven-thirty. Ted, Buddy, Jill, and Toey had decorated a table on the deck with red and white bunting. Little Russian and American flags were stuck in small Styrofoam blocks at each place setting. In the middle of the table was a replica of the America's Cup trophy made of aluminum foil and cardboard. On the base it said, "*The Age of Russia.*" It all looked wonderful. I walked up to Toey and gave her a bear hug, lifting her off her feet.

"Wow! It looks great! I know all this didn't come from Hallmark. How'd you pull it together so fast?"

"Jill helped. Teachers are good at this kind of thing, you know." She reached into her purse and pulled out eight ribbons with plastic medals. On each one they had glued crossed Russian and American flags. "We can also give them these."

"Good thinking, thanks! You guys are fantastic!" I gave her a big kiss.

"Toey says Buddy's roommate has become a gazillionaire!" Wanda yelled, as she brought me a Meyers and Coke. "Tell us about *that*, big guy." She was wearing a super-short, peasant-style dress—probably her version of a roguish Russian barmaid.

"Yeah, tell us about it, big guy!" came back the chorus.

So, I repeated the whole crazy story: how I had met with Sleak, how his men tried to kill my father and me, how Hammer had tried to kill Sleak, that the captain of *Papa's Toy* was really a cop and the owner was really a police commissioner.

As I was wrapping up my truth-is-stranger-than-fiction tale, Wanda spotted the Russian team entering the bar downstairs. They were easy to recognize—eight guys in the same outfit: white pants, polo shirts, and double-breasted navy-blue blazers—obviously not the usual Busted Surfboard attire.

They gathered around Wanda like bees to honey when she brought them to our table. As always, she handled the attention like a pro, back in minutes with another round of drinks, including two bottles of Russian vodka. The party had begun.

Monty Banks called and talked to Boris. He had worked everything out so the Russians would not have to leave: calls to the State Department, food and lodging so they could stay until the end of the America's Cup competition, and a special award in their honor, not to mention airfare home. The relieved expression on Boris's face was priceless.

Boris gave a toast. I gave a toast. Jill and Toey bestowed the ribbons and kisses on each comrade. We ate. We drank. We told stories. The Cold War was over, and we were doing our best to make sure they knew it. Somehow during the evening, Boris and I managed to exchange mailing addresses, and I knew in my heart we would stay in touch. Maybe the world wasn't ready for the new order of things, but we were.

Before we got too tipsy, Toey and I drifted away and walked across the promenade to the beach. Shoeless and arm in arm, we strolled at the edge of the ocean we both loved so much. Cool water licked at our bare feet with each wave that rolled up onto the hard, wet sand.

"I thought Monty Banks would never call. Thank heavens, he did when he did, while Boris and his comrades were still sober enough to understand what he'd done. He must have some very important friends."

"I agree. It was all very nice, Jake."

"Right now, I'm sitting on top of the world. Being a yacht captain for hire is what I really want to do for a living. Like what Ted was doing before he went to work for YachtTow. Did I tell you Commissioner Klean has offered me a job to skipper *Papa's Toy?*"

"What about Larry?"

"He's decided to go back to Fort Lauderdale. His honey talked him into it. Besides, he's got an offer to captain a 110-foot Broward. It's a move up for him and puts him close to his girlfriend."

"Then it is good for both of you?"

"Very good, you bet! I've discovered I've got some special friends— good old friends and good new friends—and enough money to pay off the loan on *Shore Loser*. What more could a man want?"

"How about *me*, Jake?"

"I love you very much. But do you think you can stand being with a boat bum who attracts trouble like a magnet?"

"Only if you can put up with a schoolteacher who is a worrywart."

"Think it'll work?"

"Yes, I do, Captain Mortensen."

Placing my hands on her tiny waist, I pulled her close; her breasts pressed against my chest as she wrapped one leg around mine, trying to get even closer. Our kiss seemed infinite.

᷎᷎ ᷎᷎

Much, much later, back in the saloon, a somewhat intoxicated Boris Ivanovich raised the aluminum foil "America's Cup" over his head as if it were the real thing. Everyone in the place started chanting, "*Age of Russia! Age of Russia! Age of Russia!*"

Watching the festivities, I hugged Toey close and mumbled the words of my tattoo: "Yep, always leave a clean wake."

# AUTHOR'S COMMENTS

What you have just read is entirely the product of a yacht delivery skipper's overactive imagination while spending too many days at sea. Sure, I've taken great liberty with real places and events, but any resemblance to actual persons, living or dead, is entirely fictional. As my friends in San Diego can testify, reality is always stranger than any fiction I could hope to write, and in the history of America's Cup competition, 1995 stands out as one of the strangest of all.

Beginning construction in the early '90s, the Russian boat was one of two intended for the 1992 competition. Only one hull was flown to San Diego, unfinished, and it is not clear whether it was ever measured to determine if it met IACC rules. It did not compete in the 1992 America's Cup, but some say it did compete unsuccessfully in the IACC World Championships and that was the end of its life. Later, the hull was seen on display along the San Diego waterfront near the *Star of India*; it had been donated to the Maritime Museum by the shipyard.

The new IACC boats developed under rules established for the 1992 America's Cup competition proved to be challenging to design, extremely challenging to sail, and—to the delight of the media—exciting to watch. Then, after several rigs were lost overboard in 1995 and a thirty-second sinking occurred, people began questioning if the technology being brought to the design table was being pushed too far. Some racing sailors and critics felt the new boats were becoming dangerously delicate.

The woman's team, *America3*, badgered by politics, male intimidation, and competitors' unsportsmanlike conduct, lost the Citizen's Cup to Dennis Conner by one point. Had they won, it would have crushed the life out of Conner's remarkable America's Cup career.

Remember, it was Dennis Conner, racing for New York Yacht Club, who lost to Alan Bond's *Australia 1* in 1983, ending NYYC's 132-year winning streak. And it was Conner who staged a remarkable comeback to claim the Cup in 1987 and return it to the United States, this time under the San Diego Yacht Club burgee, his home club. SDYC went on to successfully defend the Cup three times.

Then came 1995. In the America's Cup finals against Sir Peter Blake and his crew from "down under," Dennis Conner, San Diego Yacht Club,

194 • Douglas Danielson

and the Americans suffered a humiliating defeat. At the time, to win the most prestigious trophy in yachting, a boat must take the best of nine races. Team New Zealand's *Black Magic* won it in an incredible five straight, shutting out *Stars and Stripes*. As a result, the America's Cup was taken away from American soil for the second time since 1851. Some say it may never return.

As I write this, the US team, *BMW Oracle USA-98*, has been eliminated from competition in the 2007 32nd America's Cup Competition in Valencia Spain. *Team New Zealand* won the Louis Vuitton challenger's series and the right to challenge Swiss Defender, *Alinghi*, for the greatest prize in sailboat racing. Backstay and national participation controversies aside, frankly, I was cheering for Grant Dalton and his boys from "down under" to have the right stuff and take the Cup back to Auckland. Sailing is a national sport in New Zealand—something we seem to have lost in the United States.

Now the winner of the 32nd America's Cup has been decided. The Societe Nautique de Geneve's defender, *Alinghi*, triumphed over the Royal New Zealand Yacht Squadron's challenger, *Emirates Team New Zealand*, by five races to two, in a spectacular series reminiscent of match racing in earlier years.

That's how it should go down in the record books, but the game has changed. For the 33rd America's Cup, a new 90ft overall class will be used, with a sliding keel. Just like the demise of the aluminum12meter class, the incredible IACC carbon fiber sailing machines used in my story are now obsolete as well.


—Douglas Danielson
—July 2007, Puerto Vallarta, Mexico

1499686